REALLY
DEAD

REALLY
DEAD
A RIA BUTLER MYSTERY

J.E. Forman

DUNDURN
TORONTO

Editor: Cheryl Hawley
Design: Jennifer Scott
Printer: Webcom

Library and Archives Canada Cataloguing in Publication

Forman, J. E.
    Really dead : a Ria Butler mystery / J.E. Forman.

Issued also in electronic format.
ISBN 978-1-4597-0680-4

I. Title.

PS8611.O765R43 2013   C813'.6   C2013-900777-6

1 2 3 4 5   17 16 15 14 13

| Conseil des Arts du Canada | Canada Council for the Arts | Canadä | ONTARIO ARTS COUNCIL CONSEIL DES ARTS DE L'ONTARIO |

We acknowledge the support of the **Canada Council for the Arts** and the **Ontario Arts Council** for our publishing program. We also acknowledge the financial support of the **Government of Canada** through the **Canada Book Fund** and **Livres Canada Books**, and the **Government of Ontario** through the **Ontario Book Publishing Tax Credit** and the **Ontario Media Development Corporation**.

Care has been taken to trace the ownership of copyright material used in this book. The author and the publisher welcome any information enabling them to rectify any references or credits in subsequent editions.

J. Kirk Howard, President

Printed and bound in Canada.

The publisher is not responsible for websites or their content unless they are owned by the publisher.

Visit us at
Dundurn.com | @dundurnpress | Facebook.com/dundurnpress | Pinterest.com/dundurnpress

Dundurn	Gazelle Book Services Limited	Dundurn
3 Church Street, Suite 500	White Cross Mills	2250 Military Road
Toronto, Ontario, Canada	High Town, Lancaster, England	Tonawanda, NY
M5E 1M2	LA1 4XS	U.S.A. 14150

For D
Wish you were here to see this

The severed foot was only mildly annoying; what really pissed her off were the footprints that led to it. Against all orders, warnings, and memos, some moron had walked from the treeline to the water and then back again. The footprint trail in the sand reminded Pam of the *V* formation geese made in the sky when they were flying south for the winter. But there weren't any geese here, unless they wore size eleven or twelve men's shoes. There wasn't ever any winter here either.

The gigantic spotlight in the sky had risen above the palm trees, its barn doors wide open. The bazillion foot-candles it gave off made the white sand shimmer and scattered sparkles across the sea all the way to Great Dog Island. Pam smiled. Using the lingo of the biz was becoming second nature to her. A year earlier her meteorological thoughts would have been more along the lines of: the sun was up, there weren't any clouds blocking its rays, and it was really, really bright. Like, how boring was that? No matter how you said it, Mother Nature had sure produced one nice deserted (looking) beach. Go figure, it was a human who'd totally screwed up that whole deserted beach thing with his big stupid feet.

Hearing the blades of the helicopter chopping through the air as it flew over the island she looked up to see Adam, strapped into position with his legs straddling the gryo mount and hanging out the open side door, the big camera looking down on her. As mad as she was at whoever had messed up the beach, she was glad she didn't have Adam's job. She hated heights and there wasn't a paycheque big enough to ever get her to hang out the side of a helicopter! There was, however, a paycheque big enough to get her up at the crack of dawn on her day off to rake smooth a set of footprints on a supposedly deserted beach. Besides, she hadn't really been sleeping in, but Esther didn't need to know that. If Esther had called her room two minutes earlier Rob would have answered the phone and that would have ignited an explosion of gossip. One explosion a day was Pam's limit (unless she was being paid double overtime).

The two-way radio hanging from her belt crackled to life.

"How much longer, Pam?" Esther asked. "They're getting antsy over here."

I'll bet they are, Pam thought. She also bet that more than one camera was focused on her, watching and waiting to see how she'd react to what she'd found.

Even though the sun had only been up for about an hour it was already stinking hot and humid. Her bangs were plastered to her forehead, a trickle of sweat ran down her spine as she stood up straight. Squinting hard, Pam turned to see if she could pick out Esther in the sea of humanity that was clumped together at the other end of the long, long beach. Resting the rake on her own foot she brought the radio to her mouth. "Fifteen minutes, tops."

"Okay, thanks."

That was it? Esther was good, really good. She hadn't given anything away, but Pam knew that she was probably squirming with curiosity, wondering if Pam had seen the foot yet. Esther and her crew were going to be disappointed by Pam's reaction; she'd make damn sure of that. Pam and her crew, on the other hand, were guaranteed a big reaction to their carefully planned shocker. It was way better than Esther's stunt — gorier, too, if the blood bags had survived the night.

Most of Pam's crew were hiding behind the rocks just north of where Esther and her crew were congregated. They'd be wondering what the holdup was, but she couldn't radio them to fill them in. Operation *Albert Go Boom* required complete radio silence to safeguard the element of surprise. The sooner she finished wiping out any trace of the footprints, the sooner the fun could start.

But first she had to deal with the severed foot. It had been submerged in a tidal pool that was about the size of a transport truck's tire. The cameras on the ground couldn't see it but Adam's camera had spotted it when he'd tried to shoot the beauty shot approach to the beach.

Waves sloshed around Pam's knees as she walked into the water and bent over to get a better look at it.

"Oh, please," she said to no one but herself. "Is that the best they could do?"

The shallow water in the tidal pool blurred the tentacles of a small blue octopus tattoo on what was left of the ankle. An orange starfish had draped one of its arms, or legs, or whatevers, over the big toe. Pam lifted the foot out of the water, shook the starfish off and looked harder at the tattoo. It was just like the octopus that Kate had on her left ankle. The little-girl pink coloured chipped polish on the toenails looked like Kate's shade of choice, too. Wow, that was bitchy.

Yeah, Kate's kid-in-a-candy-shop, *"This is soooo cool!"* enthusiasm had worn thin mighty fast (like on the second day), but still. Kate was right, they did have the coolest jobs in the world — but the pros, even junior pros like Pam who'd only worked on a couple of shoots, never publicly admitted how cool they thought their jobs were. Sleeping with one of the big bosses hadn't scored Kate any points in the popularity pool either. Somebody sure had a hate on for her — the fake foot thing wasn't a love letter.

It felt clammy and it was cold. Really cold. Whatever plastic the special-effects guys had used for skin hadn't reacted well to the salt water — it was all puffed up and looked kind of waxy. Under the fake skin the red meat of muscle that circled the bones looked like a thin strip of thawing frozen steak wrapped around two wooden straws that had gunk in them. She poked the meaty bit with her finger, it was frozen meat of some sort — how unoriginal. The straws were what really gave it away. There was only supposed to be one leg bone going from the ankle to the knee, at least that's what she remembered from the song she'd sung as a kid, *the leg bone's connected to the ankle bone,* or something like that. The ankle bone — as in just one.

It was kind of creepy that the crews had both gone gross for their last stunts, but that could be because of the arrival of the incoming movie crew's special effects team. Or maybe they'd all just started to think alike. After two months on the island they were one big, happy, slightly demented, definitely dysfunctional family and Pam loved it. Production life was her crack. She'd been addicted from her very first day on her very first production.

Of course there was a down side to working with people who got to know you so well. Everyone knew how scared she was of anything creepy or crawly or gross. That's why she'd been sent to find the foot, she was sure of it. They were probably all sitting around, microphones and cameras ready and waiting for the scream. She'd show them.

Calmly, without even a hint of a girly scream, Pam threw the foot as hard as she could out into the sea. It splashed into the water and caught the attention of a passing pelican. The big bird pulled his wings into his body and nosedived into the water. She didn't bother to wait and see how the bird reacted. Instead, she looked up at Adam. He'd turned to shoot the flight path of the foot. Weird. He'd watched the foot, not her reaction. Whatever.

Adam looked around the camera and kicked his legs to wave goodbye as the helicopter banked to one side and swerved off around the point.

Pam quickly finished raking smooth the footprints that led to the treeline and then made her way to where the real action was about to happen. Quietly weaving through the crowd, she sat down in the empty folding canvas chair next to Esther's.

"Everything okay down there?" Esther asked expectantly.

"Yup, all done." Pam faked a yawn and tried to look bored.

"Quiet on the set!" the assistant director shouted into a bullhorn.

Esther stood up and walked down into the water, staying off to the side of the crew so that her footprints in the sand would be out of the shot.

Numerous camera operators shouted out a chorus of "Recording."

Esther stood in the epicentre of the semicircle of cameras and held the electronic slate board out in front of herself.

"Hang on," one of the sound guys shouted and pointed to the sky.

Pam looked up and couldn't see anything but blue. Then she faintly heard a mechanical humming sound. The sound grew louder as the propeller-driven Air Sunshine flight from San Juan came into view and buzzed over the island, making its final approach to the neighbouring island, Virgin Gorda.

"We're clear now," the sound guy gave a thumbs-up signal and adjusted his large headphones.

"I'm not," the cameraman in the chair at the top of the crane yelled. With his camera he followed the plane until it dropped out of sight behind Gorda Peak and then turned to focus back on the set. "Clear."

The assistant director pointed at Esther. "Do the slate!"

"Judy Ingram's Butler Hotel commercial, scene three, take one." She held the slate board up long enough to allow all the cameras to get the timecode, then ran through ankle deep water until she knew she was out of the shot and walked up the beach to join Pam in the shade of the leaning palm tree.

The model and her diver had been standing out where the water was chest deep. The diver put his gloved hand on the model's shoulder, handed her a mouthpiece from his oxygen tank and they both went under and disappeared from sight.

After a moment of silence the commercial director nodded to his assistant director who called for action through the bullhorn.

Like Nessie breaching the waters of Loch Ness the blonde bombshell's head rose out of the water (minus the mouthpiece and oxygen hose) and she walked slowly toward the beach. The water droplets that ran down and over her almost-translucent bikini glistened like glycerine. As she got closer Pam could see that her nipples had visibly hardened and were almost poking through the gauze-like pasty-sized cups of the bikini top. Then the good stuff started.

At first it was just a dull mechanical whine, but it got louder quickly.

"What is that?" someone whispered.

Pam looked to see if Esther had heard it. She had. She was looking at the rocks just off the shore, her eyebrows all scrunched up. Her eyes opened wide when the small skiff came out from behind the rocks and turned as if to follow the blonde babe's path. The babe just kept on strutting out of the water toward the beach.

"Who's driving that thing?" A camera assistant asked no one in particular.

"Is there supposed to be a boat in this shot?" a producer quickly flipped through the papers on her clipboard.

Pam bit her lips together to hide her smile. This was going to be awesome! The only thing that worried her was the sound of the engine. The boat looked like it was moving slower than it had during their practice run the night before, and the engine sounded like it was straining. *Come on, come on*, she chanted to herself. It only had a few more feet to go to get into position in front of all the cameras.

Finally the babe noticed that everyone was looking behind her, not at her. She turned to see what was going on.

And that's when the dummy in the skiff blew up. He blew sky high. His Styrofoam head split in two and the biggest chunk of his chest hurtled through the air, one of the staple-gun attached arms still stuck to it. A big ball of orange fire rolled up into the sky leaving behind very little smoke. The skiff nosedived and sank quickly.

The babe screamed.

Her diver popped up out of the water like a cork.

Esther ran into the water. Her big floppy sun hat flopped and then just plain drooped as it got soaked by the water she was splashing up.

The babe screamed even louder when the bloodied half-melted torso bobbed in the water beside her.

Pam slapped one hand over her mouth and wrapped her free arm around her ribcage to hold her laughter in. The torso landing near the babe had been an unexpected bonus.

Esther bent over and looked at the floating hunk of chest. She slowly stood up straight and began to march (as best as she could in the waist-deep water) back to the beach, dragging the hunk of chest behind her by holding onto the still attached arm. "This is sick. Really sick!" She tossed the imitation chest onto the beach. The arm landed with a wet thwack on the sand.

The Sharpie pen that Pam and her gang had used to identify the chest had lived up to its advertising. The black ink hadn't faded or washed out. Still clearly visible on the bloodied Styrofoam were big black block letters that spelled out *RIP ALBERT*.

Some people, most of them actually, laughed. Nobody liked Albert.

One person was royally pissed, though. Unfortunately, that one person was their boss, James Butler, the co-executive producer of the show. His face was beet red and that wasn't because of a sunburn.

He yanked the bullhorn out of the assistant director's hand and screamed into it, "God damn it! Do you have any idea how much money you're wasting on these stupid stunts? You want me to start taking that money out of your paycheques?"

The laughter stopped mostly, but a few giggles could still be heard. James' partner, Dan, was still laughing. Pam could tell it was him because of the loud snorting sound he made in between laughs.

James barked orders. Anyone and everyone in a position of authority followed suit and shouted out orders to their respective juniors.

Pam, Esther, and two more production assistants were sent out to pick up any skiff debris and remaining bits of the fake Albert. Pam didn't mind the job; it was way better than raking a beach. But Esther was not amused. "That was taking it too far, you know. Naming the dummy. It makes it kind of creepy, blowing Albert up like that."

"Hey, at least he's not here to hear about it." Using the beige hat that had blown off Albert's split head, Pam scooped up a couple of small pieces of shattered wood that were floating near her. "Kate's going to be all sad and pouty when she finds out that you put a tattoo just like hers on that severed foot."

Esther tilted her head to the side like a curious dog. "What severed foot?"

CHAPTER
ONE

My foot was killing me and I had no one to blame but myself (but I'd never admit that to Glenn). If I'd walked up the uneven stairs at a leisurely, middle-aged, sedate, boring pace I wouldn't have slipped and my foot wouldn't have jammed between two of the slabs that the Inca stonemasons had laid down over five hundred years earlier.

Glenn had done the adult thing, sticking to his methodically made plans. He was probably just landing in Toronto to return to his job so that he could continue to live up to his responsibilities. It was because of my job that I'd been offered the chance to hike up Huayna Picchu early in the morning before the trail opened to the public. The mountain rose proudly above and beyond Machu Picchu. I'd seen it a million times in the background of photographs of the ruins and had always wondered what the view was like from the other side.

While Glenn waited for his checked baggage, probably worrying that the airline had lost it, or sat stuck in a taxi during morning rush hour on the eastbound Highway 401 across the top of the city, I had Machu Picchu's main square above the clouds all to myself as I limped back to the hotel. There was no amount of money in the world that could have tempted me to trade places with him.

How could he come all this way and not want to see Machu Picchu from the peak of Huayna Picchu? He'd said he couldn't come, but that wasn't true. He could have — he chose not to. He didn't want to alter or deviate from his carefully scheduled travel plans. The unexpected private access to Huayna Picchu meant I had to change my flights too, but so what? The adventure of climbing through clouds, the strange-sounding birds, the brilliantly coloured flowers (the Dancing Lady orchid was my favourite — it really did look like a dancing lady, her yellow-and-red skirt flared out as she spun around), the feeling of being cut off from the world when a thick patch of mist swallowed up the Lost City beneath me — all of those experiences had been worth every minute of every phone call to the airlines. Even the pain in my foot was worth it.

Yet, as mad as I was at him for his stick-in-the-mud attitude, I couldn't help thinking that the adventure would have been more fun if I'd had someone to share it with. When I'd sat on the ledge of a temple ruin, my feet dangling in the air over a thousand feet above Machu Picchu and almost nine thousand feet above sea level, the powerful Urubamba River swirling around the base of the mountain hideaway, it had literally taken my breath away (and not just because of the lack of oxygen). How wondrous it was that such a gem had lain hidden beneath the overgrown jungle for so long. The jungle had been cut back, but the city was still capable of hiding when the mist rolled over it. After spending eight days almost glued to Glenn I'd turned to share a smile that said *Wow, aren't we lucky to be here*. The boulder I saw when I turned my head didn't smile back.

As I walked the length of the cultivation terraces on my way back to the hotel I passed one of the resident environmentally friendly lawn mowers, a big white llama, and his face looked like he was smiling at me. But it wasn't good enough.

Mateo, the nice man at the front desk of the hotel, smiled at me, but he lost some of his niceness when he called me *Señora*. Despite my nearing-fifty-year-old exterior, I still thought of myself as more of a *Señorita*. (Glenn thought I should act in accordance with my exterior. Apparently, there was some secret rulebook that outlined how one was to behave at a certain physical age. Having never read it, I acted the way I felt instead. I felt closer to thirty than that mind-blowing number that started with a five.)

"You have had a phone call from Canada, Señora Butler."

Had Glenn seen the error of his mouth and called to apologize? I quickly unfolded the slip of paper that Mateo handed me. *Please call your father.* Something was wrong.

I was able to ignore the pain in my foot as I ran to my room, but my aging knees wouldn't let me forget about the hike down Huayna Picchu. Despite the age of the ruins, the phone system in the hotel was blessedly modern. After a series of clicks I heard my call to Toronto go through. I wanted Dad to pick up the phone and answer in a strong and healthy voice. Instead, my niece Melinda answered.

"Where are you?"

"Still in Machu Picchu."

"You never call when you're away. What's wrong?" Mel was a very direct thirteen-year old.

"Nothing's wrong." Dad wouldn't have told her even if there was. "I just wanted to tell Dad about a spectacular hike I took this morning while it's still fresh in my mind." I hoped Mel would believe me and wouldn't hear the fear in my voice.

"Shouldn't you be writing it down instead? I figure that's what travel writers do, write about travel — not call home to talk about it."

"Thanks for the career advice, Mel. I'll make a note of it, in writing. Now will you please get Dad for me?"

"GANDY!" Mel screamed, without bothering to take the phone away from her mouth. "It's Aunt Ria. Something's wrong. She's calling from Peru."

"Mel, nothing's wrong, okay?" I wasn't sure if I was trying to convince her or me.

"Like anyone would tell me about it even if there was. Want to tell me about the birds you've seen while they're still fresh in your mind?"

Birds were the last thing on my mind but they gave me something uplifting to talk about while I waited for Dad. "I saw a Blue-crowned Motmot on the hike up the Inca Trail."

"You did?" Her interest in anything ornithological outweighed her sarcastic streak. "Did you get its call for me?"

"I was able to record it for about two minutes. You were right, they do sound a bit like owls. And, you'll be pleased to know, I even got a close-up of it swinging its strange looking blue tail feathers back and forth like a pendulum."

"Male or female?"

"I don't know. I didn't flip it over and look between its legs."

Mel sighed heavily. "You can tell a bird's sex by its plumage, Aunt Ria. Everybody knows that!"

I knew it too, but wanted to keep Mel's mind off questioning the real reason for my call. "I tried to get a close-up of a Cock-of-the-Rock but he flew away before I could get him in focus. You can see his big orange head, but you can't really tell what he is." Thankfully, Dad picked up an extension somewhere in the house just then.

"Ria?"

"Hi, Dad."

"You two want me to hang up now, right?" Mel asked. "Then you can talk about whatever's wrong."

"Nothing's wrong!" Dad and I said in unison. I hoped he was telling the truth.

"Yeah, right. Don't forget to get me some shots of Blue-footed Boobies when you're in the Galapagos. Maybe you should, I don't know, write yourself a note so you won't forget?"

"Goodbye, Mel," Dad and I spoke in unison, again.

I heard the click of her hanging up. "What's wrong?"

Dad laughed, a healthy laugh. "And you wonder why Mel's the way she is? Genetics, Ria. You can't fight 'em."

"Are you okay?"

"I'm great. I went and got topped up with a quart last Friday so I'm feeling downright perky."

Dad's lighthearted description of getting a necessary blood transfusion didn't alleviate my constant worries. "Why did you call?"

"Because someone named Roger Kerr has been trying to reach you. I gave him your work number and told him that you'll be back in Toronto in a couple of weeks, but he says it can't wait, that he needs to talk to you as soon as possible."

"I don't know anyone called Roger Kerr. Did he give you any idea why he was calling?"

"Well, I think that's fairly obvious, don't you? He was calling because he wants to talk to you."

Dad was right about those genetics. There was no denying, or fighting, the sarcastic gene in my family. "Your genius-level IQ continues to underwhelm me. Now get serious."

"Sorry, my IQ was functioning properly, but my ESP was apparently malfunctioning at the time. The only thing he was clear on was that he needed to talk to you urgently."

"His name isn't ringing any bells for me."

"Well, he won't stop ringing my telephone bell. And speaking of names, he didn't use your full name. He asked for Ria, not Maria, so you definitely know him."

I had absolutely no idea who Roger Kerr was or why he was calling me so urgently. I pulled my notebook out of the backpack

I'd dropped on the floor when I'd scrambled to call Dad. "What's his number?" The pen that was jammed in the spiral coil that held the notebook together gave me a fight, but I managed to free it while Dad found his Braille notes and ran his finger over them to get the number for me. "Where's area code two-eight-four?"

"You're the travel expert. Don't you recognize it?"

I'd travelled so much that the world was like a giant Sudoku puzzle of area codes, printed on a constantly twisting Rubik's Cube. "No. I guess I'll find out where he is and who he is when I call. Are you really okay?"

"Yes, I really am, so stop worrying."

Dad stopped talking so abruptly that I knew he had more to say. "But?"

"But nothing. It'll wait until you get back."

"What will wait?"

"It's probably nothing — but, have you spoken to James recently?"

"Who?" It had been over three months since I'd heard from my brother.

"I'll take that as a no."

"What's he done now?"

"I'm not sure, but Victoria's been decidedly distant lately. I just wondered if you knew what was going on between them."

"I'd be the last person he'd talk to about that! I'd give him an earful and he knows it." As much I loved my younger brother, he was a jerk of a husband. Even Glenn, who'd been James' best friend since kindergarten, had let a few comments slip that made me wonder if he was finding it harder to forgive some of his buddy's sins. "Last I heard he was all wrapped up in putting together a new show, and you know none of us exist when he's doing that. Why don't you call him and ask him straight out, if you're worried?"

"I don't want to stick my nose in where it's not wanted."

"Yeah, right," I scoffed. "Oh, look! A pig just flew by."

"Sarcasm is the lowest form of wit…."

"And the highest form of intelligence, or so my father says. Listen, I'm sure James will be in touch once he rejoins the human race."

"I guess so. And that should be fairly soon. They must be close to finishing their location shoot."

Talking about James' production twigged something in my brain. "Dad, the man who called me, are you sure about his name?"

"Fairly certain, why?"

"Could he have said Rob Churcher? It sounds a lot like Roger Kerr."

"Possibly."

It couldn't have been him, could it? Rob Churcher? Nah! Or … fluke of all flukes … were the gods of timing finally smiling on us? Were we both single at the same time? Maybe he was calling to ask me out? That didn't make sense — there wouldn't have been any urgent need for me to call him back (unless he was only going to be single for a very, very short time). Then there was that other pesky little issue — was I single? Damned if I knew. Even though our week in Machu Picchu had technically been only our sixth official date, Glenn and I had settled into domesticity with alarming alacrity. That settling had unnerved me and was probably one of the reasons why I'd refused to *define our relationship* when he asked me to.

"Who's Rob Churcher?" Dad brought my thoughts back into the here and now.

"He's just a guy," I heard myself say.

"I was able to deduce that from the timbre of his voice."

"He works for James; he's a cameraman." An incredibly sexy cameraman whom I'd never seen playing Lego with my little brother. I'd only known him as a full-grown man.

"And?"

"And nothing."

"Hmmm, it sounded like there was a lot of something in that nothing, but I won't push. Instead, I'll ask — how was the week with Glenn?"

"It was okay." I didn't want to talk about Glenn.

"Read that, I don't want to talk about Glenn, right?"

"Right."

"Go make your call, Ria. You know that I'm here for you, if and when you want to talk. Don't forget to pick up a *sampoña* for Mel."

"I won't." I made a note to remember to buy a Peruvian flute because I knew my brain was short-circuiting and I'd probably forget. Mel would have been proud of me for writing it down.

After giving my courage an injection of carbonated caffeine I was able to make the call. I sat on the edge of the hard chair in front of the small desk in my hotel room and looked at myself in the mirror. I'd resisted the urge to brush my hair and put makeup on. Even if — and it was a big if — the man on the other end of the line did turn out to be Rob, he wouldn't see that my freckles were more pronounced after being in the sun, my cheekbones were sticking out too much because I wasn't eating enough calories to make up for the ones I was burning, and there were more grey hairs spreading out between my ridiculously red ones than I'd noticed before. I wasn't smiling so I didn't have to deal with counting my crow's feet.

"Thank you for calling The Butler BVI. How may I direct your call?" A woman with a rich Caribbean accent lyrically asked me.

The Butler BVI? Since when did we own a hotel in the British Virgin Islands? I must have heard her wrong. "I'd like to speak to Roger Kerr, please."

"Just a moment please."

Damn. Dad hadn't heard wrong.

"I'm sorry, Ma'am, but we don't have a guest going by that name."

"What about Rob Churcher? Is he there?"

"I'll put you through to his room."

Hot damn!

"Hello?" A female voice answered.

Was that his wife? "Is Rob Churcher there?"

"Hang on." The woman dropped the phone on something hard and the resulting bang painfully pounded my eardrum. "Rob! Phone's for you. Thanks for the shirt."

I heard a door close, then another one open and the last swirl of a toilet flushing.

"Hello?" Dad had been right; there was no mistaking the timbre of Rob's voice as feminine or even effeminate.

"Hi, Rob. It's me. Ria," I added quickly. "My father said you were looking for me."

"Hey, Ria!" He sounded happy to hear from me. That was a good sign … of something. "I knew your dad would be able to find you. Where are you?"

"Machu Picchu."

"For work?"

"Yeah, and you? You're working on James' Caribbean shoot?"

"Yeah." Rob cleared his throat. "That's actually why I was calling you. Ria, something's going on here and I think James is involved."

My disappointment at hearing that his call had something to do with my annoying brother was quickly replaced by concern. "What do you mean *something's going on*?"

"It's complicated and I can't really get into it on the phone."

"Is James in trouble?"

"Not yet."

"But you think he will be?"

"Yeah, I do."

"How bad?"

"Really bad."

Our conversation was turning into a game of Twenty Questions with very few answers. "Can you get a little more specific?"

"Hang on, someone's at the door," Rob put the phone down, presumably on the same hard surface that the woman before him had, but he did it gently.

From the sound of it several people had been at Rob's door, all of them male, and all of them had come into his room.

"I'm on a call, just give me a minute," Rob said to his visitors. "You still there?"

"I'm here."

"Okay, so the thing is, I was kind of hoping that you'd be able to put me in touch with a friend of his. The guy's name is Greg or Glenn, or something like that."

"What for?" I said with more irritation than Rob deserved.

"Like I said, there's something going on." Rob, too, started to sound a bit miffed. "James told me what his area of specialty is and I think James needs some help in that area right now."

Why would James need the help of the investigative journalist who covered the crime beat for Canada's largest national newspaper? Whose specialty was solving murders, sometimes with the police, sometimes before them? "You're not saying that James is involved in a murder!"

"I could be wrong. I mean, I'm not even sure it happened, but I think it did."

"Well, either there's a dead body or there isn't." How could anyone be unsure about something like that?

"We only found a piece of it."

That stopped me cold. "You found a piece of a body?"

"Uh-huh."

My protective-big-sister genes instantly revved up to full speed and pushed the most obvious question (*Which piece?*) to the back of my mind. "James wouldn't kill anyone!" He had done an awful lot of incredibly dumb things to grab attention over the years, he was the middle child after all, but even for him murder would be taking it too far.

"I think you're right, but that doesn't mean he isn't involved."

"Jalopy's loaded and call time's in five!" someone yelled very close to Rob. "Let's go, dude!"

"See this thing I'm speaking into? I'll be out in two minutes!" He waited until some banging and male grumbling stopped before speaking to me again. "I really have to go. If you could call the guy and get him to contact me …"

"What do you want him to do?"

"Come down here, like now, but without telling James why he's come. Whether James admits it or not I'm pretty sure he's going to need someone who's on his side, someone who can find out what really happened."

Glenn was like family to James, but I was real family. If James needed someone on his side I was more suited to the job than Glenn. I didn't have his investigative expertise, but I definitely had more experience taking care of and protecting my little brother. In fact, more often than not, Glenn had been the one to get James into trouble when they were teenagers. I'd been the one they'd come to to fix it. "Are you really, really sure about this? You're being pretty vague. Can't you give me anything solid?"

"How's this for solid — why would somebody who supposedly left the island of her own accord leave her foot in a tidal pool and hide her luggage at James' place? And why, when I tried to talk to him about it, did James threaten to fire me?"

For the second time in as many days, I made a snap decision to change my flights. "I'll come."

"You?" Rob's disappointment travelled through the phone lines with digital clarity.

"Yes, me." He could have tried to sound pleased at the chance to see me.

"But —"

"James will know something's up if Glenn suddenly shows up. Let's just say Glenn's not great at making spur of the moment travel decisions." To put it mildly. "I doubt he'd even do it. And James won't be as suspicious if I show up." That wasn't entirely true, but I hoped I'd be able to come up with a believable reason for a surprise visit by the time I had to face James. "Where are you?" I gripped my pen so tightly that my fingertips turned white.

"At one of your hotels, on Soursop in the British Virgin Islands. James isn't staying here, though. He's rented a villa on Virgin Gorda. He's … ah … he's not alone there, if you get my drift."

Oh, goody. James was at it again. I wouldn't blame my sister-in-law if she pulled a Lorena Bobbit and cut off a piece of James' body. "I'll be there as soon as I can."

I sat staring at myself in the mirror for quite a few minutes after our call ended. What had the woman in the mirror just agreed to? Glenn was the investigator, not her! I gave my head a shake. I was worrying about nothing, it was a misunderstanding. It had to be. But Rob had sounded seriously worried. And something bad must have happened for James to threaten to fire his oldest and most trusted employee.

It took me less than half an hour to jam all my stuff into my carry-on bag. (Unlike Glenn, I'd mastered the art of travelling without checked luggage.) I managed to catch the next bus to Aguas Calientes and jumped on the train up to Cusco just as it was about to pull out. Four hours later I was walking the streets of Cusco, trying to find the perfect *sampoña* for Mel. My journey from cloud forest to rain forest began in earnest (and a whole lot of airplanes) the next morning.

I felt like the bouncing ball in a cartoon sing-a-long as my flights took me from Cusco to Lima, San Salvador, Miami, and then San Juan. The last flight, from San Juan to Virgin Gorda, was on the smallest plane and I had to sit squished into a little seat beside the biggest big jerk.

He was dressed entirely in beige — beige sunhat, beige short-sleeved shirt, beige Bermuda-length shorts. Even the knee-high socks he wore beneath his open-toed sandals were beige. His skin was pasty white. His entire face was tightly scrunched up — lips pursed, eyes almost closed, hooked nose wrinkled. I tried striking up a conversation with him but he just glared at me, snorted, pulled his sunhat down further on his head (hiding the few tufts of short pitch-black hair that had been visible), quickly licked his lips with a lizard tongue, and then shifted in his seat to turn his back to me. So I replied in kind by snorting, turning my back on him, and exaggerating my movements just enough to be able to *accidentally* jab his scrawny bicep with my elbow.

I stared out the window and tried, for the umpteenth time and flight, to come up with a reason for my visit that James would believe. The conniving side of my brain refused to work, because the travel writer side had gone into overdrive. Four thousand feet below me the Caribbean lived up to its advertised magical colour, darkening only when covering a coral reef. Two mammoth cruise ships were in St. Thomas' harbour, their passengers probably enjoying the duty-free nirvana of Charlotte Amalie. St. John was the next island, most of it covered in the lush green of Virgin Islands National Park. The next big island was Tortola — we'd crossed into British territory. Only slighter smaller than St. Thomas, its population density was significantly less. We passed over a small grouping of pebble-sized islands and started our descent.

Virgin Gorda's shape reminded me of a Halloween witch riding her broom. Most of her twenty-five-hundred inhabitants live in the brush end of her broom. There is another pocket of civilization in the curve of her broom handle. As we got closer to the sea I could see a secondary population of sailboats moored in her many bays.

After banking around a tall forested peak I saw the itty-bitty runway and realized that I'd run out of time. I still hadn't thought of a plausible excuse for my visit.

I let Mr. Grumpy (whom I'd affectionately named Gus) go ahead of me. His long skinny (pasty) legs strode quickly toward the lone little airport building. I walked more slowly, thoroughly enjoying being in a non-air conditioned environment, letting my skin soak up the humidity and inhaling the salt-scented air. It looked like Gus and I were the only passengers who hadn't brought checked baggage, because the people who'd filled the other four passenger seats were standing around waiting for their bags to be handed to them from the open cargo door of the plane. Gus, clutching his beige leather overnight bag, had gone through a doorway at the far end of the building. I followed him.

A uniformed BVI customs official was seated at a folding table just inside the room. "Welcome back, Mr. Black." He stamped Gus's passport, which I noticed was Canadian. (At least Gus' last name had some colour in it.)

Gus went outside through the open door on the other side of the small room. Then the customs officer looked at me and held his hand out. "Reason for your visit?" he asked as I handed him my passport.

"Why are you here?"

Same question, but with different words and coming from a different mouth.

James stood in the doorway that Gus had just used as an exit. He looked so much like our grandfather — short, stocky, with receding thick dark hair, and Grandpa's screwed up toes on display in his sandals — but he wasn't smiling Grandpa's smile. He was scowling James' scowl.

"Surprise!" I forced my lips to spread into a smile.

Holding the ink stamp in mid-air, the customs officer looked from me to James. "Is she with your production, Mr. Butler?"

"No! She's my sister and I have no idea why she's here. Go on, Ria, explain it to both of us."

"Vacation." The stupid smile was still plastered on my face.

"Right." James' lie meter, his left eyebrow, shot up.

"And where will you be staying?" the customs officer just had to ask.

"Um, I was going to, I mean, I thought I'd …"

"My guess? She'll be staying with me. You came for some family bonding time, right?"

Oh boy. "Yup, that's why I'm here."

Bang went the customs stamp onto my passport. "Enjoy your stay, Miss Butler."

"Where are your bags?" James asked.

"I don't have any."

"Let's go." James turned around and walked out into the sunshine.

I ran after him. "James, wait up!"

My brain was running as fast as my feet and I quickly threw together enough words to form a weak (very weak) excuse for my surprise arrival. But I didn't get a chance to use any of those words. I became speechless when I saw who was sitting in the Jeep that James was standing beside.

My old pal, Grumpy Gus.

"That's Albert. He's part of the production team." James heaved himself into the driver's seat. "I just have to drop him off at the marina and then we'll go to the villa."

"Nice to meet you, Albert." I gave him the sweetest smile I could muster as I contorted to get into the back seat.

His response was a nod and a tightened pucker.

A grand total of three turns and no words later, James had driven through the majority of downtown, low-rise Spanish Town. He turned into the parking lot of the Virgin Gorda Yacht Harbour and parked in one of the forty spots. Through a line of short palm trees I could see the marina itself. There were more parking spots for boats than there were for cars. Three long docks ran straight out from the shore. Sticking out from those docks like the tines on a comb were multiple smaller docks. In almost every slip there was a boat — some with masts, some with multiple engines, each of them worth more than any of the cars in the parking lot.

Albert got out of the car and, without wishing me a fond farewell, walked between the palm trees and down onto the docks.

"I just want to wait to make sure the boat's here for him," James said, his attention focused on Albert.

Under normal travel circumstances I would have wanted to take my time, look around, make note of my original impressions of the island, but these weren't normal circumstances. James, however, decided to play the part of a tour guide as I moved up to the front seat.

He pointed to single-storey building on our left. "That's the closest thing they've got to a mall," he said in a monotone. "There's a bank, a dive shop, a liquor store, and a pub called The Bath and Turtle. They make pretty good cheeseburgers." He looked to our right. "Over there's the grocery store and some showers and stuff for people on the boats."

I turned my head to look at what he was describing and pretended to be interested.

"There he goes." James nodded and started to back out of the parking spot.

Through the palm trees I saw the tallest structure I'd yet seen on the island, slowly making its way out of the marina and beyond the breakwater. Albert was apparently yachting in style — the boat he was on was three-stories high.

We turned onto the road we'd come in on, only this time we headed in the other direction and drove through the residential section of Spanish Town. After we passed the last house the Jeep strained as we headed up a steep hill. I kept having to remind myself that James was driving on the right side of the road, the left side. From my side of the car it felt like, and looked like, he was driving so close to the edge of a sharp drop down to the Caribbean that our inclusion in the fish food chain was imminent. When we crested the hill I forced myself to look up, away from the pencil-thin line of gravel that pretended to be the road's shoulder. What I saw was a postcard-perfect view of the small bay below us. Waves broke over a coral reef and then gently lapped the completely empty crescent beach.

"The villa's over there. You can have the bedroom on the top floor of the left wing for your *vacation*." James pointed at one of the two multi-level and terraced houses on the opposite hill. "I'm in the room below the main house."

I changed the topic as quickly as I could — to James' favourite topic, himself. "Why aren't you staying at the hotel?"

"I'd go insane over there, staying with the crew and everything. I can spend the day with them, but I need a separate place to find my sanity at the end of the day."

"You found your sanity? Sure took you long enough." His facial muscles didn't budge; he wouldn't be smiling or even smirking at my attempt at humour. "What are you shooting down here?"

"*Check-Out Time.*" He changed gears and let the engine take us down the other side of the slope. "This one's big. We've been picked up by one of the U.S. networks for a prime-time run." The topic change had improved his mood a bit.

"Should I say congratulations?" I already thought James was successful. He'd produced television shows and movies that had sold all over the world. Apparently prime-time U.S. network exposure was the Holy Grail of his profession.

"You should say *'Holy shit, that's great!'*"

"Okay. Holy shit, that's great." I said it with as much conviction as my exhaustion would allow. Fifty-five hours of travelling had wiped me out. "What's the show about?"

"It's a reality show. We started off with thirteen contestants, but we're down to the last two now. The prize is a one-year contract to manage the hotel. The cross promotion is a dream come true! Aunt Patti and Uncle Richard bought the island after the hotel on it was wiped out by some hurricane; they got it at a steal. They fixed it all up and our entire cast and crew have been staying there for free, which has saved me a fortune in below-the-line costs. They'll open to the public again in a couple of months, just in time for the high tourist season — and that's when the series will go to air, which'll give the hotel lots of free publicity. And, get this, I got my old boss, Dan Shykoff — you probably heard me talking about him when I started out — anyway, he's got a production company in LA now, and he signed on as co-executive producer and brought in the network boys. And he's exec producing a theatrical release that he's going to shoot on the island once we've finished shooting the series. His production's going to spend a fortune there, which'll make Aunt Patti and Uncle Richard happy. The cast and crew on the feature will be staying there for almost two months, at full price. The series is going to give his release some advance publicity," he took a deep breath, "and, if the numbers are as good as we hope they're going to be, he's going to bring me in as co-executive producer on his next feature." We went halfway up another hill, turned left on a painfully bumpy dirt road, and then swung into a short drive-way and parked. "I'm getting a shot at breaking into theatrical! Isn't that great?" He turned the car off and hopped out, burst-ing with happy energy.

"I guess so." It all sounded kind of convoluted to me, but James sure seemed happy about it. I got out of the car and walked around to join him on the driver's side.

He was bent over, getting something out from under the seat I'd been sitting in.

"It's a dream come true! All the pieces fit into place per-fectly. Well, except one — you."

His comment made me wonder where the body piece that Rob had mentioned fit in. Once I saw what James was holding when he stood up I started to wonder about something else. "Isn't that Albert's?" James was carrying the beige overnight bag.

He looked down at the bag in his hands and acted as if he'd just noticed that he was carrying it. "What, this?"

Rob was right — James was guilty of something. I instantly recognized the look that washed over his face. I'd practically raised him after our mother was killed, and could spot his guilty look a mile away. Right then that look was less than a foot in front of me. Despite the fact that he was in his forties, James looked exactly like he had when he was fifteen years old, standing in front of me with blood on the knuckles of his right hand, denying that he was the cause of the blood running out of the freshly broken nose of our younger brother, Evan.

"He must have forgotten it. I'll take it to him when we go over to the island for dinner. Come on. Let me show you the place." He stopped in front of a high wooden gate, unlocked it, and pointed at a sign on the rock wall beside it. "See? What did I tell you? It's a dream come true."

The oval sign had two artistically drawn palm trees in the middle of it. Circling around the palm trees, in red block letters, was the name of the villa — A Dream Come True.

James had always been the dreamer in our family. I'd learned, from too much life experience, that not all dreams had a happy ending. Mine usually ended when reality slapped me in the face.

CHAPTER
TWO

The stones in the stairway down to the villa had been laid more recently than the ones on the side of Huayna Picchu, and my nowhere-near-thirty-year-old knees were truly thankful for the smoother surface as I walked under an archway of palm fronds. Hot pink hibiscus flowers trumpeted our arrival when we stepped down onto the main patio. The villa was made up of two two-storey buildings, one on either side of the large patio we were standing on. Through its many windows I could see that the building on my left housed a great room on its ground floor. There weren't as many windows on the ground floor of the building on my right, so I couldn't see what was housed in it. Even if I could have, my eyes were drawn to a different view. Beyond the patio, between the two buildings, over the edge of a large horizon pool, was a priceless unobstructed view of the Caribbean that made whatever James had paid to rent the place a bargain. I instantly felt the urge to grab my camera — that was the money shot. Framed by purple-grey volcanic island shapes in the distance and brilliant red bougainvillea flowers on either side of the pool, I'd never seen the Caribbean look so spectacularly blue. The only things that ruined the view were the sparkling silver mounds that rose above the chest of the woman who was lying on a floating mattress in the pool. Her microscopic bikini top barely covered her tanned boobs. (They were too big and artificially round to be realistically called breasts.) Her blonde hair was just as bleached as the pale yellow crescent beach that curved around the bay below the villa.

She titled her mirrored sunglasses up and squealed, "Oh, hi!" when she saw me. Carefully clasping her silicone implants, she wiggled off the floating mattress and jiggled through the water to steps at the end of the pool nearest us. "I'm Mandy, Jamie's personal assistant."

I didn't know anyone named Jamie. I knew a James; he was my brother — my married brother. "I'm Ria, Victoria's sister-in-law."

"Huh?" Mandy looked confused. Her collagen inflated lower lip didn't meet up with its overly plump upper mate.

"Ria, don't," James' guilty look had been replaced by anger.

"I won't if you don't," I shot back. All he had to do was honour his wedding vows and I'd start acting like the nicest sister in the whole world.

"This tension is my cue to go get a drink," Mandy walked to the side door of the great room. "Do either of you two want anything?"

"No." We both said as we stood facing each other like two fighters waiting for the round to start.

James dropped Albert's bag on the patio and kicked it under one of the lounge chairs by the pool. "Your room's up here." He spun around and headed for the exterior stone stairway that led to the second floor of the other building.

Apparently, we were going to have our argument in private. That was fine with me. I matched the force of his stomps as I followed him up the stairs.

I'd barely closed to door behind me when James started. "What the fuck was that?"

"That was me reminding you that you're married." I tilted to the side and let my heavy bag slide off my shoulder and onto the massive four-poster king-sized bed.

"That's why you're really here, isn't it. Dad sent you to check up on me. Vic probably put him up to it. Or maybe Glenn told you to come?"

"Neither Dad nor Glenn knows I'm here. Neither does Victoria," I said with force backed by honesty. "And, for the record, Glenn doesn't control me — nobody *tells* me what to do!" It was the one and only time I'd ever said something about my relationship (or lack thereof) with Glenn to James. "I'm here on vacation. I needed a break and knew I'd find a free place to stay."

"Yeah, right! You needed a break from travelling, so you decided to do a hell of a lot of extra travelling. That makes sense. I guess it was that direct flight from Machu Picchu to Virgin Gorda that made this the most logical place for you to go?" He glared at me and then stormed across the room and flung open the doors to the room's private balcony. "Give me a break, Ria. You're full of shit and we both know it. You came here to check up on me."

"I'm not here to check up on you!" I hoped that James wasn't as good at recognizing my guilty look as I was at spotting his.

"Bullshit."

"Your bimbo isn't big news to me! It's not like it's the first time you've had one, is it? What's really bugging you? Is there something else that you're worried I'll check up on?"

"Fuck off!"

I opened my mouth to respond but my brain kicked in and stopped me from firing off an angry reply. If we kept fighting, something we'd always done only too well, I'd never find out what was going on. "Look, I haven't slept in two days, I'm tired, and maybe my crack to Mandy was a little bitchy, I'll admit that, but ..."

"A little bitchy?"

"Oh, I am so sorry if I wasn't all lovey-dovey with your slutty mistress, James. Or should I start calling you Jamie now?" So much for trying to calm things down — my mouth had over-ruled my head.

"She's my personal assistant!"

"And Victoria's your wife!" We'd completed the verbal circle and locked glares, neither one of us knowing how to break out of it.

James closed his eyes, sighed, and sat down on the edge of the cushion on the wicker settee. "Vic threw me out."

"Oh, shit." I would have sat on the edge of the bed but it was too high up. Instead, I sidestepped onto the wooden footstool beside the bed, pushed my bag over a bit and sat down.

"Glenn didn't tell you?"

I shook my head. "Uh-uh." Glenn knew? Why hadn't he told me? "Did Victoria find out about Mandy?"

"No. Mandy came in to audition for a new role on our soap the day after the blowout with Vic."

"She's an actress?"

His smirk told me that we were slowly working our way back to being brother and sister. "She wants to be, but there's one small problem with that — she can't act. Our director said hers was one of the worst auditions he'd ever seen." He leaned back and stretched his arms across the back of the settee. "So I hired her for the position of personal assistant."

I didn't want to think about the positions Mandy would get into to keep her job. "Do you care about her?"

He slapped his hands on his knees and stood up. "Grow up, Ria. This isn't about emotion. She's getting what she wants — a paycheque and production contacts — and I'm getting what I want." Thankfully, he didn't go into detail on his list of wants.

"And when this production's over?"

"We'll both move on. Don't look at me that way! Everybody does it on location shoots."

"If everybody jumped off a cliff would you do that, too?"

"Stop acting like my mother."

I somehow resisted the urge to tell him that he should stop acting like a spoiled brat. "Are you and Victoria going to get divorced?"

"I don't know. We've scheduled a meeting for when I get back, but I've heard that she's hired a pitbull of a divorce lawyer. They're probably coming up with a game plan to clean me out."

"I'm sorry, James. Really." It wasn't the time to once again tell him that I thought he'd never really appreciated how lucky he was to have Victoria.

He walked over to the side of the bed and stood in front of me. He looked like he was about to cry. "Can we be friends? I could really use a friend right now."

I smiled up at him. No matter what, he'd always be my brother and I'd never stop loving him. He looked so stressed. Some of the worry wrinkles across his forehead softened when he smiled back at me. But I had to wonder if it was just his marital problems that were making him so tense. Mandy didn't give me the chance to ask.

"Jamie! Dan's on the phone for you," she called up from the bottom of the stairs.

"I'd better take that," he said with a sigh as he walked to the door. He'd almost closed the door behind himself when he popped his head back into the room. "Oh, yeah, how did the week with Glenn go?"

"It was good." I mentally ended that sentence with one more word — *mostly*. Most of our time together had been good, verging on great even. But the bad time at the end of the week had taken the shine off of some of that good. James, however, was the last person I'd discuss it with.

I let myself fall back on the bed and stared up at the ceiling fan as it spun around above me. The bed was too comfortable. I knew I'd fall into a deep sleep if I didn't get up and soon. James had mentioned something about going over to the island for dinner and I definitely didn't want to miss that, not that I really cared about seeing the island. I wanted to see Rob and told myself that that desire came solely from my concern for James and whatever he'd gotten himself into.

I unpacked what little I had. After many tries I gave up trying to get an Internet connection on my notebook. I tried to check my voicemail on my cellphone but it wasn't getting any reception. Fighting sleep was getting harder to do by the minute so I decided to have a quick shower. The combination of the cold water and the stunning view from my open-air shower woke me up a bit. Wrapped in a towel, I lay on one of the lounge chairs on my balcony to drip dry. My eyelids lowered with the setting sun.

Stars were sparkling like diamonds scattered across the black velvet Caribbean sky when my eyes opened. I heard the rhythmic clang-clang-clang of halyards banging against a mast somewhere close by. Forgetting that I'd been wearing only a towel I stood up without holding it and it promptly fell to the ground. My instinct was to grab it immediately but then I adopted James' attitude of *why not?* No one could see me. My balcony, the whole villa in fact, wasn't overlooked by any other building. The only other villa in the bay was somewhere to my right, but if I couldn't see it neither it nor its occupants could see me. I walked over to the railing and saw the source of the halyard noises. A sailboat had anchored in the bay. Its interior lights weren't on but its mast, bow, and stern lights were; they swayed back and forth in time with the gentle waves. I could faintly see some lights on one of the islands in the distance. The glorious feeling of isolation from most of the world was momentarily spoiled when a car's headlights beamed up and over the hill we'd crested when we were driving in from the harbour. Its high-beams ran over the villa for a split second and then raced down the road that snaked along the island, finally pointing up and disappearing over the next hill.

I leaned over the railing and looked to my left to see if any lights were on in the main building of the villa. It was dark. Only the pool was lit up. Damn. I'd missed going for dinner on the island, missed seeing Rob.

When James had said that everyone did it, everyone had affairs or temporary relationships while on location, had that everyone included Rob?

A wave of impatience rolled through me. I wanted to get going. But I couldn't very well swim to Soursop, especially in light of the fact that I had no idea where it was. I tried lying down on the bed to see if I could get a few more hours sleep. The ceiling fan clicked every other turn. A cricket chirped incessantly just outside the window. Isolation wasn't as quiet as it was cracked up to be. Then I heard noises that made me move quickly.

"Ooh, Jamie! You're so big! Do it! Do it! Harder, baby, harder!"

Mandy sounded like a pretty good actress to me. She was putting on quite the performance, one that kept on going and going and going.

Given the earlier tension between James and I, I decided not to yell a friendly request — like *shut up!* Instead, I turned on the lights, pulled on a clean T-shirt and shorts, shoved my feet into my trainers, grabbed my MP3 player, and got going — going anywhere that wasn't within earshot of James' bedroom.

Mandy squealed out another "Baby, you're the man!" as I let myself out the gate at the top of the stairs. I wished she'd make up her mind — was he a baby or a man?

My eyes quickly acclimatized to the darkness and I headed down the road we'd driven in on. If the sun had set across the Caribbean from the balcony of my room, I knew it was going to rise on the other side of the island and I planned to find a spot to sit and watch it. I jammed the earbuds into my ears and clicked shuffle on my MP3 player.

By the time I found the best rock to sit on Michael Bublé was "Feeling Good," but not in a sexual way, thankfully. As he sang about the new dawn I watched the sun light up the new cloudless day. A family of goats bleated amongst themselves, a rooster crowed, the horns in Michael's song blared. ZZ Top's "Legs" pumped me up to power walk back to the villa. Emerson, Lake and Palmer's "Benny the Bouncer" accompanied me as I did some runs up and down the stairs at the villa. It wasn't until my seventh trip down that I realized there was a man standing in the great room watching me.

"Who the fuck are you?" he asked through an open window when I stopped and looked right at him.

"I'm Ria." I decided to give as good as I'd just got. "Who the fuck are you?"

"Dan Shykoff. Where's Mandy?"

"Still in bed, I guess."

"Oh. Okay. I'll go get her." He turned around and walked through the room and out the open doors that led to the covered veranda on the other side of the building.

James' partner was staying at the villa, too? It would have been nice if James had warned me.

I entered the great room by the back door and saw that Dan was leaning over the railing of the veranda at the far end of the room, but he wasn't saying anything, he was just leaning

— offering me an unwanted view of his butt. I decided to check out a different view and looked around the open concept room.

The ceiling was open to the high rafters. The gourmet kitchen shone. There was a spotlessly clean large glass dining table, surrounded by padded rattan chairs, near the picture windows that opened to the covered veranda and on the other side of the doors to the veranda there was a large seating area furnished with two padded rattan sofas. The smaller seating area across from the kitchen looked like it had been set up to watch the television, but someone had turned it into a mini office; there were files everywhere, a printer, a scanner, and two notebook computers … and Albert's bag. It was sitting beside the coffee table in front of the couch.

I heard Mandy giggle and then the sound of water running near Dan.

"Yoo-hoo! Mandy?" Dan called out, still bent over. "I hate to interruptus your morning coitus, but are you going to be long?"

"Jesus, Dan! Do you mind?" James' voice floated up from below the veranda.

"No, I don't mind at all, but it sounds like you do."

With Dan's attention focused elsewhere, I quickly walked over to the bag, kneeled down, and opened it. It was empty. The garbage can next to it, though, was overflowing with what looked like empty DVD cases.

Something electronic beeped in the kitchen, making me jerk, and I quickly zipped the bag closed again.

I jerked for the second, more startling, time when Dan asked, "Was that the coffee machine?" I hadn't heard him walk into the room. He was standing on the opposite side of the couch from me.

"I don't know." I stood up like a shot and got my first real frontal look at him. He was a slim older man with the kind of protruding belly that looked like he'd swallowed a basketball, probably in his late sixties, deeply tanned, with a small goatee and thick curly white hair that was almost too long, wearing tan loafers and linen pants, and a white silk shirt that had been left open one button too many.

"Why are you here so early?" James, wearing a terry bathrobe, his hair dripping wet from his interrupted shower, came through the doorway from the pool patio.

Dan turned around and sat on the back of the couch. "I need my morning coffee."

"What's wrong with the coffeemaker at your place?"

"I don't know how to work it and my cook won't be here for another half-hour."

"You need a babysitter more than a cook."

Dan went over to the coffeemaker and bent down to get his face close to the pot. "How do you know when this thing is done?"

"When it stops peeing into the pot." James looked at me and rolled his eyes. "I guess you two have met."

"I've met her, but I still don't know who the fuck she is."

James ignored Dan and kept his attention on me. "Sleep well? I went up to get you to come with us for dinner but you were comatose."

"I slept like a log; right up until someone felt the need to tell the world that you're the man. Congratulations on that, by the way."

"Sorry." At least he had the decency to blush. "Dan, Ria's my sister. She's going to be staying here for a couple of days."

"Actually," I decided it was as good a time as any to tell him of my change in plans, "I'm going to stay at the hotel."

"Is this because of … you know …" He was squirming, trying to find the right words that wouldn't make him look too guilty.

I didn't let him off the hook. "Pretty much."

"That'll work," Dan was still watching the coffeemaker with bizarre fascination. "We can use it. Get Mandy to call over first, like she's letting some big secret slip. She can say that another Butler is coming to do a surprise assessment of the last two players and then we can get them scrambling and sucking up on tape."

"I don't have anything to do with running the hotels, though." And I didn't want to have anything to do with the show they were making.

"So?" He turned just his head and looked at me. "They don't have to know that."

"She's not part of the show, Dan."

"She will be once she sets foot on the island. Make sure she signs a release before she goes." He walked away from the coffeemaker when Mandy bounced into the room, wearing only slightly more than she'd been almost wearing in the pool. "Thank Christ, you're finally here. Get me a cup of coffee, two creams, five sugars. And then I need you to send a couple of emails for me, carbon copied to Winnie."

"Okay," Mandy happily went about her assigned chores.

What a strange man James had chosen to work with. He made me even more certain that my decision to stay on the island was a good one. "I'm going to go have a shower."

"Ria, wait up." James followed me out to the pool patio. "You don't have to go …"

"Yes, I do." If he wanted to think my only reason for staying at the hotel was to get away from his slutty mistress, so much the better. "And by the way, your partner is a total wingnut."

"He prefers to use the word eccentric, but he's a fucking genius when it comes to distribution deal making."

"Where's his Mandy?"

"She quit," he replied a little too quickly. James' lying face flashed before me for an instant. "But she wasn't his personal assistant; she was just a production assistant working on the shoot. They hooked up after Dan flew in from LA and she moved into his villa. He's staying in the one just up the hill." He was giving me too many details that I hadn't asked for. "But I guess she didn't like it or something and she up and left, all of a sudden, without giving any notice or anything. Dan's secretary's here, too. She's worked for him forever, but she refuses to stay in the same building with him so she's staying on the island."

They both sounded like very smart women to me — one wouldn't stay with him and the other one left him.

Dan was dictating an email to Mandy when we left, but he stopped just long enough to tell her to give me a release to sign. I read it while James drove.

"Do I really have to sign this?" I asked James once we'd parked at the yacht harbour.

"Everyone on the island has to. We've got cameras everywhere and if you get caught in a shot we can't air your image without your permission."

"But I don't want my image aired."

"Please, Ria, don't cause me problems? I've already got enough of those. Just sign it and stay away from the cameras and I'll ask the editors not to use any shots that you show up in, okay?"

I begrudgingly signed my image away.

"Mandy called over to say you'd be coming, so they'll have a room ready for you. She asked for something private." James led me down a long wooden dock to a beautiful yacht. I recognized the stylized *B* on the flag it was flying — it was the Butler Hotels' *B*. Aunt Patti and Uncle Richard had gone all out with their spending! The yacht was big, really big, shiny black and multi-levelled, and it filled the slip completely. A muscular man in a white nautical uniform (with a Butler *B* embroidered on the breast pocket of his shirt) came down the steps from the upper saloon and smiled when he saw us. "Good mornin,' Mr. Butler."

"Hi, Malvin. This is my sister, Ria. She needs a ride over to the island."

"That's what I'm here for." He held his hand out to steady me as I stepped onto the large deck at the stern of the boat. "Welcome onboard."

I needed more than Malvin's firm grip to steady me when I saw Albert coming down from the saloon. He was carrying a large metal case that was labelled *Camera Originals*. I took the grunting sound that he made when he passed me as a friendly greeting and returned his pleasantries.

"Nice to see you, too, Albert." What a jerk.

"I'll be coming over later so why don't we have lunch?" James asked.

"You're not coming now?" I wasn't exactly sure what an executive producer did, but I'd assumed that they'd be there when their show was being shot. Apparently, I'd assumed wrong.

"No, I've got some stuff to do here."

I stood on the teak boards of the stern deck and watched James and Albert walk to the small parking lot as Malvin began to untie the ropes. James kept glancing back over his shoulder at me. What was he up to? Through the trees, I could see them both standing by the open back door of the Jeep.

"I forgot something." I jumped off the yacht and started running. "Be right back."

I ran down the length of the dock, across a grassy section, and then tried to hide behind the widest palm tree I could find. Albert had opened his metal case and James was flattening the empty beige overnight bag into it. When had he put that in the car? It must have been when I was in the shower.

And he must have pushed it under the seat so that I wouldn't see it. One of the first things Rob was going to have to do was give me a crash course in television production. Maybe the way they were moving DVDs around was normal? (I didn't really believe that — but I wanted to.)

Malvin was not only normal he was a fountain of information and exceptional tour guide as we bounced over the waves on our way to Soursop. I sat in the thickly padded leather chair next to his in the wheelhouse. He gave me a brief history of the British Virgin Islands, identified the islands we could see, and slowly opened up about some of what he'd seen while working for James. By the time we pulled up to the main dock at Soursop I knew that Albert's sole function on the production team was to take the discs from the cameras, the camera originals, back to the editors in Toronto. He came down a couple of times a week, spent one night at the hotel, and flew back up to Toronto the next morning. What I really wanted to know, though, was what he brought with him when he came down. Whatever he'd brought, it had stayed with James.

I also learned that the yacht Malvin was skippering was only used by James, Dan, and special guests of either the production or the hotel. The production staff and hotel employees travelled between Soursop and Virgin Gorda by a private ferry, and I was willing to bet their transportation wasn't nearly as luxurious as the yacht I was on. Their boat probably didn't have three bedrooms (Malvin called them staterooms) plus an extra bedroom for the crew, or a galley with every conceivable electronic gadget, or three marble-countered bathrooms — one with a full-sized bathtub, or a personal watercraft stored away under the stern deck, or a lower saloon that was just as nice — if not nicer — than some people's living rooms.

"When that crazy British chef came down I took him and his family out for a weekend. They seemed to enjoy that. Took them over to the Indians," he pointed to the west, "just off Norman Island, and his kids did some snorkelling. If you want to go diving or snorkelling just let me know. For overnight trips my sister comes along as the cook. Mr. Romney said she made him the best conch fritters he ever had. She still be smiling over that!"

"Nigel Romney stayed here? I thought the hotel wasn't open for guests yet."

"He be here for the show. Episode six — the kitchen challenge." He chuckled. "Between his yelling and cursing and Miss Ingram's crying it was quite a commotion. She was filleting a mahi mahi when she found out that it's a dolphinfish. Mr. Romney kept shouting 'It's not fucking Flipper, you idiotic woman!'" He looked at me quizzically. "You're not part of the show?"

"God, no! That's my brother's thing, not mine."

"So it be true, then? You coming to do a surprise inspection at the hotel?"

I shook my head and silently cursed Dan. "No, I'm just coming for a quick holiday. I don't have anything to do with Butler Hotels. Did someone say otherwise?"

"I heard a few whispers, but nobody's saying much out loud." He pointed ahead. "Looks like I'm not the only one who's heard the whispers." He geared the engines down and I looked up to see what he was talking about.

The island we were approaching reminded me of a Bactrian camel — it had two humps, only the island's humps were volcanic, not hairy. The northern hump was covered in emerald green foliage. The southern hump wasn't as green and I could see boulders poking out here and there, as well as some villas scattered on the hillside. On either side of the humps the land sloped down to the water, the island's shoreline was scalloped with sparkling white beaches. The hotel itself sat in the dip between the humps. Only four-stories high, it was fronted by a large covered veranda. A wooden walkway led to the front steps of the hotel from the dock we were pulling up to. The solitary dock was wide, wide enough to still look uncluttered despite the fact that at least six Butler uniformed people were standing in a perfectly straight line, presumably waiting to greet me, and beside them, behind them, kneeling in front of them, everywhere around them, was a swarm of television people, each person holding some sort of equipment. I tried to see who was holding the cameras, just in case Rob was one of them, but I couldn't see their faces behind the large lenses.

Two Butler employees from the line came to the edge of the dock and caught the ropes that Malvin threw to them. A small group of television people scurried along beside them. The man at the head of the line came forward.

"Welcome to Soursop, Miss Butler. I'm Ted Robarts, one of the acting managers. It's a pleasure to meet you." He had movie-star, dark good looks, in a rugged life-lived-hard middle-aged sort of way, a devilish George Clooney smile, shockingly white teeth, and startlingly blue eyes. They reflected the same ethereal blue as the densely compressed ice in an iceberg. He looked perfect for the part of a reality show winner. From what I'd seen, ugly people didn't usually make it to the final episodes.

"Hi." I felt uncomfortable being stared at by so many people. James' editors were going to have a really hard time editing me out of the shot — all of the cameras, except for the one that was focusing on Ted Robarts, were pointed straight at me.

"Andy!" Ted shouted and snapped his fingers. "Take Miss Butler's bags."

A man from farther down the line stepped forward and walked crisply toward me.

"It's okay," I said more to Andy than Ted. "I've got it." I pretended not to see Ted's outstretched hand and stepped onto the dock without assistance. Malvin handed me my bag and I heaved the strap onto my shoulder.

"As you wish," Ted almost bowed. "If you'll step this way," he waved his arm out from his body, "we can obviously forgo the formality of checking you in." He walked a deferential one pace behind me as we made our way down the dock. "I'll take you straight to your room. We've put you in Cottage 7. As I'm sure you know, it's our most private cottage."

"Watch out!" I yelled at the cameraman who was walking backwards in front of me. He was about trip over a large dock cleat. Another production person, a girl with a blonde bob and Sheepdog long pink bangs, put her hand on his shoulder and guided him around the cleat.

A shiny white golf cart was waiting for us at the end of the dock. It looked like it wanted to be an all-terrain vehicle when it grew up — there were two bench seats, plus a storage bin in the back, and it had the biggest tires I'd ever seen on a golf cart. The awning had a Butler *B* printed on it. Ted took the driver's seat. I dropped my bag in the storage bin and got in the front with him. A cameraman and his camera, someone holding a big microphone that was covered in fuzz, and the clipboard clutching girl with the Day-Glo bangs somehow all managed to squeeze themselves, and their equipment, onto the back bench. Once seated, I noticed the smaller camera mounted on the front of the golf cart, its lens pointed straight at Ted and me.

Ted commented on everything — and I mean everything — as we drove to my room. I heard about how many lights lit up the tennis courts at night, how many gardeners were needed to keep the beautifully landscaped grounds beautiful, how big a helicopter the island's helipad could handle, how many suites there were in the main building and how many cottages were scattered around the island, how many threads of Egyptian cotton were in the sheets on the bed I was going to sleep in (did someone actually count them?), how the luxury soaps in my bathroom were flown in from France, how the heated rocks that were used in the spa had been flown in from Polynesia, how my meals would be prepared by a two-star Michelin chef who was also a member of Relais & Châteaux — Relais Gourmands ... the more he talked, the more out of place I felt. I knew that the Butler chain liked to cater to the ridiculously wealthy, but I wasn't one of them and I didn't feel comfortable around them. I was more of a jeans, T-shirt, and cheeseburger kind of person. Thankfully the people we passed as we drove along the smoothly paved road looked like they were, too. (And I doubted that they cared any more than I did about how many barges had been used to bring the road construction equipment over to the island.)

Ted turned into a small driveway and the golf cart struggled to carry the weight of all five of its passengers, plus their equipment, up the short hill. With a jerk we stopped in front of a hexagonal cottage. The television crew jumped out of the cart and positioned themselves on the little veranda by the door. Again Ted let me lead the way, but this time I used it to my advantage. Using the keycard Ted had given me, I unlocked the door, opened it just enough to get one foot inside the building, and then turned around to face him.

"Thanks for the ride. I can take it from here."

He looked so disappointed that I almost felt sorry for him — almost. "Don't you want me to show you around? Point out the features of the cottage?"

I didn't want to know how many grains of sand were in each line of the grout I'd seen between the terracotta tiles on the floor. "No thanks. I'm good."

"All right," but he didn't look as if it was all right, really. "Well, if you need anything just pick up any of the phones in the cottage and you'll be connected with the front desk. They'll know where to find me."

"Thanks, Ted." I backed into the cottage and closed the door, smiling sweetly at him until I heard the bolt latch. There was pampering and then there was suffocating. Ted had taken pampering to the painful extreme.

Free of Ted, I went in search of a telephone. I didn't have to look very far. In fact, everywhere I looked there was a phone — in each of the three bedrooms, on the walls in all four of the bathrooms, on the sideboard in the dining room. There were two in the living room. I chose to use the cordless phone on the large patio, instead of the hardwired phone on the patio bar.

"Hello, Miss Butler, this is the front desk. How many I help you?" The front desk was female and her thick Caribbean accent was beautifully musical.

"I need to make an outside call."

"Certainly. I'll connect you."

I punched in the numbers of James' cellphone as soon as I heard the dial tone.

"Hello?"

"If I find one single camera in this cottage or on the patio I'm going to strip naked and give your editors nightmares for years!" I sat down at the side of my own personal infinity pool and put my feet in the warm water. The view from my patio was almost as good as the view from James' villa.

He laughed. "They wouldn't have had time to hook the room up. You're safe."

"Promise?"

"I'll call the TD and make sure. Okay?"

"What's a TD?" I thought it might mean television director.

"Technical Director. He knows where all the cameras are. Where'd they put you?"

"Cottage 7. It's huge!"

"It's the Butler BVI version of the presidential suite."

"Is this all Dan's idea? Some guy named Ted Robarts met me at the boat and gave me the royal treatment. Do they think I'm here as an owner?"

"Ted's one of the last two contestants. He's probably just trying to make a good impression."

"You didn't answer my question about Dan."

The line crackled. "I'm losing the connection, Ri…."

All I heard after that was static. I was pretty sure it was artificial static, produced by James' mouth, but it didn't really matter. By not answering my question, he'd answered my question. Everyone thought I was there to judge the contestants. Hopefully the other contestant wouldn't try to get so in my face.

She didn't. She knocked on my door, instead.

"Hello, Miss Butler. I'm Judy Ingram, one of the acting managers." Judy blew my beautiful-people-only theory about reality show finalists out of the water. She was much younger than Ted, a tall thin woman, with a synchronized swimmers' nose, a dark brown Anna Wintour bob, and an elongated chin that made the shape of her small face remind me of a giraffe's head. Like Ted, she didn't travel alone. Behind her there was a cameraman (his lens pointing at me), a sound person (his microphone held in the air between Judy and me), and another female production person who was madly scribbling notes on a clipboard. "I just wanted to welcome you to The Butler BVI. If there's anything, anything at all, that I can do to make your stay more enjoyable, please let me know."

"Thanks."

"To reach me …"

"I just pick up the phone and …" I stopped talking when the cameraman lowered his camera.

"Hi, Ria."

"Hi, Rob." With his camera pointing to the ground he didn't get to record the big smile that spread across my face.

CHAPTER THREE

Rob's smile mirrored mine, but the same couldn't be said of the flat-line lips on the face of the second cameraman who rose up from behind the aloe plant at the bottom of the steps, his camera aimed at me.

"We'll have to do another take." The dark-haired note-writing woman behind Rob angrily scratched out whatever she'd just written down. "We can take it from Judy knocking on the door."

"Sorry guys, my bad," Rob said sheepishly.

"You know each other?" Judy looked from Rob to me to Rob and then back to me.

Both Rob and I opened our mouths to answer her, but neither of us was given the chance to speak.

"Can we mike her first?" The man who held the long metal pole with the big microphone at the end of it lowered the pole, pushed a few buttons on the electronic equipment that hung from the thick strap that was draped over his shoulder, and slipped the large headphones off his head. "She must have the patio doors open. There's wind from somewhere hitting the mike and this wind sock sucks."

"Is that really necessary?" Judy tried to protest, but she

was just as invisible to the crew as I was. "I don't want to waste Miss Butler's time."

"What if she just stepped outside and closed the door?" The note-taker asked. "I don't want to stand around waiting for someone to drop off an extra wireless. Hang on." She stopped writing and grabbed the radio that was hanging from her belt. "I'm vibrating." She pushed a button on the radio. "What?"

"Esther, what brainiac put chickens under the veranda at Ariel's cottage?" A female voice crackled out of the radio.

The note-taker, who I assumed was called Esther, laughed. "Did your chickens come home to roost?"

"It's not funny! Ariel's scared shitless of birds and there's like a whole flock of them stuck under there. Listen." A loud chorus of chirps chirped out of the radio. "The mother chicken is going clucking nuts trying to get to her chicks and the chicks are screaming their fuzzy little yellow heads off. Ted's calming Ariel down, but we can't figure out how the birds got in there and we have to get them out, like pronto!"

"I don't do chickens …"

"Wait a minute, I think I see something. There's a loose board. Here, chickies. Come to Auntie Pam. No, don't run away! Damn it, come!"

"Make sure you get a credit for animal wrangling."

"Bite me."

The radio went silent just as Judy's cellphone started to ring.

"Don't forget to put it on speakerphone." The sound person grabbed his headphones, slapped them back over his ears and lifted the big microphone pole up into the air.

The cameraman at the bottom of the steps turned to point his camera more directly at Judy.

"Hello?" Judy held her phone out in front of her face and tilted it so that the speaker was pointing toward the microphone hovering above her.

"Hey, Judy. Mike here. We, ah, we have a little problem."

Rob quietly lifted his camera, put it back on his shoulder, and focused on Judy. He still bore a striking resemblance to a young Clint Eastwood, but his face had changed in the years since I'd last seen him. A scar now ran along the sharp jaw line on the left side of his face. He wasn't as tall as Glenn, barely touching six feet, and he wasn't as beefy as Glenn … what was I doing? Rob and Glenn were very different people. There was no need to compare them. The fact that Rob's dark hair was liberally streaked with greys and Glenn's lighter brown hair was still mostly brown had nothing to do with anything; nor did the fact that they both had brown eyes — Rob's were eighty-five percent dark cocoa, Glenn's were creamy milk chocolate. Was there a rule in Glenn's handbook about almost fifty year olds not being allowed to have a crush on someone? Not that it would apply to me, of course — I wasn't fifty and I'd had a crush on Rob since before I was thirty. I gave my thoughts a mental smack and forced myself to concentrate on what mattered. What was that Zen thing? Be in the moment. Stay in the moment. If you keep it moment to moment then everything is clear. It was worth a shot. What was clear was that the man who'd called Judy sounded worried.

"Chris is kind of tanked," the man continued. "Actually, he's totally wasted. He hooked up with two really hot young fans last night and their party just ended. He's passed out and —"

Judy cut him off. "I've got you on speakerphone, Mike."

"Oh. Okay. Got it. So, like I was saying … Chris bumped into an old friend from college and they've decided to have dinner together tonight, so he asked me to call you and apologize for the delay. He probably won't be finished dinner until, um, ten or eleven, so can you let your helicopter pilot know that we won't need him until then?"

"The helicopter can't bring him over after dark. It's visual flight rules only over here."

"Shit! Sorry, you'll have to edit that out." The man on the phone paused. "What about a boat? Can you send a boat for him? He's got that meeting with Christian and Dan tomorrow morning and he'd sure hate to miss that."

"Let me see what I can do. I'll call you back." Judy snapped her phone closed. "I need to get back to the office," she said to the crew. "I apologize for the unorthodox visit, Miss Butler. Again, if you need anything please feel free to call me."

And with that she turned and bolted down the steps. The entire crew, with one notable exception, had to scramble to get themselves and their equipment into the all-terrain golf cart in the driveway. Rob simply lowered his camera and stood still. It was the note-taker who noticed he wasn't moving.

"Rob? Hurry up!"

"My meal break starts in fifteen. I'll call Harry and get him to catch you pulling up to the building and he can take it from there."

The note-taker didn't get a chance to reply. Judy slammed her foot on the tiny accelerator in the golf cart and I learned something new — golf carts were capable of squealing their tires, especially if they had really big tires. The sound man had the longest dreads I'd ever seen on a white man and they waved out the back of the golf cart as it flew down the driveway and onto the island's main road.

"Give me two seconds." Rob, too, had a radio on his belt and he used it to call Harry, whoever he was. Once he had Harry's commitment to meet Judy and her travelling band of technical miscreants at the main hotel building he turned the radio off. "Let's do another take of that greeting. Hi, Ria."

"Hi, Rob." I laughed.

"Want to buy me lunch?"

"Why do I have to pay for it?"

"Because my last name isn't a brand. You're the hotel heiress."

"Yeah, right. And I have so much in common with Paris Hilton. Not! Nobody pays me to show up at parties."

"And you haven't got a sex video on the web ... have you?" He raised his eyebrows expectantly. "Because, you know, if you have, I wouldn't mind taking a look at that. Purely for cinematic reasons, of course."

"Of course."

"So, are you going to invite me in?" He didn't bother to wait for an answer and walked past me into the villa. "Hey, Will was right. You did have the patio doors open. Why don't we eat out there?" He kept right on walking, down the hallway, past the dining room, through the living room, and out onto the patio.

"Make yourself at home," I needlessly called out as I closed the front door.

Rob ordered enough food from room service to feed a small family, even though the only thing I asked for was a Diet Coke when I discovered that the refrigerator in my patio bar was stocked with Diet Pepsi. Where Rob was going to put all the calories he'd ordered was beyond me; he had a small frame with next to no meat on it, despite his appetite.

"Thanks for coming so fast. When'd you get here?"

"Yesterday afternoon. I stayed at James' place last night."

Rob had bent to sit down but froze with his butt in the air. "You didn't tell him ..."

"No, he doesn't know why I'm here."

"Good." Rob lowered himself the rest of the way into his chair. "You look great."

I sat across from him at the patio table. "You don't look so bad yourself." The lack of a ring on the fourth finger of his left hand only added to his physical appeal, but my eyes kept going back to the scar on his face. "How did you get that?"

"BASE jumping on Baffin Island. A cross draft hit me and I kissed a rock on my way down."

"You BASE jump?" BASE jumping wasn't an extreme sport in my opinion — it was a stupid sport. The risks far outweighed the thrills. Bungee jumping was my extreme limit.

"I did that day. We were up there shooting a thing for National Geographic. The guys had one more jump scheduled before we lost the light and they asked me if I wanted to try it. I figured, why not? I'd already shot their first three jumps and nothing bad had happened." Rob was sounding dangerously similar to James — justifying stupid actions by saying it was okay because everyone else was doing it.

"What did you jump off?"

"A thirty-five-hundred-foot cliff."

Rob was the first person I'd ever heard openly admit that he'd jumped off a cliff because everyone else had. Mothers around the world would have cringed if they'd heard him. "Weren't you scared?"

"A bit. Mostly of the polar bears on the ice where we landed, though. Those are some big mean bears! But I got some amazing shots, so it was worth it. Hey, that reminds me, I saw your piece in *NG* on Applecross. You're getting pretty good with the camera. I was impressed."

"Thanks." My pictures had impressed a professional cameraman. That felt good. But a different camera was concerning me. Rob's camera sat on the bar with its lens pointing toward me. "Is that thing still on?"

He went over to the bar and turned the camera around. "Nope, and it's not a thing. It's my constant companion. You may call him Icky."

"Icky?"

He smiled and winked as he sat back down. "It's an Ikegami."

"And that means something to me because…?"

"Like you, it's a brand."

"You can stop that now. It's wearing thin." He had already doubled my usually allowed quota of one Butler Hotels joke per conversation.

"Sorry, I couldn't resist. That was the last one." He relaxed back into his chair.

"Maybe now you can tell me what's going on?"

He nodded slowly. "Why don't I just give you a sound bite about what's been happening and then you can ask questions. Deal?"

"Deal."

He took a deep breath. "Okay, here we go … just before Ted's team blew up Albert, Pam found a severed foot. Pretty well everybody thinks it was a fake foot, but I'm not so sure, especially since the rest of Kate has been conspicuously absent from the set ever since the foot was found."

I waited for him to go on, but his mouth stayed closed and he just smiled at me.

"That was one heck of a sound bite!" An incredibly effective sound bite, too. My curiosity had been detonated. "Who are Pam and Kate?"

"Pam's one of our production assistants, although she might be adding chicken wrangler to her list of credits now. She's the one who radioed Esther a few minutes ago. Kate was a PA, too. After hours she moonlighted as Dan's location slut."

I instantly thought of James' Mandy. Location slut was an accurate moniker for her, in my humble sisterly opinion. "You don't like Kate."

"I don't respect Kate. Or, if I'm right, I should say that I didn't respect Kate. She seemed like a nice enough kid, and she wasn't a bad PA, but she had too many stars in her eyes. She had an encyclopaedic knowledge of almost every television show that's aired in the last thirty years. I mean, really, who actually knows all the lyrics to *The Flintstones* theme song? Kate did. And she had a severe case of fan-itus extremis."

"How old was she?" I'd picked up on Rob's use of the past tense so quickly and easily that it worried me.

"Early twenties? Pam would know."

Would James end up like Dan — a sixty-plus man having sex with someone who was young enough to be his grand-daughter? He was well on his way down that road with Mandy; she was young enough to be his daughter. "Was she using Dan for his production contacts?"

Rob shook his head. "Kate didn't think like that. Have you met Mandy yet?"

"Unfortunately, I had the displeasure of meeting her yesterday."

"Yeah, she's a piece of work. She's a professional user, but Kate was too naive to think that way. She didn't go after Dan the way Mandy sunk her claws into James. She was impressed by Dan's resume and maybe she even liked him, God knows why, but I don't think she was using him. The use and abuse went the other way. Dan's always likes having a sweet young thing in his bed — and he likes to brag about it, about how he's got more stamina than Hugh Hefner, without needing Viagra. A few of us old-timers have worked with Dan a couple of times over the years and more than once he's shown up on the set with a new fiancée, as he calls them. The engagements, paid or otherwise, usually last the duration of the shoot. This time he showed up alone and didn't get engaged until the third day he was here. Whether or not Kate knew she was just something to do on location is anybody's guess."

"Maybe she figured it out and left?"

"Leaving behind her foot and her luggage?" Rob shook his head. "I may work in fantasy land, but that doesn't mean I believe it."

"You said something about Albert being blown up right after the foot was found. What did you mean by that?" Maybe *blow up* was a technical TV term? Albert didn't look like he'd been explosively blown up to me.

"That he was blown up. With explosives. How else would you blow somebody up?" Rob shook his head as if he couldn't believe that I'd asked such a dumb question. "They strapped him into a skiff, loaded the boat up with explosives, drove it by radio remote until it was in the middle of a shot, and blew him up."

"But I've seen him. There isn't a scratch on him."

"They didn't blow up the real Albert!" Again, he looked amazed by my apparent stupidity. "They made a dummy, and named him Albert. He's not exactly the most popular guy on the shoot. It was a cathartic blowing up for all of us."

"Maybe the foot was a cathartic foot, not a real one?"

"That's the problem, no one knows for sure. Pam threw it away. She swears it was a fake, but it's mighty coincidental that Kate suddenly left the production at the same time. And the special effects guys aren't bragging. That, in and of itself, is strange. They like to brag about their stuff if it's good. If it's bad, they blame it on materials or the production crew."

My thoughts started to get dizzy trying to keep straight what was real and what was fake. "Why didn't you get it out of the garbage to look at it more closely?"

"It's not in the garbage. It's fish food now. Pam threw it out to sea." The doorbell rang. (I didn't even know I had a doorbell.) Rob stood up and started to walk into the villa. "Adam was in the chopper doing beauty shots when she tossed it and he says he caught her throwing it away."

A few minutes later he came back onto the patio, pushing a wheeled table. There were three covered dishes on it, two glasses, a bucket of ice, and six Diet Pepsis.

"Are you sure you don't want any?" he asked after sitting down and lifting the lid off one of the covered dishes to reveal fries, coleslaw, and the largest bacon cheeseburger I'd ever seen.

"It's only ten thirty ..."

"My shift started at six."

I stood up to get the cordless phone from the bar. "They screwed up the drinks order. You asked for Diet Coke, right?"

Rob nodded while he chewed his first bite of hamburger. "But Donnella wasn't there. She's the one with the secret stash of Coke."

"You make it sound like it's something illegal." I read the label on the back of the phone to see what number to dial for room service.

"It pretty well is around here." He scooped up a forkful of coleslaw. "Dan signed some mega product placement deal with Pepsi. Name the Pepsi product, Doritos, Lays, Mountain Dew, Ocean Spray, those you can get. But Coke products? Nada! Dan banned them from the island for the duration of the shoot because he didn't want them accidentally showing up in a shot." The coleslaw finally made it to its destination.

"But I don't like Diet Pepsi and I'm not part of the show." I put the phone back down on the base. "How do I find this Donnella person?"

"She's the head of housekeeping, but she won't give you the Coke unless I talk to her first. She could get in real trouble if Dan found out about her stash."

"I wouldn't tell him." I returned to the table and dejectedly opened a can of Diet Pepsi.

"She doesn't know that. All she knows is that your last name is Butler — ergo you either work with James on the production or you're here to check up on the hotel." He wiped a drop of mayonnaise off of his lower lip. "I'll talk to her, but you have to promise to never tell Dan where you got it and to only drink it here, in your villa. There are cameras everywhere and if you're walking around with a Coke product you'll ruin every shot you're in."

"Promise," I said with my fingers crossed behind my back. I'd keep the name of my Diet Coke dealer secret, but had absolutely no intention of keeping the second half of my promise. In fact, I planned to go out of my way to break it. Once I scored I was going to make darn sure that I had a can of Diet Coke in my hands at all times. "Let's get back to Kate. What makes you so sure that it really was her foot?"

"Kate had a little blue octopus tattooed on her ankle and Pam said she saw part of a tattoo just like that. And Kate's gone. The thing is, Kate never would have quit, even if she'd figured out that Dan wasn't after her for her personality. This job meant everything to her, especially with the movie crew just coming in. That's what she really wanted, to move to LA and work in features with the big stars."

"Maybe she got offered a job in LA?"

"Uh-uh. This was her first production job. She didn't have any experience, never mind enough experience to get a job on features." He pushed plate number one aside and started in on the large Caesar salad on plate number two. "She tried getting friendly with the DOC ..."

"DOC?"

"Director of cinematography. He flew in with the second unit." My face must have given away the fact that I, once again, had no idea what he was talking about. "The special effects guys, they came in early to test stuff out."

"James said you were shooting a reality show. What do you need special effects for if it's reality?"

Rob didn't do a very good job of hiding his laughter. "Careful, I'll have to start calling you Virginia if you keep talking like that."

"Virginia?"

"Yes, Virginia … hate to break it to you, there isn't a Santa Claus, and as for reality TV, well, it's real TV — a product that's produced to entertain."

"So the explosion, the blowing up of Albert, that the special effects guys did, that was part of the reality show?"

"Technically, yes, it happened while we were shooting the reality show, but what we were shooting was the commercial crew who flew in to shoot the commercials that the last two contestants had to make as their second-last challenge. The special effects guys are here for the movie, not the television show."

"And not for the commercial, right?"

"Right. They had to come down early because, go figure, the airlines won't let you transport explosives on their flights, so they had to source as much as they could locally and they weren't sure what kind of explosions they'd get out of the stuff they found down here."

"What do you mean the kind of explosions? Things either go boom or they don't."

"And some explosions have big booms, some have little booms, and sometimes a director wants an orange flame, sometimes he wants a whiter, hotter looking one, he might want black smoke or he might want white smoke …"

"And sometimes he is a she. There are female directors, too, you know."

Rob ignored my comment. "Sometimes a car is supposed to burst into flames and flip in the air, sometimes it's supposed to just smoulder …"

"Does this lesson in special effects have anything to do with Kate?" If not, I wanted it to end. I liked going to movies and letting myself believe the stories I watched (even though I knew they were fiction).

"Not really, except for the foot. If it was a fake, it would have had to been made by the special-effects makeup crew. A prop like that would be expensive. Way too expensive for a joke."

"But they did blow up Albert, right? Why? They aren't even working on the television show."

Rob shrugged his shoulders. "For fun? I bet Dan had something to do with it, though. He's a media whore and an outtake like that would definitely get airplay on a show like *TMZ* or *Access Hollywood*, and a simple boat explosion wouldn't cost much. Dan could anonymously make sure the clip got leaked and then sit back and enjoy the free press promoting the show. He's been behind a bunch of the jokes that the crews have pulled on each other."

"Which crews? The television people, the commercial people, or the movie people?" I felt like I was standing between three mirrors in a house of mirrors at a carnival, surrounded by a multitude of distorted images of reality.

Rob picked up my glass and took a sip of my drink. "How do you drink this carbonated stuff? It's awful!" He went over to the bar, bent down, and then stood up holding a can of iced tea — Lipton Iced Tea, presumably a Pepsi brand. "Let me give you a synopsis of who's doing what down here."

"Please!" People were blowing up, but they weren't. There were crews and teams and units, all of whom were shooting something or other, but no one had been shot.

"First off, forget about the commercial crew. They came, they shot, they left. They were only here for a couple of days and we were pulling long shifts, so Kate didn't get a chance to know any of them. Now for the reality show, James came up with the series idea. He put it together and brought Dan in. He did that partly because of Dan's distribution connections with the U.S. networks and partly to get himself into features with Dan — theatrical releases, the movies shown in theatres. We, the television crew, have been here for a couple of months and we're almost done. James' company hired us, but we technically work for Dan, too. Once we're out of here, Dan's company is going to shoot a feature on the island. His producer hired that crew out of LA ..."

"But I thought Dan was the producer of the movie?" A few more mirrors popped up in my mental carnival.

Rob shook his head. "Uh-uh. He's the executive producer. He makes the deals; for financing, distribution, stuff like that, and executive producers have final approval on the director, the leads —"

"The what?"

"The stars. The producer, or producers, there's usually a couple of them, take care of actually making the show. They hire the crew, but the director, hired by the executive producer, usually has final say on the big-ticket crew members, like the TD, DOC, senior editor, people like that. The producers hire the regular crew, arrange for craft services, transportation, rent the equipment, and stuff like that." Rob stopped talking and started laughing — at me.

"What?"

"Your face! Now I know what dumbstruck looks like. It's really not that complicated, you know."

"Maybe to you! To me, it's like you're speaking a foreign language. You're using terms that I've only ever seen on the movie screen when I'm leaving the theatre. Nobody reads them and I guarantee you most people don't have a clue what they mean."

"Okay, how's this — you don't know exactly what everyone in a shoelace factory does, right?"

I nodded and resisted the urge to ask what shoelaces had to do with anything. For all I knew shoelace was a technical term for yet another complicated aspect of television or movie production.

"All you care about is that shoelaces are made and you use them. They're a product, right?"

Another nod, with very little actual comprehension propelling it.

"We, all of us working on this island, either for Dan or James, we're just shoelace factory employees. We work on the line, making a product. You don't have to know or understand what each one of us does. All that matters to you, the consumer, is that we do it and that you can go out and buy shoelaces whenever you want."

"But we're not talking about shoelaces! We're talking about movies and television shows."

"They're the same thing when you get right down to it. They're products. The only difference to the audience, or consumer, is that movies seem a lot more glamorous. To the guys who actually work on them, they're not. We show up, punch in, do our shift, go home at the end of the day, and the product gets made. We light, look, and listen. That's it. And we probably have more fun doing our jobs than the guys in the shoelace factory. I mean, look around! I'm getting paid to be here — it really is a sweet job. Upper management, the exec producers, make sure that the right product gets made, based on market conditions or what the consumer wants, and find store shelves or movie screens to sell the product from. Middle management, or the producers, make sure that the production line runs smoothly, on time and on budget."

The mental mirrors in my head were sort of, almost, starting to come into focus. "The shoelace thing, that helped, a little."

Rob checked his watch. "I'm running out of time, so it'll have to do for now. Can I get back to what's going on here? Are you good on who's doing what?"

"Mostly, but I do have one question."

"Shoot."

"What's a gaffer?"

"They're like the aglets."

"The what?"

"Those hard bits on the end of shoelaces that hold all the strings together."

"So gaffers hold everything together on a production?"

"Yeah," he chuckled for a reason I was so far from understanding that I didn't even try to get him to explain. "They hold it together with gaffer tape." Rob broke into real laughter. "Damn, that was a good one."

I let him laugh at his own joke. Maybe it actually was funny?

"Gaffer tape?" He kept on laughing. "Get it?"

"No." I popped open a second can of Diet Pepsi, mainly to give myself something to do while Rob enjoyed his own humour.

"Hey, that reminded me of something else that's weird about that morning Kate's foot was found."

I'd almost forgotten about Kate and, for some strange reason, started to wonder if she (or her foot) was wearing a shoe and if it had shoelaces or was a slip-on.

"A big bag of gaffer tape rolls disappeared the night Kate disappeared. Could mean nothing, but it might mean something."

"What's gaffer tape?" I didn't want to know, but knew I had to ask.

"It's tape, strong tape. Oh, hell, what's the name they use in hardware stores ..." Rob tapped his foot at a rapid pace and looked at the stones on the patio. I immediately recognized that he was having what I called an *old-age moment* — the word he was looking for was just beyond the tip of his tongue. His foot stopped tapping, his fingers snapped once, and he looked at me. "Duct tape! Gaffer tape is duct tape!"

"Finally, a product name I understand! Don't you dare tell me how it's made."

The radio on Rob's belted squawked to life. "Rob, we're heading to the north end," a female voice said. "Judy's doing some final prep on Chris's place and then we're going over to St. Thomas to pick him up. We're supposed to shoot his arrival on the island, but if he's still too wasted we'll re-do it tomorrow. We get to go for a ride on the fancy boat! Sweet, huh?" She didn't stop talking long enough to let Rob reply. "And it'll mean overtime, because we won't be back until late. Even sweeter! Do you have a ride or do you want me to send someone to get you?"

Rob unclipped the radio. "Send somebody. Actually, send two carts. I'm still at Ria's place and she'll need a cart to get herself around the island."

"You're still there? Well, excuse me! La-di-da. Aren't we moving up in the world. Does she want the Bentley or the Rolls Royce golf cart?"

"She can hear you."

"We'll be there in fifteen."

I wished that my last name was Smith.

"Back to our shoelaces," he lifted the lid off the final plate. A small mountain of chocolate chip cookies had stayed warm under the domed lid.

"Please, no more shoelaces," I privately resolved to only buy slip-ons in the future.

"I'm almost done. I brought them up for a reason. They're how I break down the two types of people who work in production. There's the people who see shoelaces, and then there's the people who see stars. Kate saw stars."

"And that means?" The cookies smelled so good that I almost started to drool. Instead, I reached over and grabbed two of them before Rob could empty the plate.

"One of Dan's favourite lines is *'It's called show business and business is the big word for a reason.'* The people who see the stars only see the show. The people who see shoelaces understand that it's a business, just like any other business. Kate was, or maybe she still is, so totally hooked on the fantasy that there's no way, no way at all, that she'd walk away from it. She was in, just where she'd always wanted to be. And, according to Narc —"

"Who?"

"The DOC on the movie. His name's really Mark, but everybody calls him Narc — I'll let you guess why — anyway, he told me that Kate was talking to him about how to get a job on the movie crew."

"But she already had a job with Dan. Wouldn't that have kept her here for the movie?"

He shook his head as he finished chewing a bite of cookie. "Dan won't stay for the whole shoot and, knowing Dan, he would have been extra careful to avoid even hinting at the possibility of taking her back to LA with him."

"And Narc, or Mark, or whoever, didn't give her a job, right? So maybe I was right, maybe she figured out she was being used by Dan and she simply decided to go back home early?"

"Maybe. She and Dan did have a big fight the night before her foot showed up, but I don't think even that would have made her quit. She could have just moved her stuff back here, to the hotel, and kept on working the shoot. Remember, she worked for James' company, not Dan's. The thing is, she was positively gaga about Chris coming in today. He's one of the leads in the movie and Kate couldn't shut up about how much she was looking forward to meeting him. Seems she's had a major crush on him ever since he did *Silent Lucidity*."

I almost choked on a chocolate chip. "Chris, as in Chris Regent?" He was barely in his thirties but he'd already won two of the three Oscars he'd been nominated for, in between his well-publicized stints in rehab.

"One and the same. He's who we're heading over to pick up on St. Thomas. Nobody was supposed to know that he was coming, but it slipped out a couple of weeks ago and when Kate heard about it she went nuts." Rob stood up and walked over to his camera. "She was over the moon about Ariel coming, but she would have circled Pluto to meet Chris."

"Ariel? As in Ariel Downes?" She'd only won one Oscar. "That's the Ariel who was freaking out about the chickens?"

"Yeah. She just did a remake of Hitchcock's *The Birds*, which Dan exec produced, and then she gets here and, gosh and by golly, someone let some birds get trapped right under her veranda. What a shocker, huh?"

"Dan?"

"I bet they got some great footage from that." He pushed a few buttons on the camera. "And it'll get some promo airplay for the Hitchcock remake, the show we're shooting, and his next feature." He turned around and looked at me. "Kate didn't leave here voluntarily, Ria, I'm sure of it. And that foot was put where it would be found, where it would be caught on camera when it was found."

"You think Dan did that?"

He nodded. "I'd bet your inheritance on it."

I ignored his inheritance jab. "Where does James fit into all of this?"

"Don't take this the wrong way, okay? James is Dan's boy. Most of the time, he's a shoelace guy. We've worked together for a lot of years and he's never paid much attention to the glamour and glitz. But Dan's dangled some pretty shiny stars in front of him on this production and he's changed. Something's really changed in him. I went to him, one on one, with my concerns about Kate. When the police showed up —"

"Someone called the police?" If they were involved, why had Rob called me?

"No, they came over after Albert was blown up. Nobody thought to get a permit for the explosion and I guess somebody on Virgin Gorda called them. They came over to find out what we were up to and I think Dan might have been fined for it. While they were here, Pam —"

"The one who found the foot? The lady with the chickens?"

"Right. Anyway, Pam said something to them about the foot so they went off with Dan and James to discuss it. Rumours were building, big time, about what might have happened to Kate and then, on Saturday, two days after she disappeared, Dan held a crew meeting and told us that the BVI police confirmed with the police in Toronto that Kate was back home. Most people bought it, but it still didn't sit right with me or Bear …"

"Bear?"

"Our TD."

"Technical director."

"Nicely done, you're getting the hang of it!"

"So this Bear person doesn't think she quit, either?"

"No. He and I agreed that I should be the one to talk to James about it; I've known him the longest. So, I went to James and told him I wasn't buying it. He got pissed — really pissed. Being his sister you probably haven't noticed this, but he gets this weird look on his face when he's lying." Rob picked up his camera. "I've worked with him long enough to recognize it, and he got that look."

"I know the look you're talking about."

"He swore up and down that Kate had quit, that he'd seen her leaving Dan's villa with all her stuff on Friday morning, the morning the foot was found. I could tell he was lying, but I couldn't prove it. Then he told me to drop it if I ever wanted to work again. He said that to me! The guy who's worked with him the longest. That's not the James I know."

I stood up and started to stack the plates on the tray. "He can't fire somebody without just cause. You could sue him for everything he's worth." What I didn't say was that my brother, at least the brother I thought I knew, would never have threatened someone like that — unless he was really scared. But of what?

"He wouldn't have to fire me, or anyone else on the crew who asked too many questions. We're not salaried, we're all freelance. Once this shoot is over we're unemployed and it's up to us to find another gig. If word gets around that you've caused trouble on a shoot you won't find another gig." He stood and watched me for a minute. "You know you have staff to do that for you, right?"

I slammed the last dome down on the plate that had held the cookies. "Stop with the rich jokes!"

Holding his camera in one hand, he walked over to me and draped his free arm around my shoulders. "I'm sorry. Really. I won't do it again. But it's just so much fun to see you get all huffy!" He gave my shoulders a squeeze.

Despite my physical attraction to him the close physical contact hadn't done anything for me. In fact, it felt more paternalistic than erotic. I mentally shook off my brush with disappointment.

The doorbell rang and we walked together through the villa.

"Bear might be out there. He's really ticked off at me for calling you. He doesn't want to lose his career either, and he'll want to check you out before he opens up to you about what he knows." Rob stopped just as we got to the door. "I don't think James had anything to do with Kate's disappearance, but I know for a fact that he's covering it up. When I was leaving James' place the housekeeper was in the little room under the stairs of the building across the pool from the main house. She was doing laundry, the washer and dryer are in that room, but I saw something else in there. Piled up against the back wall is all of Kate's luggage. And before you ask me if I'm sure about it being Kate's, I am. She had two *Partridge Family* lunchboxes that she used as makeup cases. Both of them were sitting on top of her *Around the World in 80 Days* suitcase. I saw all that and called you. The thing is, if something's happened to Kate it doesn't matter if James was involved in it or not. Dan is the living definition of conniving. I could see him doing just about anything, to Kate or anyone else, but he's smart enough to twist everything around to make it look as if he's innocent. And he's sneaky enough to lay the blame quite visibly at someone else's door ... like at James' laundry room door."

A shiver shot through me, knowing that I'd slept in the room above Kate's suitcases.

Rob opened my door and waved at the people sitting in one of the two golf carts.

There was only one person sitting in the other golf cart and he immediately jumped out of it when he saw me. He was wearing a black chauffeur's hat and I tried to stare at it instead of at his unusual appearance. He looked like the by-product of a conjugal visit between a biker gang member and an Ewok. He was short, wide, overly muscled and tattooed (those muscles and tattoos clearly visible because of the wife beater T-shirt he was wearing), and covered in lots of excess hair — on his body, his face, and his head. He ran up the steps to the villa, whipped off his hat, and bowed in front of me, dangling the key to the golf cart from the hand he held outstretched.

"Your Highness," he stood up straight (his eyes coming level with my chest), "your chariot awaits."

"Can the royalty crap, Bear." Rob stepped outside. "Ria, meet Bear, our TD."

"Who doubles as a golf cart jockey when the need arises," Bear smiled up at me, but it wasn't a warm, welcoming smile. It was just something for his lips to do while his eyes looked hard into mine. "Nice meeting you, Ria."

"Hustle it, dudes!" The woman I now knew to be Esther yelled from the other golf cart. "We're on the clock in less than a minute and Dan and James won't be off island much longer."

I watched them pull away. Bear, who really should have been nicknamed Cub, had hurled his body into the storage bin on the back of the golf cart and then sat up on it so that he could face me as they turned out of the driveway. I wanted to laugh when a politically incorrect thought popped into my head, but stopped myself and felt ashamed instead. (But he really did start to resemble a garden gnome as the golf cart got farther away.)

My footsteps echoed through the empty villa as I walked back out to the patio. Now what? What the heck was I supposed to do now? I sat down by the pool again, dipped my feet into the water, and tried to think. Unfortunately, one thought was blocking out all others — *what would Glenn do?*

I tried to push Glenn out of my thoughts.

Dan told everyone that the Toronto police had confirmed that she was there. Was she really? If so, why did she leave her luggage behind and why was James hiding it? Had Dan made up the Toronto police story to keep people from asking too many questions? I knew Toronto was where I should start (and maybe even end), but to do that I'd have to call Glenn; he was the one with friends on the force.

No matter when or where our next conversation took place it wasn't going to be an easy one. Our last words to each other hadn't exactly been those shared by a happy couple and Glenn hadn't made any effort to apologize. (Neither had I, but that was because I had been in the right and didn't owe him an apology.)

I didn't want to call Glenn. He'd ask me about where I was ... and why, and my answers sure wouldn't help to smooth things out between us. On top of that, I didn't want to have to admit to him that I needed his help. But did I have any other options?

I couldn't confront James. He was more than capable of lying, especially when he felt trapped or about to be caught doing something wrong by his big sister.

I couldn't very well call up the Toronto police force and say, *Hi, you don't know me and I can't tell you why I need to know this, and I don't know who would have the answer, if they have the answer, but ...* They'd either hang up on me or transfer my call to the closest psychiatric hospital.

Glenn would know who to call. That thought irritated me — a lot.

Glenn would call his golf buddy Cam. He was a detective sergeant in the homicide unit and I'd met him a couple of times through Glenn. Why couldn't I call Cam myself?

I stood up and walked into the cottage, on the hunt for my cellphone. Cam's number was stored in my address book.

G lenn had never really noticed how loud the silence in his condo was — it was deafening. The walls and windows were so well insulated and double or triple glazed that it was almost as if he was embalmed in a residential cocoon. The sounds of the city streets far below him never made it into the condo. When propeller planes took off from the Toronto Island airport Glenn only knew about them if he happened to be looking out the window at the right time. An ice cube clunked out of the icemaker and landed in the plastic bin on the inside of the freezer door. Damn, the ice-cube maker was loud. Why hadn't he ever noticed that before? He sighed and heard the air enter and exit his body. Was this what it was going to be like? He turned away from the floor-to-ceiling window in the living room and went to the kitchen to use one or two of the ice cubes that the freezer had made so loudly. He wanted a scotch but given the time of day and the fact that he didn't really like the taste of scotch he poured ginger ale on the rocks he'd let fall into his glass. But it still felt like an *I-need-a-scotch* moment.

He'd known for ages that Brandon was going to go to Perth, Australia, to do a foreign exchange semester. He'd dealt with the mixture of sorrow and joy — knowing that even though he'd miss Brandon like hell he'd be happy for him to be having such a great experience. He'd been fine with it. Really. Besides, come Christmas everything would be back to normal again. Brandon would be home, living in the condo again, going to classes, not doing the dishes, and forgetting to buy food, life would be good. That was the plan. It was the plan Glenn had known about, prepared for, and accepted.

Then everything went to rat shit when Brandon was invited to enter the Butler Hotel's Internship program and Glenn had to slap a big smile on his face and nod and say things like "That sounds great!" and "What a terrific opportunity!" while inside his head he was thinking *Don't go!* His little bird wasn't taking a tentative step out of the nest, he was thinking of hurling his body out, taking flight, and never looking back. Glenn didn't want to have to deal with empty nest syndrome. Not yet. Not ever, really. Yeah, Brandon would eventually set up a life of his own, but did he have to do it now? The kid was barely twenty years old! To make matters worse, Glenn had either James, Ria, and/or their father to blame for it. All it would have taken was one phone call from Doc Butler to guarantee that Brandon got the internship.

The old guy did own a third of the hotel chain. He had clout — major clout. Especially since his two partners were only owners because Doc had given them each a third of the company. What kind of nutjob just hands over two-thirds of the hotel chain he inherited when he finds out his father made babies with his two mistresses? Doc Butler, that's who. Talk about an overdeveloped need to do the right thing! Doc's half-sister ran the whole operation out of Sydney, Australia. And it was someone in that head office who'd called Brandon and offered him the six month position in Sydney. Those six months would come right after his four months in Perth. Put them together and that was almost a year. A year of living alone. A year of only the occasional phone call and impersonal emails sent whenever Brandon had the time. *Don't go!*

Was his fear of losing Brandon the reason why he'd pushed Ria so hard about their relationship? He gave his head a shake. He'd been spending too much time with Doc Butler if thoughts like that were popping up in his head. Even though Doc had retired from his career as a psychiatrist long ago, he still had a knack for getting into someone's head.

He chugged down the last of his ginger ale. The half-melted ice cubes clanked loudly when he dumped them out into the stainless-steel sink. After putting his glass in the dishwasher he walked purposefully back to his home office. His cellphone started to ring just as he was sitting down.

"Cooper."

"Do you want to tell me why your girlfriend's calling me about some missing girl in the Caribbean?"

Glenn dropped into his chair. "What?" He and Cam had known each other so long that they never wasted words, but the few words that had just come out of Cam's mouth didn't make any sense.

"You and Ria are officially dating now, right?"

"Yeah. Sort of. I think so."

"So that would make her your girlfriend, right?"

"Yeah." Cam sure found it easy to define their relationship! So why couldn't Ria? *Get back on track, Cooper.* "But she's not in the Caribbean. She's in Peru. I mean she was. She's in the Galapagos Islands by now."

"No, she's not."

"Yes, she is."

"No, she's not. She left me a voicemail, asked me to check something out and then call her back. I got the information she was looking for and then did a search on the phone number she left. She's in the British Virgin Islands. I don't have the time or clearance to get involved in some international thing so I thought I'd call you to find out what's going on."

Glenn opened his mouth, but didn't know what to say. The British Virgin Islands? That's where James was shooting. Oh man, if Ria had found out about the woman James was shacking up with down there she'd be furious! Furious enough to go blast James in person. He wondered if she'd ever be able to see James as an adult, irresponsibly responsible for his own life, instead of as her little brother. (He didn't let himself wonder if that was one of the things that was messing them up because, if he went down that thought path, he'd have to admit to himself that sometimes it was hard to think of Ria as a woman — not James' big sister.) But if Ria had gone there to blast James, what possible reason would she have had for calling Cam? "What did she want you to check out?"

"Uh-uh, I asked you first. What's going on?"

Glenn reached for his pack of nicotine gum, but tossed it in the garbage can under his desk instead of popping a piece out of the package. He yanked open the bottom drawer and grabbed a pack of cigarettes from his emergency carton. Ria was one of the main reasons he'd been trying to quit. Ria was the reason why he suddenly wanted a smoke so badly. "Cam, you've got me. I don't know what the hell she's up to." A blast of hot summer air hit him in the face when he opened the door to the balcony. A police car's siren assaulted his ears as he stepped outside and lit the cigarette, but its sound was nothing compared to the alarm bells that were going off in his own head. "Your turn. Go."

"She wanted me to find out if our guys were contacted about a missing girl, and if they were she wanted to know if they'd found the girl here in Toronto."

"Did she say why?" The smoke scratched its way down into Glenn's lungs. It hurt like a bitch. He took another drag.

"No."

Who was missing? James' mistress? "Who's the missing girl?"

"Kate Bond. Ever heard of her?"

"No." Glenn tried to remember the name of the woman James had told him about — Melanie, Margery, Mandy ... something like that. Definitely not Kate.

"Well, she's not missing. I did some digging. A call did come in from the British Virgin police — do you think they're all virgins, or something?" Cam didn't stop talking. "Two uniforms went to her apartment ..."

"Address?" Glenn tossed the cigarette into one of the potted plants and went back inside to get a pen.

"I can't give you that."

"Yeah, it's against the rules. That's nice. What's her address?"

"I mean it. I can't give you that. I don't have it. Listen, Glenn, this isn't my department. I had to pull a favour just to get the information I got. If I start asking too many questions people are going to start wanting answers from me and I don't have any."

Me either, Glenn thought. "Did the uniforms find her?"

"Yeah, she was there. They talked to her and reported that she seemed fine. You really don't know what this is about?"

"Haven't got a clue!"

"You want me to call Ria back with the info or do you want to handle it? I don't want to get in the middle of whatever's going on between you two."

"I'll call her. What's the number she gave you?" Now, more strongly than he'd wanted it in Peru, Glenn needed to find out what really was going on between them. Even Cam seemed to have given up the definition he'd had at the beginning of their conversation. And now Glenn, who was supposedly Ria's boyfriend, was asking someone else for his girlfriend's phone number. Bloody Butlers! He wrote down the number that Cam dictated. "Thanks for calling me on this one, Cam."

"Bros before hos, right? Not that Ria's a ho, mind you. You know what I mean."

"Yeah. Is that it? Is there anything else I should know before I call her?"

"One more thing."

Glenn cringed.

"She asked me not to tell you that she called."

Glenn went back out onto the balcony, inhaled as deeply as he could, and exhaled every single thought he'd ever had of apologizing to Ria for pushing her so hard about their relationship.

"Thank you for calling the Butler BVI. How many I direct your call?"

Of course. She and James were staying at one of their hotels. One of the hotels that was part of the chain that was about to swallow up his only child. "Is Ria Butler there?" Glenn tried not to sound too angry, but knew he'd failed.

"I'll connect you to her room, sir."

She answered on the fourth ring. "Hello?"

"Hello." Really, what else was there to say?

"Glenn?"

He chomped down hard on the nicotine gum in his mouth. "Yup."

"Oh, boy. Cam called you."

Glenn wasn't in the mood to waste words. None were required in response to Ria's enlightenment about Cam's call. None were offered.

"I can explain."

He leaned back in his chair, put his feet up on his desk, and twirled a pencil around between his fingers. "I'm listening."

Masticating his gum, squeezing every last drop of nicotine out of it, he listened to Ria's attempt at an explanation.

As she went on he put the pencil down and started to click around on the Internet to find out exactly where the British Virgin Islands were — east of the U.S. Virgins. It took a while, but he finally managed to find a map that showed the island Ria was on. Soursop was less than a pinprick, in between Tortola and Virgin Gorda, just east of a collection of islands called The Dogs. He changed his screen's background from the map of the Galapagos Islands to the map of the BVI.

Ria's explanation left a lot to the imagination, Glenn's imagination in particular. She said she hadn't wanted to bother Glenn if it turned out there was nothing to worry about. That was the lamest part of the explanation, but he let her go with it. What it came down to was that she wasn't where she was supposed to be and she wasn't doing what she was supposed to be doing — all because of one phone call from some guy Glenn had never heard her mention before. Sure, they were just getting to know each other as equal adults, but the core person hadn't changed much in either of them over the years. Ria liked to come across as spontaneous, verging on impulsive, but Glenn knew that she never made a move without carefully thinking it through first. Only one part of Ria was truly spontaneous, her heart. She'd pull a one-eighty at the drop of a hat if someone she loved needed her help. While she started out by saying she'd gone to the British Virgin Islands because James was in trouble, his name sure wasn't coming out of her mouth very often. Another name kept coming out: Rob.

Who the fuck was Rob? He wasn't just some cameraman who worked for James, that was for sure. He was the guy who was pulling a scam on Ria, involving a fake foot and a not really missing girl.

No matter how much she tried to distance herself from the family business, Ria was a hotel heiress. She'd be worth a lot of money someday. Then again, she was so much like her father that she'd probably give it all away to a home for stray relatives. But Robbie wouldn't know that. Was the money what this Rob guy was really after? Or did he just want Ria? Either way, you had to give the guy points for originality. A severed foot. Nice. Too bad for him, Glenn was going to put an end to his scam. As mad as he was at Ria, and hurt by her actions, she did sound sincere in her concern for the girl. She was buying what Rob was selling.

"Ria," it was the first time he'd spoken since she'd started her fast-talking explanation, "the girl's not dead. She's here, in Toronto."

"Are you sure?"

"Positive. Two cops went to her apartment and talked to her."

Now it was Ria's turn to go silent; a rare occurrence indeed. It meant she was really confused. "But the suitcases, Rob saw her suitcases, why would she ..."

"Have you seen the suitcases?"

"Well, no, but ... you think Rob's lying, don't you. Why would he make something like that up?"

To get you to Soursop, that's why, Glenn thought but didn't say. Why did Bobbie want Ria there? Was he going to pull off his scam right under the nose of her brother? It wouldn't be hard to do. James had a self-centred streak that made him almost as blind as Doc Butler sometimes. When it kicked in any person or situation that didn't directly affect him barely blipped on his radar. "I don't know why he's doing it. I don't know anything about him. All I know is that the girl is alive and well and in Toronto."

"Something's not right about this ..."

"I'll say!"

Ria ignored his comment. "Rob isn't lying, Glenn. I'm sure of it."

"Well, he's not being entirely accurate, either."

"Look, I know we have a lot to sort out between us and this trip hasn't helped things any ..."

Talk about an understatement!

"... but I know — know — that something is going on down here. I haven't even told you about Albert and whatever he brought to James, or James lying to me about it. Glenn?"

Uh-oh. That was Ria's *I'm about to ask you for a favour* voice.

"Would you go talk to the girl yourself? See if you can find out something, anything, about what happened down here?"

He listened to her breathing.

"Please?"

Her request was a simple enough one to handle, if she gave him the girl's address, but Glenn wasn't so sure that he wanted to do it. Would it have killed her to let him know that she'd changed her plans before she took off to the Caribbean? "I'm kind of swamped right now, Ria." He glanced around his home office at the multitude of papers that were spread everywhere. The most important ones were on his desk, but to narrow it down to those important papers he'd had to do one hell of a lot of research and that research had generated the paper waste-land that eradicated his usually neat home office. "Why don't you just ask James, straight out?"

"Because it would get Rob in trouble. James told him that he'd lose his job if he didn't drop it."

Like Glenn gave a rat's ass whether or not the guy kept his job! He could always call James himself to find out what was really going on, but their last conversation hadn't gone too well. Not well at all. He doubted James would even answer if he saw that it was Glenn calling.

"Are you still there?"

"Yeah, I'm here. I was just thinking. "

"So, will you? Go to her place and talk to her?"

"I'd need more information first. Why don't you get Bob —"

"His name's Rob."

"Fine, Rob." Rob, Bob, Bobbie, Dickhead, whatever. "Why don't you get him to call me? He can give me some more background info and I'll see what I can find out, but it's a backburner thing right now. Remember that story I told you about, the one on white-collar criminals who never even get charged?" Ria didn't say anything so he kept on going. "Bob —"

"Rob!"

Glenn took a deep breath and counted to two. "No, Bob. My editor?" Again, no response from Ria. "Bob," he stressed both B's, "loved the idea and you won't believe the stuff I've dug up on this one guy in British Columbia." Glenn built up steam as his thoughts refocused on the thrill of a chase. "He tells everybody that he's a retired FCA, which is some kind of high honcho accountant, and he's socially connected up the whazoo. He's on the finance committees at a couple of big name charities, handling all their money. But get this — the slime bucket pleaded guilty to stealing over a million bucks from some of his clients, was expelled from the accountant association and striped of his FCA, and he had to swear in an affidavit that he'd never accept another position of financial authority ever again. His only punishment was a small fine and the only press his expulsion got was a tiny little announcement in an accountant's magazine with limited readership and a microscopic announcement in Canada's other national paper, and he tried to stop even that. He said he'd kill himself if his accounting parents scolded him in public. Because practically nobody saw those announcements, his high-society friends still see him as some sort of paragon of financial authority, but in reality he's nothing more than a well-dressed crook. Can you believe it? This grown-ass man tried to keep his crimes secret by threatening to hold his breath until he turned blue in the face and died."

"I'm not asking you to do a complete background check on the girl. I'm just asking you to talk to her."

What Glenn had wanted to hear was *"Wow, that's unbelievable,"* or, at the very least, *"Who is it?"* but Ria wasn't hearing a thing he said. "And if she won't talk to me or if she says everything was hunky dory down there? Then what?"

"Then I guess I'll come home, or maybe I'll see if I can get booked on another cruise to the Galapagos. I haven't thought that far ahead. Why does it matter?"

Because it matters to me, Glenn thought. *It matters that I'd like to see you, talk to you, sort out whatever's going on between us.* The only thing that apparently mattered to Ria was that Bobbie kept his job. "Never mind. Get Rob to call …"

"What do you need to know?"

"Her address would be kind of helpful." He heard the sharp edge in his own voice and did nothing to smooth it out. "A photograph wouldn't hurt either."

"Is that it?"

"It's a start."

"Does this mean you'll be able to squeeze a visit to her place into your hectic schedule?"

What the hell was she getting mad about? He wasn't the one who'd crossed a continent to "help" someone of the opposite sex! "I'll do what I can."

Ria's terse *"thank you"* met Glenn's brusque *"you're welcome"* and the call ended, leaving Glenn angry, hurt, and disappointed, and probably some other emotions that he didn't want to think about, let alone deal with.

He tried to get his head back into the story he'd been working on, but couldn't shake the mental image of a severed foot.

What kind of sick mind would come up with something like that, real or fake? He vaguely remembered something about a foot floating up on the shore of Vancouver Island. Maybe that's where the idea had come from? He Googled "foot on shore British Columbia." Sure enough, he found page after page of articles about six severed feet that had washed up on various shores around the Vancouver area. The unusual nature of the story had garnered it a lot of press coverage. The BC feet had been in the water a long time, long enough for the skin, muscle, and ligaments to decompose or wash off, or get eaten by some sea critter. *"Through a process called disarticulation, the feet appear to have separated naturally from the body."* Glenn shuddered as he read the more formal description of why the feet had come off. No matter how you said it, it was disgusting. He closed down his web browser, not wanting to know any more gory details.

Bobbie would call and Glenn would slam him for messing with Ria's mind with his cockamamie story and the whole thing would be over and done with. With the exception of the Bobbie issue.

"Men!" I tossed the cordless phone onto the rattan sofa. A cute little speckled green gecko popped up from behind the sofa and hung on the wall, looking at me with his head tilted to the side. "Testosterone is a highly overrated hormone," I told my new gecko friend.

With a jerk, he quickly tilted his head to the other side. I took that as a sign of agreement. It must have been a female gecko.

Could Glenn have been any more obvious? I hadn't lied to him. I was upfront and honest about everything (if you didn't count me asking Cam not to tell Glenn about my call). I'd come to Soursop because there was a very real chance that

James was in trouble. The fact that I'd heard about it from Rob wasn't important. I'd come for James. (And if I repeated those thoughts in my head often enough I just might start believing them wholeheartedly.)

I wasn't going to allow myself to feel guilty, because I hadn't done anything wrong (mostly).

And, my thoughts weren't done with me yet — my silent rant continued, even if I had had a few less than faithful thoughts involving Rob, none of them had turned physical.

And even if they had, Glenn and I weren't married. We weren't living together. We were dating! Seeing each other. We'd made no commitment to each other. Our relationship was so new that we hadn't defined it yet.

(Yet, wasn't that exactly what Glenn had asked me to do? A little guilt crept in and I deliberately decided to ignore it.)

Given his mood there was no way I was going to let Glenn talk to Rob. I was going to get the information on Kate and I was going to be the one to call Glenn with it. And I knew where to find it.

Despite my repeated claim about not having anything to do with Butler Hotels I knew a lot about how they were run. The privacy and safety of their guests was handled the same way at every hotel in the chain. No one came or went from the property without being checked through security. Somewhere, on some computer, there would be a list of all the people allowed on the island — complete with a photo of their face and their personal information. All I had to do was find that list.

I found a map of Soursop in a folder of information on the table in my front hall. It showed where the roads were, the many villas and blocks of hotel rooms, the beach bars (there were four of them), the helipad, the docks (there was a big marina on the west side of the island), the tennis courts, the dive shop, the spa, the gym, the movie theatre (what did they need a movie theatre for? I'd already read that each room had a flat-screen TV with satellite reception), and the Internet café. The island was much wider than I'd thought and the road system looked as if it had been designed by a crayon-wielding child in the middle of a major sugar rush; brightly coloured roads squiggled, swooped, and zigzagged all over the island. If I took the blue crayon line, turned right at the red one, and then left on the orange one I'd hopefully end up in front of the main building.

As I drove along, taking only two wrong turns, I quickly learned how to tell the difference between hotel employees and television or movie personnel. Both groups wore a uniform, of sorts, but only the Butler employees had my second initial embroidered on their shirts. The television and movie people, who seemed to travel in small packs, wore a uniform of a T-shirt or loud Hawaiian shirt with jeans or shorts. No one, working for either employer, looked at me as I drove past them. They glanced at me, but quickly turned their gaze when I looked at them.

One person seemed out of place, not fitting into either group. She was dressed entirely in thin white crinkled cotton. With each step forward her pencil thin legs pushed against her wide-legged pants. The tunic top that she wore hung loosely over her torso. Even her hands were covered up, with white gloves. On her head sat a white sunhat with a brim wide enough to protect three people from the sun's rays. I couldn't see her hair, she had it wrapped up in a white scarf under her hat. The lenses of her sunglasses were Jackie Kennedy Onassis big and black and John Lennon round. She walked so slowly that it almost looked as if she was hovering just above the paved road, floating along at a ghostly pace. In her right gloved hand she held a thick stack of papers which were held together on one side by two brass studs. I slowed down as I passed her and looked hard at the papers. All I could see was the top sheet — *Rebecca's Story*. It wasn't a title I recognized. Maybe it was the title of the movie they were going to shoot? She was so covered up that I couldn't tell if she was Ariel Downes. She didn't turn to look at me. In my rear-view mirror I saw that she didn't stop to say hello to anyone she passed, nor did they stop to talk to her. If that was Ariel Downes she was doing a great Greta Garbo impersonation — everything about her silently screamed *I want to be alone*.

I parked under a large Flamboyant Tree in the small parking lot in front of the main building. Looking up to admire its vibrant green leaves and brilliant red-orange flowers I noticed something strange — a little red light in the *V* of its trunk. It was above the lens of a carefully camouflaged camera that had been wedged into the *V*. Big Brother (or, in my case, Little Brother) really was watching everything, everywhere. It gave me the creeps.

When I entered the lobby Little Brother himself was standing at the front desk talking to Ted, both of them surrounded by a television crew.

"… she's not answering, Mr. Butler. Do you want me to send someone down to her cottage?" Ted picked up a cordless phone from behind the counter.

"No, she's probably swimming or running or doing something physical. Ria likes that crap. Just leave her a message that I'm looking for her."

Ted spotted me. "I think you can tell her that yourself. She's right here!" He sounded oh so happy to see me.

James turned around and smiled. "Hey! I came over earlier than I thought. Feel like an early lunch?"

"Okay," I said with noticeable uncertainty. James sure noticed it, he looked hurt. "But can you give me a few minutes?

I have to … do something." Hopefully, it would only take me a few minutes. If I'd read Ted right he'd move extra fast to impress a Butler.

"Come find me when you're done. I'll be out by the pool."

James walked away. I smiled at Ted. Ted smiled back. He really did have a sexy smile. I stared at his shiny white teeth while I silently rehearsed the performance I was about to give.

"May I help you with something?"

James was out of earshot but the television crew had shifted positions to include me in their shot.

"Can you guys hold off for a minute?" I looked directly into one of the two cameras and used my friendly-but-in-charge hotel owner voice. "This discussion isn't part of your show." It seemed to do the trick, they lowered their equipment. "I need to see the guest registration information."

Ted knew the rules, only hotel management was allowed to access that information. I wasn't management, but I was a Butler. Sometimes the name came in handy. It opened doors.

"May I ask why?" He looked nervous, he was blinking too fast.

I switched to my friendly voice. "It's sort of personal. Can we talk in there?" I pointed to the closed door behind the front desk which hopefully led to the front desk manager's office. Even though they'd pointed their cameras away from me I couldn't be sure that the television crew had turned their microphones off.

"Certainly, Miss Butler. Right this way." Ted held open the swinging gate at the side of the reception desk and I followed him into the office.

It was a standard, boring, beige-and-brown office with file cabinets, a desk, and chair. Ted closed the door and looked at me expectantly.

"This is kind of embarrassing," I started. Ted's shoulders

relaxed a bit. I didn't like the storyline I'd come up with but it was all I could think of — mention *female troubles* and most men of a certain age would bend over backwards to get you to stop talking. "On top of the night sweats, hot flashes, and mood swings, I'm having more and more old-age moments, as I call them, and I've just had a big one. I saw someone I know I should know on one of the television crews when I was driving down here. He shouted hello and, I feel like an idiot admitting this, I can't for the life of me remember his name. I just want to scroll through the guest photos to put a name to his face and then I won't feel like I'm a dotty old lady when I bump into him again."

Ted laughed, an annoyingly condescending laugh. "We all have those moments."

It was a good thing he hadn't added *"deary"* to the end of that sentence! I would have kicked him in the shin with all the velocity that my non-geriatric legs could muster.

He walked over to the desk, put his hand on the mouse, and started clicking.

I quietly slipped into the chair and watched the screen.

After a few clicks, the screen filled with rows and columns of little headshots. Underneath each one was the name of the person. The names were in alphabetical order. Finding Kate Bond would be easy.

"Let me know if you see him," Ted started to scroll down the page painfully slowly (probably because he doubted I'd be able to focus quickly through my cataracts), but stopped at Agnelli when we both heard someone yelling in the lobby.

"… I don't pay you fuckers to sit around contemplating the lint in your belly buttons! Why aren't you shooting? Where's Ted?" The door to the office burst open and Dan came marching in. "What the fuck are you doing in here?"

Ted jumped to attention. "We're just …"

"It's hotel business." My hotel owner voice lost some of its confidence after being confronted so suddenly.

"And it takes two of you to do it? We're making a show here and footage of a closed door isn't something I need a lot of. Do the hotel shit on your own time."

Ted looked torn, not knowing whether to stay and help the old lady (who might be an owner of the hotel he wanted to work at) or go with Dan (who was one of the bosses of the television show he was working on).

"I can handle this, Ted. It'll only take me a minute."

"Are you sure?"

"She said she'd handle it, didn't she? So get back out here and do something screen worthy! I hear you had a poultry problem at Ariel's villa. Have you called maintenance to nail up the loose board?"

"Not yet."

"Now might be a good time to do it, don't you think? And show some anger, some frustration, when you're talking to them. Their screw up upset the star you're supposed to be making happy, it made you look bad. You want that board fixed immediately!" Dan pointed to the front desk.

Once Ted and Dan were out of the room I pulled the chair in closer to the desk and quickly scrolled through the few remaining As to the Bs and Bond. As I double clicked on Kate's name I could hear Ted acting very upset as he spoke to someone on the phone. He wasn't a bad actor. If I'd been the one at the other end of that call I'd have believed he was really upset. I wondered if he found it as interesting as I did that Dan, who hadn't even been on the island when it happened, knew all about the chickens and the loose board.

The next screen to pop up was a full page with Kate's information. Her photo filled the right side of the screen; her personal information was listed on the left.

She looked so young. If I hadn't seen her birth date I would have guessed her to be a teenager, not twenty-four years old. She had shoulder-length brunette hair and wore too much makeup. Her lips didn't need the heavy coating of lipstick she'd put on; she had a beautiful smile — the kind that made you want to smile back at it.

My lipstick-free lips curved down into a frown, though, when I saw the person listed after her — Maria Butler. I opened my information page and saw myself staring back at me. When had my picture been taken? I was wearing the same T-shirt, so maybe they took a frame from the video that had been shot of my arrival? James was listed as my immediate family contact, and he was identified as my brother. But they got my mailing address wrong; they'd used the address of the head office in Sydney. They had my marital status right, though: Divorced. I closed my file down.

While the printer spewed out Kate's information, I decided to look up one more person and scrolled up the *B*s. There wasn't a picture or even a listing for Albert Black. The only way I was going to get more information on him would be through James, and I doubted he'd be eager to open up about whatever Albert was transporting to the island.

With the page of Kate's information safely tucked in my pocket, I closed the computer program down and went back out to the front desk, mouthing *thank you* to Ted and giving him a thumbs-up signal as I closed the office door behind me.

"See that you do!" He shouted into the phone just before slamming it down. "Did you find what you were looking for, Miss Butler?" He asked me in a very calm and friendly voice.

I wasn't sure which voice was coming from Ted the person, not Ted the actor. "I sure did. Thanks."

"Who was it?" Ted threw me a curveball I hadn't been expecting.

I blurted out the first name that came to my mind. "Rob Churcher. He's worked for James for years. I can't believe I forgot his name."

"He's working with the other contestant and I believe they're off island now."

"I'm sure I'll see him around. Thanks again." I wanted to get out of camera range and started to walk away from the reception desk, but quickly spun on my heels to face Ted one last time. "I just remembered that I have some papers I need to send to head office." Glenn would have loved knowing that I'd figuratively made his condo our head office. "Is there a scanner in the Internet café?"

"There are two of them, actually. Our guests require all the business services that they have at hand in their own offices and we pride ourselves on being prepared to meet their needs. If you need any IT assistance just pick up the phone on the desk by the door of the café and someone will come right away." He'd obviously studied the Butler employee manual well.

"Okey-dokey." I spun around with a spritely youthful skip and went in search of the café.

Glenn was on the phone with his editor asking for an extension when Ria's email came in.

"No problem. You can work on something else and I know exactly what. You won't believe this one! Somebody got hold of my social insurance number and used it to set up an account with Quebec Hydro in my name! Now there's a debt collector hounding me and the wife and they've put a lien on my house — my real house, not some bogus place in Quebec. I've never even lived in Quebec!"

Bob's story suggestion didn't interest Glenn. "Identity theft is old news."

"Not when it's happening to me it isn't. We can do a series, highlighting individual cases ..."

"I might have something more current to work on. I have to check out a few leads, but there could be a story in it." Glenn didn't really believe that there was a story in Bobbie's scam, not one that would sell papers anyway, but he definitely didn't want to get saddled with a series on identity theft when he was right on the verge of blowing the white-collar story wide open.

"Story in what?"

"Some strange stuff's happening on the set of a reality TV series and I'd like to check —"

"Forget it! It's a fluff piece. Give it to someone in entertainment. In the meantime —"

"It might involve a murder and severed body parts."

Bob went silent. Glenn could hear him breathing heavily. "You've got a week. If nothing pans out I want you on the identity-theft piece."

He had a week to expose a scammer — either the white-collar slime or Bobbie. Glenn opened Ria's email. Her words didn't give him a warm and fuzzy feeling.

Here's the info on Kate. R

He got more pleasure out of looking at Kate's picture. She had a beautiful smile. He picked up the phone and dialled the number listed on her information sheet. Her voicemail kicked in after the fifth ring.

"Hi, I'm on location in the Caribbean for a couple of months so don't hold your breath waiting for me to call you back. I'll check my messages every so often, but my per diem won't cover a lot of long distance calls so I'll only call you back if it's super important. Thanks. See you in the movies!"

Odd.

Glenn hung up at the beep and stared at her picture on his computer screen. She sounded so happy as she boasted about working on location, even throwing in the bit about her per diem. As a production assistant she probably didn't get much of a per diem, just enough to cover her laundry expenses, meals, and a couple of phone calls home, but she'd sure sounded thrilled to have one.

If Kate had left the production over a week ago to come home, why hadn't she changed her phone message? He felt the tingle of the hairs on the back of his neck standing up. They only did that when he stumbled onto a story worth telling. Could be something. Might be nothing. It was worth taking the next step.

It was a nice day for a walk along the lakeshore anyway. Kate's place was only about ten or twelve blocks west of his condo building. What Glenn hadn't counted on, though, was the heat and humidity. His body liked the air conditioning in his condo. It didn't like the wall of thick heat that slammed into him as he walked past the Hockey Hall of Fame. He hoped there'd be a breeze off Lake Ontario and went two blocks farther south than he really had to. Queen's Quay was packed with tourists and office workers out for a midday stroll. He weaved his way through and around them and gave up any hope of a breeze by the time he was walking past the CN Tower. The lake was mirror flat. Man, it was hot! He mentally quoted one of his favourite movie lines. Matthew Broderick said it in *Biloxi Blues* — "It's like Africa hot." Glenn had never been to Africa, but he figured it was always hot there. He'd never been to the British Virgin Islands, either. He hoped it was worse than Africa hot there.

Kate's apartment was on the top floor of a building that used to house a coffin-making factory. It was in the west end of the city, down by the lakeshore, in an area that was in the process of changing from industrial to high-end condos and lofts. The meat packing plant at the end of her street had only closed down a few months ago. Good thing, too. On hot days the smell coming from that place had been horrific. Glenn worked a murder investigation in the plant right after being hired by the paper. It gave him the willies just being near the place again. Somewhere between the blood of the slaughtered animals and the blood of the slaughtered little girl he'd permanently lost his ability to control his stomach in gory situations, much to the amusement of his coworkers and his buddies on the homicide squad.

Kate's building had yet to be upgraded and to call it gritty would be a compliment. It wasn't air conditioned and Glenn was sweating like a not-yet-slaughtered pig by the time he finished walking up the four flights of stairs. Someone was watching Dr. Phil at full volume in the apartment next to Kate's. He knocked on Kate's door just as Dr. Phil asked *"How's that working for you?"* Glenn was paying more attention to the softly spoken response to Dr. Phil's question than he was to Kate's door so when it opened it caught him off guard.

"Kate? Kate Bond?"

"Who wants to know?" She must not have worn all her piercings when she had the photo taken of herself for the shoot in the BVI. Glenn hadn't seen any in that photo, but the woman standing in front of him had five studs in her left ear, one in each eyebrow, one on the side of her right nostril, and he caught a glimpse of one in her tongue.

He fumbled in his pocket, hoping to find one of his business cards to add legitimacy to his visit. "I'm Glenn Cooper." She read the wrinkled card he handed to her. "I'm doing a piece for the Entertainment section on what it's like to work on a television show and I heard that you've just come back from working on one that was shot in the British Virgin Islands. Have you got a few minutes?"

"No." It was hard to believe that such a harsh response had come from the same person who'd sounded so cheerful on her answering machine.

"No, you don't have a few minutes, or no, you didn't work on the show?"

She started to close the door. "I don't want to be interviewed, okay?" A black cat bolted out through the almost closed door. "Crap!" She threw the door open and ran after the cat. "Salem! Help me catch him," she yelled to Glenn.

Great. Glenn wasn't a cat person. But if catching the cat would get Kate to open up, maybe even answer a few questions about good old Bobbie, then he'd catch the damn cat.

They eventually cornered the cat in the stairwell. Backed into a corner, literally, he puffed up and hissed angrily.

"He's declawed. He won't scratch you," Kate informed Glenn, while staying a good distance away from the cat.

Glenn was a dog man. Dogs he could understand. Cats not so much. It was hard to like a species when you knew most of them were smarter than you. And black cats just plain freaked him out. If this one had really been declawed why was Kate staying so far away from him? He got his answer when he picked the cat up. Salem still had all of his teeth. His extremely sharp teeth.

He could feel blood dripping from his hand as he carried the cat back to Kate's apartment, but he refused to look at it. (What was it with blood in that neighbourhood?)

"Come in. You can rinse that off and I'll find you a bandage." Kate once again stood a healthy distance away from the cat as she held the door open for Glenn.

Salem flicked his tail three times in short jerks once Glenn let go of him, and then proceeded to curl up on the couch and give himself a bath. He was probably licking off Glenn's blood.

Standing at the kitchen sink in the bachelor apartment, his hand under running water, Glenn looked around (instead of at his hand). The place was plastered in movie and television-show posters. There were so many of them that he couldn't see what colour the walls were painted. One wall was devoted to sitcoms from the eighties. A *Kate and Allie* poster was smack in the middle of the wall, with the other posters fanned out around it. Glenn recognized most of the shows and smiled when he saw the one for *Packham Inn*. He and James and their university dorm mates used to get high and watch that show all the time. The pot made it hysterically funny. It had been about a family, kind of like the Partridge Family, who ran a small hotel in LA. They sang (sometimes on key), they danced (those bits were really funny if the pot was strong enough), and each week mayhem and madness ensued with the characters who stayed in their hotel. Glenn and James had decided that most of the visiting characters must have been recent escapees from an insane asylum and often wished Jack Nicholson had stayed at the hotel in character as R.P. McMurphy. They understood why it was a hit in Canada, one of the kid actors was Canadian, but the only logical explanation for the show's long-running success in the U.S. was that the audience there was just as high as Glenn and James. The guy who'd played the big brother was a teen heartthrob right up until he drowned in his own vomit after a wild night of partying. That killed the show and the careers of the other child actors on it. The little sister went on to an illustrious career in porn. Because of the success of the show in syndication the precocious freckled-faced, blonde-haired, blue-eyed middle brother had never been allowed to grow up into adult roles. He and his syndicated musical siblings still pretended to play instruments in the wee hours of the morning on television sets all around the world.

Glenn glanced at a *Sabrina, the Teenage Witch* poster and then understood why Kate had named her attack cat Salem.

A scan of the rest of the apartment revealed that the furniture was all pretty ratty, but the big flat-screen TV was new and expensive.

Kate came out of the bathroom with a box of bandages and joined him at the sink. "That doesn't look so bad. One should do."

From the pain and the amount of blood Glenn had felt he was surprised to hear that he wasn't going to need stitches.

"Thanks for grabbing Salem. He's a real pain sometimes."

"Tell me about it." Glenn stuck the biggest bandage from the box over the gaping wound on the back of his hand. Then he made the mistake of looking down at the sink. His blood had mixed with the water and there looked like there was a lot of it, an awful lot of it. He quickly looked up and walked away. "I can see why you work in television. This place is like a shrine to TV and movies." There was a stack of autograph books on the coffee table and from the look of the worn pages they'd been flipped through many, many times. On the table next to the couch there was a digital picture frame. The images kept changing yet, at the same time, remained the same. They were all head and shoulder shots of Kate (minus her piercings) with someone famous; stars like Brad Pitt, John Cusack, Catherine Zeta Jones, George Clooney, Colin Farrell, and Zac Efron. All of them had shot movies in Toronto. "You've met all of these people?"

She nodded as she walked toward the door. "Just because you helped me catch Salem it doesn't mean I'm going to answer your questions."

"Even though I got injured in the line of duty?" Her smile made him hope that he was making some headway. He stood his ground, trying to think of a way to soften her up even more. The next photo in the digital picture frame was of Kate with an old guy who Glenn didn't recognize. But he sure recognized the guy in the next photo. "That's James Butler."

Kate stood by the door, her hand on the handle. "Who?" She turned and looked at Glenn as she opened the door. "Oh, yeah, him."

Glenn didn't budge. Why didn't Kate know who James was? She'd supposedly been working for him for the last few months. "Which show was he in? I know his face, but can't remember the show."

If Kate had had an Adam's apple it would have bobbed when she swallowed hard. "*Corner Gas.*"

At least she'd picked a Canadian show. But James hadn't acted in it. He'd never acted in anything. It wasn't even a show that James' company produced. Glenn continued to stare at the picture frame but barely registered the next three pictures of Kate with a man Glenn didn't recognize but, from his perfectly straight and white teeth and his masterfully manicured dark eyebrows, he looked like a movie star of some sort. The man in the shots didn't look happy to be in any of them. Glenn wasn't happy, either. Ria was right — something wasn't adding up. Then it switched to a picture of a younger Kate with Steve Irwin, the Crocodile Hunter.

"I guess it's gone back to the beginning of the loop. That picture was taken years ago, obviously. Anyway, like I said, thanks for helping out with Salem."

Glenn smiled. "No problem." He started to walk toward the door. "Can I ask just one question?"

"You can ask, but that doesn't mean I'll answer."

"Were you lying to me about not recognizing James Butler, your boss from the show you were just working on, or were you lying to the police about being Kate Bond?"

CHAPTER
FIVE

Even though I couldn't hear what they were saying, I knew from the expressions on their faces and the way they emphasized their words with jerky hand movements that James and Dan were arguing. Sitting at a poolside table, their chairs turned to face each other, they were definitely facing off about something. Whether by choice or by accident, their table wasn't near any of the other occupied tables. All of the other people around the pool were laughing loudly and obviously enjoying each other's company. Dan and James were speaking in hushed growls.

Dan was drinking some sort of frilly Caribbean holiday tourist drink; the liquid was bright red, there was a pineapple chunk slipped over one side of the frosted glass, and a little green umbrella poking up beside a skinny straw. James' drink was more basic — scotch, neat. I recognized the golden liquid instantly. It had been our father's anaesthetic of choice (and abuse) during the hellish years after our mother's death. Seeing James suck back a big gulp of it made me mad, made me sad, made me ill. What was he trying to wash away?

Their argument stopped when James looked up and saw me walking around the pool to join them. The welcoming smile on his face was in stark contrast to the curious stares I felt scanning me from every other direction. A noticeable hush swept over the pool patio like a wave as I walked to James' table.

The pool, like James' drink, was basic; a large rectangle. The far end of it melded into the infinity of the Caribbean blue beneath it. I weaved my way through the two rows of padded lounge chairs that faced the shallow end near the door I'd come out and then walked a straight line behind the rows of lounge chairs that ran the length of James and Dan's side of the pool. I kept my eyes on James, not wanting to meet the questioning eyes of the lounging tanning people on my left who'd turned their heads to watch me, or the people seated at the tables on my right under the awning that ran the length of the pool. I wished James and Dan had chosen to sit on the other side of the pool — there were fewer people over there. Only the tables and lounge chairs closest to the doors were occupied. The table directly across the pool from James and Dan had been blocked off by a line of orange plastic cones that were spaced out on the flagstone patio. That lone table had been set with silver and crystal on linen for one diner, but the diner wasn't there.

As I took the chair that James pulled out for me I saw that the pool was set on the edge of a cliff. Below us was a marina that looked much more businesslike than the solitary wide dock Malvin had brought me to when I'd arrived on the island. It had multiple rows of docks that were big enough to classify as wharfs. A barge was tied to the end of one wharf and people were scurrying in and out of the large container on it. They went into the container empty handed, they came out in pairs, their hands working together to unload the heavy equipment that the container contained: massive lights, coil after coil of what looked like thick black electrical cable, silver metallic boxes the size of trunks (some of them on wheels). The movie crew was moving in.

"What'll ya have?" James handed me a menu.

"What I'd really like is a Diet Coke, but apparently I'm not allowed to." I looked at Dan.

"Pepsi, Coke, they're all the same." He lifted his glass and held it out for me to take. "Try some of this. It's a Soursop Shirley Temple."

"I'll pass, thanks." I turned and made a point of looking at James' glass. "What are you having?"

"The crab salad." He deliberately lifted his glass and gulped down another mouthful of scotch. "It should be here any minute."

"Cue the waiter!" Dan yelled and snapped his fingers.

Dan had powerful fingers. The reverberations from his snap had barely dissipated when a waiter carrying a tray on his shoulder came out of a side door and headed for our table. He delivered James' crab salad (and a second glass of scotch), Dan's steak, and took my order (James' crab salad looked delicious).

"So, Mz Butler," Dan sounded like a bee as he emphasized the z, "why are you here?"

"Because James invited me to join him for lunch?"

"That's not what I …" Dan didn't finish his sentence; his attention was focused somewhere else.

I turned around in my chair to see what he was watching so intently. The ghost lady was floating along the pool patio, following a waiter who was showing her to the empty table directly across the pool from us.

The hush over the entire pool area didn't come in a slow moving wave for her entrance, it landed like a lead anvil. It was as if everyone around the pool was momentarily frozen in time, slow-motion time. She melted into the chair the waiter pulled out for her and then slowly removed her large sunhat and gloves.

"That's star power," Dan said admiringly. From the tone of his voice I could tell that Dan wasn't seeing a product, he was seeing a star.

"Is that Ariel Downes?" I wasn't a big movie star fan, but even I felt a quick trickle of excitement run through me.

"Yup." James polished off the last ounce from his first glass and then picked up the recently delivered refill.

"What movie are you making, Dan?"

"Did you ever read *Rebecca*?"

"Yes!" Daphne du Maurier's book was one of the few books that I actually re-read just for the sheer pleasure of it. I must have read it at least ten times and still hadn't been able to decide if Rebecca had been a villain or a victim.

"We're doing an updated version, based on that book and mixed in with another book called *Rebecca's Tale*."

I hadn't heard of that book. "Did du Maurier write that, too?"

He shook his head. "No, some broad named Sally Beauman wrote it. It's a continuation, of sorts, of du Maurier's book."

"Dan's going through a Hitchcock phase," James interjected in a less-than-impressed way. "First *The Birds* —"

"Which was based on a short story by du Maurier," Dan added.

"— now this." James began impaling pieces of his salad with his fork.

"What part's Ariel going to play?" She certainly didn't seem right for the part of Mrs. Danvers, the weird housekeeper who worshipped Rebecca in a psycho sort of way, and she had too much presence to play the mousy unnamed second Mrs. de Winter.

Dan carved a paper thin slice off his steak. "Rebecca, of course."

"But Rebecca isn't in the book. She's dead."

"Well, she's alive in the movie."

"Who's Chris Regent playing?" I could see him as Maxim, Rebecca's husband.

"His character is based on the Terence Gray character."

I'd read *Rebecca* so many times that I knew every character's name by heart, even the minor ones, and there wasn't a character named Terence Gray in du Maurier's book. He must have come from the other book Dan mentioned. "Why are you shooting it here? The story was set in Cornwall."

Dan finished chewing another sliver of steak and dabbed at his mouth with a napkin before answering. "Cornwall Schmorm-wall! It's too fucking cold and wet and depressing there."

Personally, I'd always liked the climate of Cornwall, which was only sometimes cold and wet, and never depressing.

"Besides, what kind of press could *Check-Out Time* give my movie or your hotel if we shot in Cornwall? You don't own a hotel in Cornwall, do you?"

"I don't own any hotel anywhere."

"Which brings me back to my question — why are you here?"

James put down his fork, leaned back in his chair and watched me closely. My answer had to be good.

"Vacation."

"Interesting," Dan's eyes closed to slits. "You were travelling for your work, but then decided to take a vacation by travelling some more. That doesn't sound like much of a vacation to me."

James smirked, ever so slightly, but I caught it.

"It sounds like a vacation to me. I can relax. No one's expecting an information-packed, entertaining, well-written article, with photos, when I get home."

"So, it's a vacation because you don't have to do any research?"

"That's one way of looking at it." My crab salad arrived and I chose to look at it, not Dan or James.

"Yet, when I saw you in the office, you were doing research and I have to ask myself why — why were you researching information on Rob Churcher when you'd just spent almost an hour with him at your villa?"

Little brother's partner was watching me a little too closely. I chewed a piece of crabmeat so long that it turned to pure mush, but I kept on chewing — desperately trying to think of an answer that would sound believable.

There was a scurry of activity behind me, feet running along the stones of the patio.

"Mr. Shykoff," Ted said breathlessly as he ran up to the table, followed by the ubiquitous television crew, "we might have a problem." He stood beside Dan's chair, but turned just enough to be facing the cameras.

"What sort of problem?" Dan asked.

"Miss Downes ordered a —" Ted stopped himself and thought for a minute or two, "— she ordered a brand of soda pop that the hotel doesn't currently carry."

"So?" Dan didn't look very concerned.

"Well, I know how some movie stars are and I wanted to make sure that there's nothing in her contract about it."

Dan's eyebrows rose up. "Good point. Where's Winnie?"

"I believe she's in her office."

Dan bent over and reached for something under the table and I thought I heard James whisper *Plug your ears.*

Before I knew it, Dan was holding a megaphone in front of his mouth and the sound person who'd been standing beside my chair was madly fiddling with the dials on his equipment.

"WINNIE!" Dan bellowed to the sky. "I NEED YOU! NOW!"

I looked over at Ariel Downes to see how she was reacting to Dan's blast. She'd lowered her sunglasses just enough to get an unfiltered view of Dan over the top of them.

Dan looked at his watch and started to tap his fingers impatiently on the table. "What part of now do you think she didn't understand?"

So little time had passed since Dan's blast that Winnie, whoever she was, couldn't have made it to our table even if she'd been sitting at one of the tables across the pool from us (unless she was capable of transporting herself from one location to another like a character from *Star Trek*).

"That blasted woman. I don't know why I put up with her insolence." Dan brought the megaphone back to his mouth. "What took you so long?" Even though he hadn't screamed, the decibel level of his voice was still painful.

A woman, who looked like the quintessential spinster in her fifties and from the fifties, was walking toward us from the main building. Her chunky high heels thumped against the flagstones. She was wearing a suit, a tweed suit — despite the heat, the skirt went just below her knee, the short jacket was buttoned up, and her legs were covered in thick stockings. Her hair was a mix of black and white, the strands contrasting as sharply as a skunk's stripe, and it was all twisted up in what looked like a long braid that had been rolled around and around into a tight bun on the back of her head. "I was on the phone." She stood in front of the cameras, her back defiantly to them, clutching a couple of small slips of pink paper.

"Is there a clause in Ariel's contract about what drinks we have to have here for her?"

Winnie immediately closed her eyes and just stood there.

"Photographic memory," Dan said to me. "You wouldn't believe some of the things agents wrangle for their clients in contracts. That idiot Regent has a whole clause about red flowers. Red flowers! Who's scared of red flowers, I ask you? Every single arrangement for his villa had to be …"

"No," Winnie's eyes popped open, "nothing about drinks. Her assistant has a peanut allergy though, so the island has to be peanut free for the duration of the movie shoot. I sent the head chef a memo about that weeks ago."

"There you go, Ted my boy, problem solved. Now go get her order put together and don't let one of the waiters deliver it to her, you do it. And make a point of apologizing for the delay." Dan pointed his megaphone at the girl who was standing behind the crew. I recognized her, and her pink bangs, as the girl who'd been shooting me when I arrived on the island. "Who's covering your team, Pam?"

She looked surprised at being spoken to. "Norbert."

"Tell him to get a shot from a second-floor balcony, with the movie crew unloading the equipment down below in the background, when Ted's delivering Ariel's food."

"Howie just told him to go over to —"

Dan cut her off. "I don't care where he sent Norbert. I'm telling you where I want him!"

"But, like, Howie's kind of the director and isn't he supposed to say where the cameras go?"

"Does Howie sign your paycheque?" Dan said through his clenched teeth.

"No." Pam took a deep breath and blew out the air with enough force to make her bangs lift off her forehead.

Dan leaned back and relaxed a bit. "Right. Who does sign it?"

"Well," she bobbed her head from side to side slightly, as if trying to make up her mind how to answer Dan's question, "James does, actually."

Dan froze, only his eyes expressed his anger. It was an

intense (and kind of scary) anger. "Do you want him to keep signing your cheques?"

Pam nodded. "That'd be nice. And, in return, I'll keep showing up for work."

"James?" Dan didn't take his glare off Pam.

James' shoulders slumped. He looked, and sounded, the part of a spineless lackey. "Pam, tell Norbert to get a shot from the balcony. If Howie gives you grief, tell him to come talk to me."

Pam shrugged her shoulders and pulled the radio off her belt. "Okay." She spun around on one heel and walked away from our table.

Dan turned on James. "For the second time, I'm telling you to fire her. She's nothing but trouble."

James sat up just a bit straighter. "For the second time, no. Pam's a damn good PA."

Little brother had one or two vertebrae left after all.

Dan aimed his anger and frustration at Ted. "What are you waiting for? GO!"

Ted nodded and bolted to the doors at the end of the pool, his crew running right behind him. Winnie, on the other hand, didn't budge.

"We're done," Dan waved her away and lifted his glass. "That's all I wanted."

"We're not done yet. I came out to give you two phone messages. One," she handed him the top piece of pink paper, "Harvey Levin wants to talk to you." She looked up at Dan. "I leaked the clip of the Albert incident this morning. Do you want to call him back?"

Dan shook his head and handed the paper back to Winnie.

Winnie folded the slip of paper and then handed the one beneath it to Dan. "Two, you have to deal with this — quickly."

Dan's face fell as he read whatever was written on the paper. "Shit!" He scrunched it into an extremely tight ball. "It's the insurance company," he said to James.

James' forehead instantly creased with multiple worry lines.

"How did they find out?" Dan was struggling to control his voice.

"First guess, someone told them." Winnie didn't appear to be having any problems staying calm. "They've called twice now. I told them you were off island and that you wouldn't be back until later this afternoon."

"Is this about —" James started to ask.

Dan shot James a look that screamed *"shut up"* just as loudly as it would have if he'd been using the megaphone.

"They know about Chris Regent's night on the town in St. Thomas. They're threatening to cancel the policy." Winnie sounded bored.

Dan re-inflated and fired off orders. "Call his agent and read him the riot act — his client will be in breach of contract if he does it again, the sobriety clause is two fucking pages long! Remind him that I can replace the little fucker at the drop of the hat. Val McCubbin would give his left nut for this part. Tell Regent's agent that!"

"His manager's with him, remember?" Winnie took advantage of the pause while Dan inhaled. "Mike's babysitting Chris until he gets to location."

"Well, he's doing a shit-ass job of it! Make sure he knows that. And send someone to Regent's villa before he gets here. No! You go, go over the place like the sniffer dog I know you are. I want your personal guarantee that he hasn't got something stashed away in there, waiting for him. Flush everything you find down the toilet. And call Judy, she's on the boat going to get him, tell her to take every bottle on it and toss it overboard. Chris better damn well show up sober and stay sober."

"Anything else?"

"When are the speedboats supposed to be getting here?"

"Now," she pointed to the sea below us.

Dan spun around in his chair and looked down at the marina. "They're blue!"

I had to sit up as straight as I could and lean at a strange angle to see what he was talking about. Two identical big speedboats, both blue, were barrelling and bouncing over the waves, heading straight for the marina. They reminded me of the speedboats that were used in the opening montage of *Miami Vice*.

"They're fucking blue!"

"Unless you're going to ask me to go paint them some other colour, I'm done here." Winnie turned around and stomped on her square heels back to the building.

"Cheeky bitch," Dan muttered under his breath as he turned around and looked at James. "Blue! Who puts a blue boat on blue water?"

"What's wrong with blue boats?" I asked James more than Dan.

"No contrast against the water." He finished his second drink. "They'll stand out more in the shot if they're yellow or red …"

"I don't care if they're fucking polka dot, as long as they're not blue!" Once again, Dan's frenetic attention shifted. Someone had run down the other side of the pool and was moving the orange cones that separated Ariel's table from the rest. Dan stood up and spoke in a much calmer voice. "Time for me to make my cameo. I'm going to officially welcome my star."

Dan had timed his welcome to coincide with the delivery of Ariel's food — both of which were going to be shot by the television crew that was following Ted as he carried a large tray on his shoulder from the main building to Ariel's table.

He unloaded the plates and full glasses from the tray so professionally that I had to assume he'd started his hospitality career as a waiter. While Ted set the food on the table, Dan slipped into the chair next to Ariel's. He was all smiles and had left his megaphone behind at our table.

"Is he clinically insane?" I asked James. Our father had been a highly respected psychiatrist but even he would have thrown his hands up in defeat if he'd had a patient like Dan.

"No, he's just Dan. You get used to him after a while."

"Is Winnie his secretary?"

James nodded. "She's been with him since he started out."

The blue boats slowed down and pulled up next to one of the docks in the marina. "Why does he need two identical speedboats in his movie? Rebecca died in her sailboat."

"She's going to blow up in Dan's version. One of the boats will be used in travelling shots and close-ups and the other one will be rigged up with radio remote and the explosives."

I didn't say anything right away; I wanted a minute to think. There were many possible responses running through my head. I chose the explosive one. "Like the boat they blew up with the dummy named Albert in it?"

James looked surprised. "How'd you hear about that?"

I fiddled with what was left of my salad and tried to sound nonchalant. "Rob mentioned it."

"Oh yeah?"

"Yeah."

"What else did he mention? You two sure hooked up fast enough." The anger in James' voice killed my appetite.

"He came to my door with one of your contestants and I invited him to stay. He told me that he thinks you're stressed out and working too hard on this production." I forced myself to meet his glare. "He's worried about you. And, I've got to tell you, so am I. You look awful, you're drinking, and …"

"Of course I'm stressed out! Do you have any idea how much is riding on this show for me?"

"Is that all it is? The show?"

"Isn't that enough?" His lower lip was quivering and his eyes started to get watery. "If this show flops, I'm screwed. I'll lose my shot at features, Dan'll never team up with me again, which will mean I'll lose his distribution contracts for any shows I make after this. Aunt Patti and Uncle Richard will be angry if they don't get the promo they're expecting. Even if the show flies they'll probably be mad at me. Dan just told me that he wants one contestant to win and Aunt Patti's already told me that she wants the other one to win, so no matter what happens someone's going to be pissed. And," he stood up with a jerk, "while all of this crap is going on, my wife is threatening to destroy me financially. Other than that, life's just peachy. You sure picked a great time to stick your nose in my business, Ria. Family interference is that last thing I need!"

"How about some family support? I'm on your side, James. You know that."

"Right now, the only thing I know for sure is that I have to go talk to one of my producers about how we're going to deal with the budget overruns that Dan's stunts have caused." Those few remaining vertebrae were having a hard time holding his spine straight. "Dinner's at seven. Dan's set up a special dinner for you and Ariel." He looked and sounded as if those few remaining vertebrae had collapsed on themselves.

I wanted to run after him and give him a great big hug but knew, given his mood, that he'd just push me away. How the heck was I going to get him to open up to me? He was in one of his *the-world's-against-me* moods and until that mood eased off he wasn't going to let me in.

On the other side of the pool Ariel and Dan were in the middle of a heated argument. Ariel had her script open and kept jabbing at it with the arm of her sunglasses. Dan looked like he was trying to reason with her, touching her arm and smiling a lot — but his actions weren't calming her down any.

It seemed like the only people who were actually enjoying themselves in the Caribbean paradise were the off-duty crew. They were laughing and splashing like a bunch of kids at summer camp. Even the working crew on the docks below the pool deck were enjoying themselves, their laughter and friendly shouts were carried up to me by the onshore breezes. I could hear one of them whistling while he worked and, from my vantage point, they did look like the seven dwarves times five.

"Fine!" Ariel's strong voice startled me. "I'll play it your way, but you're wrong." She didn't float away from the table, she marched — quickly.

I decided to follow her lead. I'd lost my appetite anyway.

Kate, or whoever she was, closed the door slowly, leaned her back against it and crossed her arms over her chest. "Can't you just find someone else to interview? There must be hundreds of people who work on television shows and movies in Toronto. Why are you so interested in Kate?" The corner of her mouth slid up into a sly smile. "You're not doing an article about just any production, are you? You're looking for the inside scoop on Kate's supposed disappearance. He's good, I'll give him that."

Glenn forced his lips to stay together. Yeah, he had a million questions screaming through his head and wanting to be let free, but sometimes not asking them left the person he was interviewing wanting to fill the silence in the air with more answers than they normally would have given.

"Listen, there's no story here, okay? Honest. Kate's fine. He's just using this as a publicity stunt." She waited for Glenn to say something. He stayed silent. "Kate left by choice and I guarantee you she'll reappear in a big way very soon."

Salem started to purr in his sleep. Dr. Phil continued to talk in the next apartment. Glenn finally broke the impasse of silence. "Why did you lie to the police about being Kate?"

"Because I don't want to be me right now. That's why I'm actually staying here, not just coming over to feed Salem."

"And you are?" Glenn already knew the answer. It was obvious that she was Kate's twin. He never would have guessed her name, though.

"I'm Allie," she pointed at the *Kate & Allie* poster on the wall. "Our parents watched way too much television!"

"Why are you hiding in Kate's apartment and identity?"

"It's a matter of wanting all my body parts to stay attached, okay?"

Glenn immediately thought of the unattached foot. "You're scared of someone hurting you? You think the police would hurt you?" Maybe there was a real investigative piece here after all?

She shook her head. "Not them, but my ex did some less-than-legal things and they want me to testify against him. He'd do whatever it took to make sure I couldn't talk."

"The police could protect you." Glenn said with little conviction. The police would do all they could to protect her, but often it wasn't enough to guarantee safety.

"That's what my lawyer says, too, but I'm still not convinced." She pushed herself off the door, walked over to the couch and sat down tentatively, as far away from the sleeping Salem as was possible. "It's a long story. I don't want to talk about it."

Glenn sat on the torn arm of one of the padded chairs. "All right, let's talk about Kate then."

Allie crossed her legs under herself. "If I answer your questions, will you promise not to tell the police that I'm here?"

Even though he didn't feel comfortable about promising something like that, he couldn't very well claim to be Mr. Honesty when it came to the police. More often than he liked to admit, he'd been less than one-hundred-percent forthcoming with some of the information he came across during his investigations. His sources told him things because they knew they could trust him to keep their identities anonymous. That's all Allie was asking for. "Promise."

Allie stared at him for a few minutes. "What do you want to know?"

"Where's Kate?"

"I don't know exactly where she is, but I have a pretty good idea. I can't believe he called the police to report her missing, though. Slip the story to the press, like you, okay, but call the police? That was taking it too far."

"Who's he?"

"The old guy, what's-his-name, the producer."

"James Butler is the producer on Kate's production ..."

"Yeah, you already said that, but he's got a partner." She jumped off the couch and went over to the table where the digital picture frame was. After pushing a button on the back of the frame several times she stopped the picture show at one of the first photo's Glenn had noticed. "Him. He knows damn well she's not missing. His secretary even called me last weekend, the day after the cops came, and she asked me to let Kate know that they'd deposited her final payment into her bank account."

Glenn's right hand involuntarily formed a fist — the fist he wanted to shove down Bobbie's throat for messing with Ria. "How did she know to call you?"

"Kate had to give them the name and number of a family member, you know, in case of emergency. But Pooh Bear wasn't calling about any emergency. She was just making sure that Kate knew she wouldn't be getting any more money from them."

"Pooh Bear?"

"She said her name was Winnie Pavlovich, like Winnie the Pooh, right? Movie people are all weird. I don't know how Kate stands them."

"So, you're saying that the old guy called the police to report Kate missing just for publicity? How could having one of your employees go missing be good publicity?"

Allie put the picture frame back down and Glenn watched James' face come onto the screen next.

"Kate told me some of the stuff he's done for publicity. He doesn't care if it's good or bad, just that it is. When Kate left he must have decided to use that to his advantage, too. He's a real dirt bag. He's who you should be doing a story on."

"Do you know him?"

"I know his type. Kate shacked up with him down there. He made all sorts of promises about taking her to Hollywood when the show was over, but she knew he was full of it. He just wanted someone to get his rocks off with someone young enough to make him feel less ancient. Kate said he was wrinkly all over. It kind of made her ill."

"Is that why she left?" Glenn wasn't sure who had been the user in that situation, Kate or the older man.

Kate shook her head. "In her last voicemail she said she'd found her golden ticket."

"You mean like a Willy Wonka golden ticket?"

"No, her ticket wouldn't come in a chocolate bar. Her ticket would be a person, someone who actually would take her to Hollywood."

Kate sounded like a real piece of work. Not only was she sleeping her way up the cinematic ladder, she'd also inadvertently given Bobbie his opening to start a scam on Ria.

Nice people James worked with. Glenn stood up. He'd heard enough. There was just one more detail he wanted from Allie. "Any idea who her ticket is?"

"She didn't say, but my guess is it's Chris Regent." She opened the door.

Even Glenn, who rarely watched TV and went to maybe two movies a year, knew who Chris Regent was. "Why is Chris Regent doing a reality show?"

"He's not." Allie kept an eye on the still lounging Salem. "The old guy is making a movie on the same island and Chris Regent is starring in that."

"So, Kate left with Chris, who took her to Hollywood once he was done working on the movie."

"Yup. She'll probably send some photos of herself with Chris in the next day or two. If you want, I could sell you copies of them. An exclusive like that would be worth something to your paper, right?"

Glenn's paper wouldn't care about the photos, but Ria would. They'd be something physical, tangible. She couldn't continue to buy into whatever Bobbie was selling if she saw proof that Kate was okay. "Are the photos time stamped?"

"Yeah, and so is the file they come in." Glenn's complete lack of technical comprehension must have been plastered like a billboard all over his face, because she went on to say, "Kate takes them with her cellphone and then emails them to the picture frame."

"That would work," he supposed. He'd get someone in the IT department to explain it to him, if necessary. "Actually," it never hurt to get everything, there was no such thing as too much information, "could you email me the pictures she's already sent from the islands? I don't know if my boss will want to use them, but he might."

"You'll pay for anything you use, though, right?"

"Oh, for sure."

"Okay. And I'll email you the Chris Regent pictures when she sends them."

"Great."

Don't be mad at Ria, don't be mad at Ria, Glenn chanted to the beat of his feet marching along the pavement as he headed to his condo. *But it's okay to feel a little bit hurt.* It had been her choice to come a runnin' when Bobbie called her. That was the bit that hurt. But she couldn't be blamed for falling for Bobbie's scam. Bobbie probably knew, just as well as the old guy did, that Kate had up and left with their star. That meant James probably knew, too. But Bobbie had been clever enough to make sure that Ria wouldn't question James.

"Ooo, I'm scared he'll fire me," Glenn said in a high whiny, wimpy voice that came out louder than he'd planned it to just as he walked past a woman wearing a homemade aluminum foil headdress and a sign that read THEY'RE COMING! She looked at him as if he were the crazy one.

He was going nuts, torn between hurt and worry. What was Bobbie up to? Glenn sat down on one of the park benches along the lakeshore to calm his thoughts before making the call to Ria. One thought refused to be quietened, though. What if Ria chose to believe Bobbie over him?

CHAPTER
SIX

Puffy white cotton-ball cumulus clouds floated slowly across the robin's egg blue sky above me. They reminded me of the opening of an episode of *The Simpsons*. Looking south, there were clouds with rougher edges. They were taller, darker, wider, and flatter on the bottom. I swam over to the side of the pool, rested my elbows on the infinity edge, and watched the straight column of rain that was shooting down from the biggest cloud. For the second time that day I thought of *Star Trek*; the rain column was so perfectly formed that it looked like the brightly lit tube that Captain Kirk and his buddies had been beamed up in. The column moved east, south of Soursop, and slowly crossed over the southern tip of Virgin Gorda, soaking everything in its path. Rays of sunshine beamed out from behind the clouds, like spotlights pointed to the sky to advertise something.

Looking down over the edge of the pool I could see four two-storey buildings below my villa. The back of the buildings looked like cell blocks, the doors to the ten rooms on each floor lined up in uniform precision. A woman wearing only a towel, carrying what looked like a bottle of shampoo, came out one of the second floor doors in the building directly under mine, ran down the outside stairs, and then went into the room underneath hers.

"Brad, I'm using your shower," I heard her call out, presumably to the inhabitant of the room.

I rolled over onto my back and floated into the middle of the pool. I felt completely useless.

"Idle hands are the devil's workshop." With my ears submerged, my muffled voice sounded deeper than normal. I wondered if there was a saying about idle minds. Not that my mind was completely idle, it just didn't know which thoughts to concentrate on. Should I try to think of a way to reach James and get him to open up to me? Should I maybe try to understand and solve the tension between Glenn and me? Nope. Didn't want to think about that one. There was no point in trying to figure out what had happened to Kate. Not yet, anyway. The person I wasn't letting myself think about would tell me if she was really missing. If she was, I'd let her consume my thoughts. A cloud floated into my line of sight and I decided to set my mind to work on thinking of what its shape reminded me of. After several minutes, as it moved off into my peripheral vision, the only thing I could come up with was that it looked like a cloud.

"It is what it is," my muffled voice told its audience of one.

That saying had always annoyed me. Of course it was what it was. What else could it be but it?

My ears heard a sound, but my brain didn't want to recognize it. The ring of a doorbell wobbled through the water. A doorbell in a pool? Was that what it was? I lifted my head up and heard it ring again, this time without watery distortion. Of course, how silly of me. In the pampered world of Butler luxury a guest would just take for granted that there was an underwater speaker hooked up to the doorbell of their luxury villa. It was what it was.

I pulled myself out of the pool and grabbed one of the perfectly folded beach towels that were stacked in open shelves near the patio bar. The towel was the size of Tortola and it took me until I was standing by the front door to get it completely unfolded. Once I was suitably wrapped in Egyptian cotton (probably brought to the island by the direct descendants of King Tut himself), I opened the door.

A Butler-uniformed, middle-aged woman, whose width far surpassed her height, stood on my threshold, her arms authoritatively crossed over her ample bosom. She looked me up and down and made me feel like I was being X-rayed. Just enough of her name tag poked out from under one of her crossed arms for me to be able to figure out who she was. I read "Donne" and knew I was looking at Donnella, the head of housekeeping, the Diet Coke dealer.

"Rob tells me you be wanting something different to drink."

"Oh, yes please!"

"You're really not working with your brother, Mr. James, on the show?"

"Nope."

"You're not working for Mr. Dan, neither?"

"You couldn't pay me enough to do that!"

She smiled. "And you got nothing to do with running the hotel?"

"Nope, I'm just a non-paying guest."

She tilted her head slightly to the side and looked at me hard, with a razor-sharp stare that felt as if it could dissect a lie as skilfully as a scalpel. "Why are you here?"

I had one slow blink of her eyes to decide how to answer her question. "Rob asked me to come to try to find out what really happened to Kate Bond."

Donnella pursed her lips and nodded slowly. "All right then. I got a delivery for you. Come help me get it out of the car."

I tied the towel on tight like an over-sized toga, shoved my feet mostly into my sandals, and ran down the steps after her.

Donnella's car was a pygmy pickup truck. Sitting in the back of it was a canvas-covered rectangular box. She looked around before lifting the edge of the canvas sheet and I caught a glimpse of the contraband stash — two beautiful cases of Diet Coke. Forty-eight fixes, just waiting to be chilled.

"Bless you," I said as I bent over and picked up one of the cases.

"Just don't be getting me into trouble! There be eyes everywhere."

"I promise, no one will know where I got these from." I walked up the stairs, into my villa, and turned into the kitchen and only then realized that Donnella hadn't followed me with the other case. Leaving the first case on the kitchen counter, I went back outside. She was leaning against the open back gate of the pickup truck, talking into a walkie-talkie.

"… he's just trying to stir up trouble. Did he ask you in private or in front of those cameras?"

"There were two cameras," a young female voice answered.

"You tell him to talk to me about it. Nobody's been stealing his shoes and he knows it. Besides, who's going to see a little sand on his shoes anyway? Seems to me he's always sticking his face in front of the cameras, not his feet." Donnella didn't wait for a reply. She shoved the walkie-talkie into the deep pocket on the front of her skirt, shaking her head.

"Troubles?" I picked up the second case of Diet Coke.

"That Mr. Ted, it's always something with him. I told Ms. Whitecross my opinion on who should be managing this hotel, you can be sure of that! And it wasn't Mr. Ted."

"You know my Aunt Patti?"

"She hired me. Asked me to keep an eye on those last two. Your brother got all these cameras all over the place, but she knew I'd see more with my own eyes."

I wondered who was backing Ted as the eventual winner of the hotel manager's job — Aunt Patti or Dan. But it wasn't my worry. As I kept telling everyone, I didn't have anything to do with running the hotels. "Well, thanks so much for the Diet Coke, Donnella. You're a godsend."

She snorted like a horse. "Tell my husband that."

The refrigerator in the patio bar could only hold eighteen of the cans (and two of those really didn't fit and would probably fall out the next time I opened the door). I put the remaining cans in the full-sized refrigerator in my kitchen, saving one to stick in the freezer for a quick chill. Ice clunked into the ice maker bucket on the inside of the freezer door when I closed it just as the doorbell rang again.

Ariel Downes' mesmerizing hazel eyes met mine when I opened the door.

"Hi, I'm Ariel."

As if there was anyone on the planet who didn't know who she was! "I'm Ria." Chances were she wouldn't have a clue who I was.

"James' sister, right?"

"Yes." It struck me that I'd never thought much about how James had worked with, heck, employed so many famous people.

"Can I come in for a minute? I have a favour to ask." Ariel Downes was inviting herself into my villa. Did James ever get used to everyday, run-of-the-mill conversations with A-listers?

"Sure." I stood back to let her float into the villa.

She was still sheathed all in white but, then again, so was I — only my white sheathing was absorbent while hers was diaphanous.

"I'm in the villa up the hill and I saw that you just got a delivery of Diet Coke. I know we're not supposed to have it on the island, but could I buy a couple of cans from you? I promise I won't drink it out in the open."

I had to laugh. I had something in common with one of the most famous movie stars in the world. "I was just about to pop open my first one. Why don't I open two? I can send you home with a care package, too."

"That sounds heavenly." Ariel took off her sunhat and gloves and started to untie the white scarf that was wrapped around her head.

Her lengthy legendary hair fell down around her shoulders, but the legend had changed. Instead of her famous golden locks, her hair was now black. She was stunningly beautiful — the cameras that focused on her hadn't lied. Her resemblance to a young Audrey Hepburn was startling, especially with her new dark hair. And she was surprisingly petite. I was used to seeing her on an eight-foot high screen, not standing less than two feet in front of me. "Why don't we take these out onto the patio?" I asked as I took two glasses (probably Waterford Crystal) out of the cupboard.

"Is it covered?" Ariel tidily put her hat, gloves, and scarf on the kitchen counter. "I can't get a tan. It'll screw up the continuity."

"The what?" I felt my taste buds tingle with anticipation as the Diet Coke bubbles fizzled while I filled the glasses.

"You're not with the TV show or the movie?"

I shook my head and handed her a glass. "Cheers." We clinked glasses and both took a big gulp.

"Ah!"

"I couldn't have said it better. Come on, there's a sofa under the awning. You should be sun-free there. Why is it you can't get a tan?" I asked as we walked outside.

"Continuity. We don't shoot the scenes in chronological order, so I have to have an even skin tone throughout the entire production. If I start tanning now I could end up being darker in the first scene than in the last, and that wouldn't make sense to the audience."

"So that's why you cover yourself up."

She nodded. "Dan's orders. He's good at giving orders."

"I noticed."

"Are you with the hotel? One of the owners?"

"No, I'm just a non-paying guest on vacation."

"Must be nice."

I felt my defences instantly fire up. Was I once again going to hear the *Gee, your life must be perfect* jab?

"Lucky you, you don't have to deal with Dan. But your brother does. Is Dan being a jerk on the TV show, too? Stupid question. Of course he is. Why? Because that's who Dan is — an egotistical, vainglorious, domineering, duplicitous, sexist jerk. I bet he killed that girl."

I almost swallowed an ice cube, whole. "What girl?"

"Some PA who's gone missing." She looked straight at me. "You haven't heard the gossip? Oh that's right, you wouldn't have. You're an outcast, just like me, only people usually use the word recluse to describe me."

That's exactly what I'd thought when I'd seen her floating along the road to the main hotel building. "Why am I an outcast?" I'd never been called that, then again I'd never felt as blatantly excluded as I had when I'd walked across the pool patio.

"Because you're not part of either family — the television one or the movie one. Your brother probably knows the whole story, but he's teamed up with Dan so he's not going to tell you if it's true or not. Something like that would kill his show. Then again, it might triple his ratings, but he'd have to leak it to the press piece by piece to build up interest."

Piece by piece? Like maybe leaving a foot in a tidal pool? James wouldn't do something like that and he wouldn't condone it. I hoped. "Did people open up to you because you're part of the movie family?"

"Hell no! I'm a star — with a capital S. I'm difficult to work with. I'm reclusive. I'm too high and mighty to mingle with the peons. At least that's what everybody says about me. Don't you read the tabloids?"

I shook my head. Sure, I'd glanced at the front covers of the tabloids whenever I was waiting to pay for my groceries, but I'd never really paid attention to them. "If you're an outsider, how did you hear about a girl getting killed?"

"I was doing my morning yoga on the beach and was in the middle of a *Kapotasana* pose when two guys from the television crew came down to talk about it, but they didn't see me."

"What did you hear?" I tried to sound nonchalant, as if I was only mildly interested.

"They were arguing. The tall one told the short one that he'd asked someone to come to the island to investigate her disappearance — that's the word he used, *disappearance*. The short one was angry about it. He didn't trust whoever the tall one had hired to do the investigation. But they agreed on one thing — they both think Dan killed her. I could see Dan doing something like that. He doesn't just fire people, he destroys them. From the way they were talking, it sounded like Dan was screwing her. She and Dan had a big fight and the next morning she wasn't around."

"You heard all that?" She must have been holding her yoga pose for a very long time.

Ariel nodded. "I'm good at people watching. I do it all the time, it helps me develop characters. I sit on the sidelines or meld into the background and watch and listen. Maybe that's why people keep saying I'm reclusive? You wouldn't believe how many times I've been compared to Greta Garbo."

I believed it — I'd done it. "You mean the whole '*I vant to be alone*' thing?"

"What she actually said was '*I want to be left alone.*' There's a big difference. Anyway, if you're really interested and want to know more about the missing girl, blend into the background and listen when the short guy's around. You won't be able to miss him. You aren't the investigator his tall friend hired, are you?"

"Ha!" I laughed too loudly. "Yeah, right."

"The tall one was in your villa and had room service delivered here." Add Ariel to the ever-growing list of eyes watching me.

I'd already guessed that Bear was the short one, and now knew that Rob was the tall one. "You mean Rob?"

"I don't know his name, just what he looks like. Sort of like Clint Eastwood."

"Rob and I have been friends for years, we were just visiting, that's all. I'm a travel writer, not an investigator."

"I thought you said you were here for a vacation."

"I am."

"A vacation from travel writing? And you travelled here to do it?"

I should have come up with a more believable excuse for coming to the island. "Travel writers need vacations, too."

"I never thought of that. Huh. It must be a fun job, exploring new places … BIRD! BIRD! BIRD!" Ariel started flapping her delicate little hands as quickly as a hummingbird's wings and quickly flipped her legs up onto the sofa.

Sure enough, a bird had landed on the patio and was in the process of waddling toward us. "That's just a white-crowned pigeon." My niece would have been proud of me for identifying it so quickly. Of course, the white crown feathers on the top of its head had made my job easier. The little patch of iridescent green on the back of its neck told me that it was a male pigeon. "They're harmless."

"Harmless?" Ariel was almost hyper-ventilating. "Pigeons are the worst! They're Fascists!"

Pigeons had political views? I didn't get a chance to ask Ariel how she'd determined that the birds were so right wing.

"That's what Dan used in *The Birds*." She pointed at the pigeon. "Kill it!"

The pigeon wisely chose that moment to take flight.

"God, I hate those things! There was a flock of something trapped under my veranda this morning. It was horrendous! Ted — have you met Ted? He's one of the contestants on the TV show and he's a real sweetheart. Anyway, Ted was wonderful and he got rid of the birds for me. I hope he wins the job here. I'd come back for a vacation. It's a beautiful spot, so isolated. The paparazzi wouldn't be able —"

The cordless phone started to ring and shimmy across the glass topped coffee table in front of us. "Excuse me." I reached over for the phone. "Hello?"

"Hi." Glenn's greeting wasn't over enthusiastic.

"Hi." I replied with an equal lack of affection.

"Your friend Rob," at least he got Rob's name right this time, "is wrong. The supposedly missing girl isn't missing at all. She left the island by choice."

Without her luggage? I wanted to ask but couldn't. Ariel was intently people watching — and I was the people she was watching. "Are you sure?"

Glenn sighed, loudly. "Positive. She's gone to Hollywood with Chris Regent."

"But that's impossible. Chr —" I stopped myself. "Um, can I call you back? I've got someone over visiting right now."

—>—

Someone over visiting? Glenn had a pretty good idea who that someone was — and he didn't like him. Correction. He detested him.

One way or another he was going to expose Mr. Bobbie Dickhead. But first he had to find out more about him.

He punched the numbers for his paper into the keypad of the phone on his desk. "Entertainment desk, please."

He didn't know the new kid who answered the phone, but the new kid sure knew who Glenn Cooper was. His byline had been on the front page of the paper so many times that there weren't many people at the paper, let alone in Canada, who didn't know who he was. "I need information on some people working on a reality show that's shooting in the British Virgin Islands."

"You're talking about *Check-Out Time*, right?" she asked.

"You've heard of it?" Not that surprising, really, given that entertainment was her beat.

"Some footage was leaked from the set that's pretty explosive."

"Can you send it to me?" Maybe he'd catch a glimpse of Bobbie.

"Sure. What's your email address? I'll send it right now."

Glenn gave her his address.

"It should be there any minute."

"Thanks." He clicked on Send/Receive. Nothing came in. "While we're waiting, I need info on a crew member." It was then that Glenn realized he had no idea what Bobbie's last name was. "I don't know his last name, though." Idiot. Whatever happened to getting as many facts as you could? "He works for James Butler …"

"Who's executive producing the show with Dan Shykoff. What's the first name of the person you're interested in?" He could hear her tapping the keys on her keyboard.

"Bo … Rob."

"What does he do?"

"He's a cameraman."

"Okay." Glenn listened to her tapping a keyboard. "I think I found your guy. There's a Robert Churcher who's worked for James Butler on most of his shoots."

"Where are you getting this from?" Glenn was impressed by how quickly she'd found Bobbie.

"IMDbPro. It's an online database of information about people who work in the business. It lists filmographies, has biographies, the usual stuff, on just about anyone who's worked in production."

Glenn didn't know what information to ask for next so he clicked on Send/Receive again. "I just got your email. Give me a minute to watch it."

Glenn opened the attachment and watched the video play. A small dinghy, driven by a man dressed entirely in beige, came out from behind some rocks. It was heading toward a beautiful woman who was walking out of the water toward the beach. The shock of seeing the dinghy suddenly explode into a ball of fire made Glenn jerk. "What the …" The woman in the water screamed and the screen went black.

"We don't know if it's real. Remember, this is reality TV we're talking about, the biggest oxymoron of the twenty-first century. Do you need anything else?"

When in doubt, go for everything. "You'd better send me the link to the database, I might have to check out a few more people. Will I need a password?"

"You can use mine. I'll put it in the body of the email with the link. You'll find info on Shykoff's movie personnel, too. His company's producing a theatrical, once the television show wraps."

"Isn't it the other way around? Didn't they do the movie first?"

"No, principal photography hasn't even started on the movie yet. They aren't scheduled to start for another couple of weeks."

Glenn didn't like the way his stomach felt. It was sinking. If the movie hadn't been made yet, Chris Regent wouldn't have left the island yet. "Did Chris Regent come in early to shoot his stuff first?" It was worth a shot — a long shot.

"He's not even on the island. He's been seen partying in St. Thomas for the last week. Ariel Downes is there, though. Rumour has it she and Dan aren't seeing eye-to-eye. Do you need anything else?"

"Can you do a quick check on one more name while I've got you on the line — Kate Bond?"

"Are you sure about her name? There's a Kathy, a Karen, and a Kathleen Bond. Oh, and a Kathryn Bond, but she was an actress back in the silent movie days. There's a Kate Pond, the last thing she worked on was a production in 1997; she was the script supervisor."

"Keep looking. See if there's a Kate Bond who's worked on something more recent."

"Kathleen Bond was an accounting clerk on *Revolutionary Road*. Could that be who you're looking for?"

"No." Was James' show the first production job Kate ever had? Allie would know. Ria probably knew, too. Yet another piece of information Glenn had failed to ask for. He was batting a thousand. "Hang on." A beep had signalled another call coming in. "Cooper."

"Hi."

"Hey!" Glenn sounded almost glad to hear my voice.

"I just had drinks with Ariel Downes!" I hoped that I hadn't sounded too much like a star-struck fan. "I didn't want to talk about Kate in front of her. Glenn, Kate couldn't have gone anywhere with Chris ..."

"I know."

Huh? "But you said ..."

"I was wrong."

The temperature in Hades had just plummeted. "Why did you think she'd gone to Hollywood?"

"That's where her sister thinks she is. I went to her apartment and her sister was there. Her identical twin sister."

Kate had a twin? "Oh my God, that's who the police talked to! But why would her sister tell the police that she's Kate?"

"Can I call you back? I'm on the other line with the entertainment desk. We're looking for info on Kate, but we can't find a listing for her on the entertainment database."

"That's because this was her first job." A fact Glenn would have already asked for if he'd taken me seriously to begin with. But he was taking me seriously now. I could hear it in his voice. "Look up another name — Albert Black."

"Who's he?"

"It's a long story. I'll explain it to you later." We both had a lot of explaining to do ... later.

"Hang on." The line went quiet for a few minutes. "Ria?"

"I'm here."

"She found three of them; a composer, a broadcast engineer in Scotland, and an actor in South Africa. Which one is your guy?"

"None of them."

"What does your guy do?"

"He's a camera original courier."

"I'll ask her to check again."

He was gone for less than a second.

"Her guy is a camera original courier. Can you look up people by their jobs instead of their names?"

"It's still me. You pushed the wrong button."

"Shit. Be right back."

The line went quiet for so long that I started to wonder if Glenn had cut me off.

He came back. "Louise Flavelle was just killed by a hit and run driver!"

"Seriously?" I'd never seen any of her movies, but had seen her smiling face on the posters for too many romantic comedies to count. Chris Regent had been her co-star in one of those movies.

"Seriously. The newsroom's going nuts!"

"What about Albert? Did you find him?" I felt bad for Louise Flavelle, especially for her infant daughter, but she wasn't real to me. Kate, even though I'd never met her, was real. And Albert was too real — really creepy.

"Oh, sorry, the newsflash came in while we were talking about him. Hang on, I'll see if she found him."

The line went quiet — and stayed that way. Glenn had disconnected me, instead of putting me on hold.

It wasn't quiet below my veranda, though. I heard someone crying and then a woman yelling *Did you hear about Louise?* Doors slammed. Feet pounded up and down the wooden staircases on the back of the cell blocks below me.

Bad news sure spread fast in the world of production. So why hadn't news of Kate's disappearance spread like wild fire?

Because nobody realized that she'd really disappeared.

CHAPTER
SEVEN

Our call time for dinner was seven o'clock, but the digital clock on my patio changed from 7:34 to 7:35 just as Ariel rang my doorbell. The delayed departure had given me the chance to hang out with my gecko friend on the patio. She'd clung to the wall and agreed with everything I said. Neither one of us thought I should be the one to call Glenn — he'd hung up on me, the onus was on him to call me back. Both of us wondered why he hadn't.

"Wow," I exhaled when I saw Ariel. She was sheathed again, but this time in a flowing gossamer gown. She looked red-carpet ready and I was tempted to ask her who she was wearing.

"You like?" She asked as she did a sultry pirouette on my front patio.

She'd worn her hair loose (but I bet it had taken a lot of work to make it look so naturally wavy). It flowed with the dress as she spun and lifted enough to show me that the dress didn't have a back. (If she'd been wearing a thong I would have seen most of the small back triangle of material.) The dress didn't have any straps or sleeves and the front was split open from her belly button to show a widening estuary of chest flesh. How the heck was it staying on? The deep, rich periwinkle colour made her thick dark hair look dramatically darker and her white skin look like alabaster. Around her delicate neck hung a glittering diamond necklace that must have cost more than the gross domestic product of some countries. Looking down, I saw that she was wearing sparkling sandals and that her toenails were painted the exact same colour as the dress; a tiny, shiny gold star had been painted in the middle of each toenail.

I was wearing my cleanest T-shirt, most comfortable jeans, and brown leather sandals. The only jewellery I wore was the multi-ringed silver ring I'd bought from a prune-faced old lady on the miniscule Greek island of Kythira a few months earlier. The last time there'd been paint on my toenails had been when I helped my niece paint her bedroom and some of the black trim colour had dripped onto my feet. My hair was pulled back into a high ponytail. To say I felt underdressed would have been like saying Hugh Jackman had no sex appeal.

"You look amazing," I said with conviction.

"Thanks! You look okay too." Even with her considerable acting skills she hadn't been able to make that last line sound believable. "Ready?"

"As I'll ever be." I locked the front door to my villa and we walked down the steps to my waiting chariot/golf cart.

"Thanks for giving me a lift. Dan doesn't know it yet, but he'll be bringing me home, so don't feel as if you have to wait for me. I'm hoping this get up will make him more willing to see the Rebecca character the way I do."

If she wanted Dan to see Rebecca barely half-dressed then she was wearing the perfect *get up*, as she called it.

"Did you hear that we lost Louise Flavelle today?" Ariel asked.

"I did." I drove slowly, not wanting to take the curves too fast and risk rolling one of Ariel's breasts right out of her almost dress. "It sounded like a lot of people on the crew were really upset about it. Did you know her?"

"We worked together once. It was a nightmare. She was a bitch!" she said with venom.

I held the steering wheel extra tight to stop myself from swerving.

"And she couldn't act her way out of a paper bag. She auditioned for the role I had in *The Birds* and it was laughable. Not that she ever had a chance of getting the part. Dan had to go through the motions of auditioning other people, though."

"Oh." What else could I say? I'd been planning on telling Ariel that I was sorry for her loss of a co-worker, or maybe even friend.

"I wonder if her baby was affected by all the coke she was constantly snorting? Gerrard's life will definitely be better without her. We hooked up just before I left to come here and he was miserable. Louise getting killed has saved him a fortune — Hollywood divorces are insanely expensive. And speaking of killing, have you heard anything else about the PA?"

"Nothing." Unfortunately, it was true.

"Well, that's boring. Every production should have a least one melodrama. And tonight's party won't be much fun if the crew's all mopey because of Louise. I guess the TV crew won't be, though. I don't think she ever worked in television, especially Canadian television. Maybe if they get liquored up they'll talk about the PA? That'll at least make the night interesting."

I was liking Ariel less and less by the minute. At first I'd thought she was a nice person. The person she was showing me as we pulled up to the hotel's main building wasn't very nice at all. She wasn't interested in "*the PA*," who was a real person named Kate. She was only interested in the thrill of the gossip.

The pool area had changed, too. It had been transformed sometime between my tense lunch with James and our arrival for dinner. A long table had been set up on what looked like a floating floor that hovered across the far end of the pool. Tall metal towers of scaffolding had been built on both sides of the pool and they had big lights attached to them that were all pointing at the table. The table was covered in a big linen cloth, but there were no place settings on it.

Circling the area where Ariel's lunch table had been there were more lights on individual tripods. Those lights were on, illuminating the white-tuxedoed members of a band — a big band. Only one thing remained fairly unchanged, the groupings of crew personnel, in various stages of undress and casual dress, who were lounging and laughing in the unlit areas. I recognized Bear; he was sitting beside Pam, the girl with the pink bangs.

The band leader tapped his baton and the band started playing a tune that sounded vaguely familiar. The clarinet player stood at the front, the horn players rocked from side to side in unison behind him in time to the music.

"Name that tune!" Bear yelled out to his group.

People starting calling out possible answers.

"Johnny Dorsey?"

"It was Tommy Dorsey, you moron."

"Benny Goodman?"

"Wrong!" Bear added his own rendition of the incorrect answer buzzer from *Jeopardy*.

"Ooh! I know!" Pam shouted happily. "'Next Stop Pottersville!'"

A couple stood up and starting dancing. "Who cares what is it, let's jive, man!"

"Hep cat, all the kids are doing it." Another couple joined them on the dance floor.

It did have an infectious beat; my right foot was tapping of its own accord.

"Wasn't 'Next Stop Pottersville' from a *Seinfeld* episode?" asked the guy who'd been holding the big poofy microphone when I was first met by Ted at the dock.

"Episode 94, 'The Mom and Pop Store,'" another crew member shouted.

The swinging doors to the kitchen burst open and Ted came strutting out onto the patio. "There you are! Mr. Shykoff has been waiting for you."

"Haven't you heard, Teddy? It's good to keep a man waiting. It makes him want you more," Ariel ran her fingertip down the length of Ted's tie in an extremely sensual manner and then jitterbugged her way to the door and disappeared into the kitchen.

Even in the poor lighting I could see Ted's blush.

"Are we eating in there?" I asked.

"Yes. We had to change everything around because of Chris' … I mean, Mr. Regent's delay. You were supposed to be eating there, with the sun setting in the background." He pointed to the floating table. "The big dinner party scene, with the leads and senior production staff for the movie. And you, of course." He sounded disappointed.

I wasn't disappointed at all! Nobody had told me I'd been invited to a dinner that was going to be part of a television show. If they had, I wouldn't have come — and not just because I didn't have anything that even came close to matching the apparent dress code of the evening. Hanging out with the crew I would have done gladly. I looked like one of them. I felt like one of them, too. I would have much preferred to jitterbug or jive with them than dine with Dan.

The drummers started tapping out the opening to Tommy Dorsey's "Song of India" and I gave one last longing glance to the happy people I was about leave behind.

"Did you hear that we lost Louise Flavelle today?" Ted's question only hammered home the point that I was probably about to eat with some of the people I'd heard crying earlier.

"Ariel and I were talking about it on the way over."

Ted held one of the doors open for me. "Doesn't Ariel look lovely tonight? She embodies everything about the word star. And she's nothing like I expected."

"You mean the whole Greta Garbo '*I vant to be alone* thing'?"

"Miss Garbo didn't actually say that, you know. What she said was '*I want to be left alone.*'"

"And there's a big difference," I repeated the line Ariel had used.

There was no difference to the scowl on James' face. He was sitting with Mandy at a chef's table in the kitchen, nursing yet another scotch. Mandy's dress was so tight and low cut that she looked as if she should have been nursing (twins).

Dan and Ariel were standing by one of the long stainless counters, looking down at the skinned carcasses of five small birds.

"Finally!" Dan didn't sound happy to see me. "Now we can get down to business." He then proceeded to tie a big white apron around and over Ariel's exposed bits. "I think you're going to enjoy this. Did you know that I started off in the business with a cooking show?" Dan tied his own apron on and picked up a huge cleaver while I went over to the table and sat on the non-Mandy side of James.

Ted stood still for a few minutes, as if waiting for orders, and then backed out through the swinging doors.

I was so looking forward to a nice cozy evening, just the five of us. There were several Butler uniformed kitchen staff working farther down the line from Dan and Ariel, and I seriously wondered if I could get away with going down there to hang out with them. A waiter lifted a loaded large tray up onto his shoulders and pushed his way through the swinging doors to the patio. I wanted to scream *"Take me with you!"*

James nodded at me. "Hey."

"Hey."

J.E. Forman

"Shush! I want to hear what he's saying." Mandy pointed at Dan.

Our warm friendly sibling greeting had irritated her.

"… so I thought I'd let you get some payback. You just hold the leg out like this and then," Dan brought the cleaver down with a whack, "you chop it off." He held the tiny leg up for all to see.

"What kind of birds are they?" Ariel, too, now held a cleaver.

Dan's smile gave me the creeps. "Squab."

Dan gave me the creeps. What kind of sick joke was he trying to play on Ariel? "Um, Ariel? Do you know what squab is?"

"No."

I was glad to be sitting so far away from her. She still held the cleaver and I didn't want to be near it when she heard my answer. "Squab is a fancy name for pigeon."

Ariel slowly looked from me to Dan, then down at the dead bird in front of her. She gripped the cleaver with both hands, raised it high above her head and brought it down hard on the spine of the corpse, splitting the bird carcass in two. "Take that, you motherfucker!" I didn't know what kind of workout she did, but whatever she lifted it was working. Her delicate arms hid some powerful guns.

"I knew you'd enjoy it. Do you want to do the rest of them?"

Ariel gently rested her cleaver on the stainless counter, dusted her hands off as if they'd been covered in flour (not splattered bits of dead bird), and started to untie her apron. "No, thanks. But that was fun."

She joined us as the table while Dan gave a monologue as he mutilated the remaining fowl corpses.

"So, as I was saying, I started off with a cooking show on CJOH in Ottawa. Graham Kerr did his show there, too, but he's much older than I am."

148

"You mean *The Galloping Gourmet*?" From the look on Dan's face I knew I wouldn't make the mistake of speaking again.

"He was like the first TV chef, right? Kind of like the Gordon Ramsey of the seventies?" Mandy made the same mistake as I had, but she went on to make it worse than I had. "My grandma loved him."

"I was the first TV chef!" he bellowed. "Kerr started after me and I've never been second to anyone." His cleaver hit the next bird with such force that its split legless body flew off the counter. "A lot of us got our first really big break on the CBC," he said more calmly.

"What's the CBC?" Ariel, the American in our midst, asked.

"Canadian Broadcasting Corporation, the biggest network in the country at the time. Lorne Green, Ben Cartwright on *Bonanza*, started out with CBC Radio. Alex Trebek, whose real name is George by the way, started out doing news and sportscasting." Dan laughed. "One of Bill Shatner's first TV gigs was as Ranger Bob in the Canadian version of *The Howdy Doody Show*."

"I didn't know any of that." Ariel crossed her legs, letting the slit in the front of her dress open up to show the world ninety-nine percent of the surface area of her left leg.

"That's nothing. A lot of current big names in LA are Canadian."

"Who else?" Was Ariel really as captivated by Dan's dissertation on Canadians who'd made a name for themselves south of the forty-ninth parallel as she was acting? It sure felt like an act to me.

"Jim Carrey, Michael J. Fox, Ryan Reynolds and Ryan Gosling, to name a few. Even America's first Sweetheart, Mary Pickford, was Canadian." Dan tossed the now desecrated birds into pans of heated oil. The birds sizzled. "And we're not just in front of the cameras. Doug Sellars was in charge at Fox Sports …"

"I worked with Doug, back in my *Hockey Night in Canada* days. He was a rarity in this business, one of the kindest, most truly decent guys you could ever meet."

Apparently Dan didn't care, because he just glared at James and kept right on talking. "… Arthur Smith produces *Hell's Kitchen* and *Kitchen Nightmares* …"

"You Canadians sure like your cooking." Ariel was allowed to interrupt Dan's soliloquy without having to suffer an angry glare.

"… and we've even had one of ours serve as president of the Academy of Motion Picture Arts and Sciences, Arthur Hiller."

No wonder James so desperately wanted to break into the U.S. market. Dan wasn't mentioning any Canadians who'd done well for themselves at home.

"I met Arthur at the Governor's Ball a few years ago. I think you were there that night, too. You and Reese were …"

I had nothing to add to Ariel and Dan's conversation and wanted nothing from it. James and Mandy weren't included either. Mandy tried to join their conversation a couple of times, but they never let her in. James drank. I tried to count the number of threads in the linen tablecloth. The only good part of the evening was the food. Dan was an excellent cook.

I faked a yawn. "Well, it's been a long day and I'm really tired …"

My dinner companions all suddenly felt the same exhaustion (or desperate need to be anywhere else) and we were soon standing out on the pool patio, making polite thanks-for-the-lovely-meal conversation, when Judy burst through the double doors from the lobby of the hotel and headed straight for Dan and James.

"Mr. Butler? Mr. Shykoff? Might I have a word with both of you?" Her suit was wrinkled and some sort of yellowy-green liquid had been spilled down her white skirt long enough ago to have dried to a crisp that crackled when she walked.

"Oh, good! You're back. How's our boy doing?" Dan looked around Judy to see if anyone else was coming out of the hotel.

I looked, too, but didn't see Rob.

"That's what I want to talk to you about," Judy said through clenched teeth.

"Problem?" James asked.

"I agreed to come on this show with the understanding that it was a legitimate application process. Mrs. Whitecross herself assured me that she was seriously looking for the right candidate to manage this, her newest hotel." Judy took a deep breath. "I, at no time, signed up to be one of the acts in a circus, however!"

Dan leaned over and spoke closely into James' ear. "Why aren't there cameras on this?"

James shrugged his shoulders.

"Because I told them to stay away. And, just in case you've got cameras hiding out here, I took the liberty of disconnecting this." She reached into her pocket and pulled out an electronic looking pack that was about the size of a deck of cards. Dangling from it was a thin wire that had a small microphone at the end of it. "I'm not a performer! I'm a professional in the hospitality and tourism industry and from here on in I expect to be treated as such. No job is worth what I just went through."

"If Chris gave you a hard time I apologize on behalf of my entire production," Dan's voice was as smooth as room temperature butter. "I give you my word that he'll smarten up and sober up for the remainder of the shoot."

"I'm sorry, Judy." James sounded more sincere than Dan.

"But, really, you should know how hard it can be to deal with difficult guests. It's part of the job. I bet you've dealt with …"

Judy began to noticeably shake. "I have never!" She was starting to screech. "Ever! Had a guest shove his tongue down my throat, right after he'd deposited the entire contents of his stomach on my lap!"

Dan's well-cooked dinner didn't feel so good in my stomach anymore.

"I want your assurances, in writing, that not one second of that ever gets broadcast! Anywhere!"

"I'll get Winnie to write something up first thing tomorrow morning and we'll both sign it, right James?"

"Absolutely," James nodded.

"The bitch hit me! The fucking bitch hit me!" The infamous Chris Regent sauntered through the doors from the hotel, closely followed by Rob and the rest of his crew. Chris' Hawaiian shirt looked like it had been torn open. His low-rise board shorts had slid down to X-rated depths.

It wasn't until Chris was standing right in front of us that his rapidly darkening black eye became visible.

"She touched the face, Dan! Fire her! I don't want her on my set!"

"I'll take that," Bear's voice suddenly came from right beside me. He held his hand out to take the microphone pack from Judy. "We'll hook you up with a new one tomorrow."

Chris' jaw dropped and he stared at Bear in shock. "Midgets?" I detected a hint of an Irish accent in Chris' voice. "They're filming midgets?"

"Listen, jackass, you're not in Bruges, and you're no Colin Farrell." Dan went over and stood face to face with Chris. "Go to bed. I'll deal with you tomorrow."

"But the night is young, Danny." Chris smiled his world famous smile and then began to sing, off-key, with a bad fake Irish accent. "Oh, Danny boy!"

"Security!" Dan bellowed, this time without a bullhorn, but his non-amplified blast was just as effective.

Two large Butler-uniformed men came running out from the kitchen. "Miss Winnie said you needed us?"

"Would you please escort Mr. Regent to his villa? And make sure he stays there, inside, all night."

Chris sang himself out as the security guards carried him into the hotel. Winnie held the doors open for them.

A second camera crew had scampered into position to capture Chris' involuntary trip to his villa, leaving Rob and his crew behind. They shut their equipment off and I heard Rob sigh heavily as he lifted the camera off his shoulder.

Winnie joined us on the pool patio. She was carrying a Butler bathrobe which she draped over Judy's shoulders. "Here, let's get you inside and cleaned up. I've already told housekeeping to have a new uniform sent to your room."

Judy followed Winnie obediently.

"Mike's in my office, Dan" Winnie said over her shoulder. "I told him you needed to speak to him about his client."

"Do I have to do that tonight?" Dan asked.

"Yes." Winnie let the doors swing closed behind her.

"Can it wait?" Ariel asked. "I need to talk to you, in private."

"Anything for my leading lady," Dan slid his arm around Ariel's slender shoulders. "Bear, make dubs of the discs from the cameras that shot the fiasco on the boat. I'll give them to Judy to keep her happy. Give Winnie the originals. James, how are we going to handle reshooting Chris' grand arrival? We should get Malvin to —"

"He's booked tomorrow, Albert's coming in. I'll see what I can do about juggling the schedule to bring him in on the helicopter." James turned to Mandy. "What time are you meeting Albert?"

"I can't go get Albert. I'm going to be in hair and makeup all afternoon."

"No, you're going to be picking up Albert." The take-charge tone in James' voice surprised me.

"But I can't!" Mandy's whine reminded me of nails on a chalkboard.

"I'll let you two sort this out amongst yourselves. Come along, Ariel. Goodnight children," Dan called over his shoulder as he and Ariel went into the hotel.

"I'm not going for Albert, Jamie. You and Dan were the ones who decided to change the dress code for the dinner to vintage thirties. I've got a one o'clock booking for my final fitting and right after that I'm going to hair and makeup."

"Change your appointments." James said firmly.

"That's not fair!" Mandy stomped her foot hard enough to send very noticeable shock waves wobbling through her silicone implants. "You promised me air time, Jamie!"

I decided to let the children, as Dan had so accurately called them, sort it out amongst themselves. I didn't want to go back to my villa to sit around conversing with a reptile, but I wasn't sure if I was brave enough to just invite myself to join the small party of production people who were still on the patio. Rob looked like he was about to join them.

They'd pulled ten chairs around one circular table. The band had gone for the night. Standing a few feet away from the table, Rob was talking to Pam. He handed her a small package that she apparently liked very much. She liked it so much that she threw her arms around his neck and gave him a great big kiss.

Right, then. Back to my villa it would be. Maybe there'd be a message from Glenn?

I lifted my foot to take a step, but gently put it down in the same place it had been when I overheard what the crew members were talking about.

"… I'm telling you, dude, it was a straight out of a *Law and Order* episode, season four, episode fifteen or sixteen, I can't remember exactly which one," the sound man from Rob's crew said. "They found a woman murdered and her foot was missing."

"Episode sixteen, 'Tortured.'" Bear added more detail. "I remember, because they made a technical goof. The medical examiner says something about the nine metacarpal bones in the wrist. She should have said there were eight carpal bones. The metacarpals are in the palm, not the wrist, and there are only five of them."

"You're both wrong," Esther, the girl from Rob's crew, had sat down beside Bear. "*Law and Order,* season seven, episode fifteen, part of the 'Risky Business' trilogy — the head of a major studio is found with her head, hands, and feet cut off. There's the television tie in."

"Yeah, but our victim was only missing a foot." Rob took one of the two empty chairs.

Pam took the other one.

I hid behind a potted palm.

"Kate isn't our victim! She isn't anybody's victim. She left because she couldn't hack Dan, and can you blame her?" I couldn't see who'd spoken and I didn't recognize the voice.

"Face it, the foot was a fake, one of Dan's stunts. I'm out of here. I've got an early call."

"Yeah, me too."

Chairs scraped against the flagstones. A chorus of Walton-esque goodnights went round the table.

The party was breaking up. I watched several people going through the doors to the hotel lobby, but I didn't see Rob, Bear, Esther, or Pam leave. What I didn't expect to see (and wasn't pleased to see) was Mandy coming back onto the pool deck. Even worse, she saw me.

"There you are!" she so loudly that Rob and his friends couldn't have missed it. "I need to ask you a huge favour!"

I wanted her to do me a favour, too — go away. "What?" I walked out from behind the potted palm as nonchalantly as I could.

"Can you pick up Albert for me tomorrow? All you'd have to do is meet him at the airport, drive him to the marina, and then leave his bag at our place. That's it. Will you do it? Please? Jamie won't let me ask anyone else to do it."

"Does he know you're asking me?"

"Well … no, but you're family. Why would he mind you doing it?"

I could think of many reasons why James wouldn't want me to do it — the primary one being that he knew how nosey I was, especially when it came to my family. Unwittingly, because she didn't have many wits, Mandy had done me a huge favour — she'd given me the perfect opportunity to find out what Albert was bringing to James. "Okay."

"Really?"

Why did she have to squeal like that? "Really. When should I…?"

"They're scrambling to reschedule tomorrow because of Chris' screwed up arrival scene. The call time hasn't been set yet, so I'm not sure when Malvin and the boat will be ready to go. I think Albert's flight gets in around five. You can leave his bag under the couch by the printer. You know, sort of out of sight. Jamie wouldn't want anyone snooping through it, for obvious reasons." She winked sloppily, as if implying that I already knew what would be in the bag. "I'll leave the keys with Malvin. Thanks!" She blew me an air kiss and jiggled her way through the doors and into the lobby.

"Are you going to hide behind the plant again or do you want to join us out in the open now?" Rob and his friends laughed at his own oh-so-humorous question.

I blushed and hoped that the lighting wasn't bright enough to show the red patches that were spreading across my cheeks and down my neck.

A waiter bought us a round of drinks and cheeseburgers for Rob and Esther.

"How as your day?" Rob asked me in between mouthfuls of burger.

"Okay, I guess." To me, the day had been bizarre. To Rob, it would have probably sounded like just another day at work.

"Did you guys hear about Louise Flavelle?" Pam asked Rob and Esther, who both shook their heads and kept right on chewing. "She was killed by a hit-and-run driver."

"No shit?" Rob asked.

"No shit."

"Did they get the guy?" Esther asked.

"They haven't even got a description of the car," Bear answered. "The way I hear it the police interviewed the people who saw it, but all they saw was the star in their midst. Nobody noticed the car."

"They'll get something from the CCT cameras." Rob reached over and stole a handful of Esther's fries.

"Back off!" She swatted his hand away.

"You should have heard the movie crew," Pam rolled her eyes. "They were all 'Oooh, we've lost Louise, boo-hoo-hoo,' as if they were her immediate family members. It was so fake. Sure, some of them probably worked with her, but ..."

"We'd feel like we'd lost a family member if somebody

died on this shoot." Esther smacked Rob's hand away from her fries, again.

"Nobody felt that way when Kate disappeared," Bear opened just the line of conversation that I'd been hoping would open.

"Two reasons for that." Esther held up two fingers. "One," she pulled down her index finger with her other hand, "Kate didn't get killed and two," she left her middle finger up in the air, "nobody liked her enough to care when she left."

"I liked her," Pam protested. "And we don't know what really happened to her. But Bear says that's what Ria's going to find out for us."

Esther gave me a long, questioning look.

"Can we maybe have this conversation somewhere else?" Rob asked. "I can point out three cameras and two microphones that I can see from here ..."

"Chillax!" Bear sloughed off Glenn's concern. "Everything out here's disconnected. I thought Ria might come out after her dinner with Dan."

"Listen, guys, you saw one side of Kate and I saw the other. You thought she was sweet and innocent. The Kate I saw was sneaky, conniving, scheming, shrewd ..."

"Careful, you'll run out of adjectives soon." Bear cut Esther off and tapped some tobacco into his pipe. "Besides, who she was doesn't really matter. Whether she was a victim or a villain is unimportant. What's important is finding out what really happened to her." He turned to look straight at me. "How's that going?"

"I'm still fact gathering." I didn't want to admit that I'd gathered next to no facts. Then again, I'd only been on Soursop for what, a day? Had it really been such a short time? So much had happened in those few hours that I felt as if I'd been there for weeks. "Pam, would you be willing to describe what you saw to someone for me?" Hearing the crew discuss metacarpals and carpals had made me think of Dad. He'd know if the foot was real, if Pam could give him a good description of what she'd seen.

"Okay. Who?"

"My father. It's too late now, but maybe you could drop by my place tomorrow morning and we can call him from there? He's a doctor."

"Sure, but I'm pretty sure the foot was fake. I think it was a red herring, like those fake clues they have in murder mysteries. Maybe she even put it there herself? Maybe the real mystery is why did Kate fake her own death?" She looked around the table. "What? Why are you all looking at me like that?"

"That sounds plausible. I know that I never travel without a personalized replica of a severed limb in my carry-on. You never know when you'll need one." Bear shook his head.

"Face it," Esther said, "this isn't a mystery. Kate left. Bu-bye. End of story. Roll tail credits."

"So, what's with that doctoring thing?" Bear turned to me. "Is it a hobby, or something? Your father owns the majority of this hotel chain, so it's not like he had to work or anything."

I wanted to give Bear a swift kick to the groin.

"And what about you? You flit around the world on someone else's dime, staying at places like this without having to worry about paying for it. Even if you did have to pay for it, you could afford it with the Butler billions padding your wallet. Must be nice, huh? Never having to work. Sweet life, if you can get it. We really appreciate you slumming with the likes of us."

"Oh boy," Rob cringed.

I could have answered calmly but I'd heard one too many snide comments and supposed jokes about my presumed wealth and perfect life. That irritation mixed with my concern about whatever was going on between Glenn and me, and my confusion about whatever was or wasn't going on between Rob and me and/or Rob and Pam, and my disappointment in and anger at James, and the repulsion I felt for Mandy, and the resulting sympathy I felt for my sister-in-law — combined, those emotions were explosive. If this was Bear's way of checking me out he'd regret it. Rob had been right to cringe. I figuratively threw my manners muzzle to the ground and set free years of resentment, whether Bear deserved to have them hurled at him or not. "You're right, Bear," I said as if I was actually going to agree with his assessment of my life. "Money does buy happiness. Like when I was fifteen and my mother was killed, we were really happy about the fact that we could put her in the nicest coffin money could buy. Sure, Dad lost his eyesight in the same accident, but he could afford to buy more than enough Chivas and Glenfiddich happy juice. And he can still sit around counting his dough — there are Braille dots on all the Canadian bills. He'll never see his grandkids, though. That's kind of a buzz kill …"

"Ria," I heard Rob say.

"I was super happy on my wedding day, because of the money of course. It's why my ex married me. Boy was he ever unhappy when he found out that I don't own a single share of Butler Hotels and that I've never asked for or received one penny from the company." I stood up so angrily that my chair went skidding across the patio behind me. "Just for the record, the money that's in my wallet got there the good old-fashioned way — I earned it. I'm so happy we could have this chat, Bear."

Only then did I take my eyes off Bear. Pam and Esther were both staring at me with their jaws dropped and eyes opened wide.

Any hope I'd ever had of fitting in with these people had been shot to hell. I wasn't just a rich person anymore; I was a crazy rich person.

"I deserved that." Bear stood up, walked over to my chair, picked it up, and carried it back to the table. "And I apologize." He motioned for me to sit back down. "Of all people I should have been more sensitive. I know what it's like to be judged based on what people see, not what they actually know. You heard Chris earlier — I'm a midget. Other names I've been called include: Ooopma Loompa, Munchkin … you get the drift. None of those identify who I am, though. Looking at me nobody would guess that I'm a classically trained pianist, but I am. Unfortunately, due to my longitudinally challenged fingers there are some pieces that I can't play.

"I liked getting to see the real you. Friends?" He held out his hand for me to shake.

"You can do better than that, Bear!" Esther slapped his arm. "That girl needs a hug."

"You should sell your story." Pam instantly started giggling. "You could get rich off it!"

I felt more accepted by the people around that table, most of whom I'd only met that day, than I had in any grouping of people in years. Maybe I should have shaken off my manners muzzle earlier? "Friends." I shook Bear's hand and he pulled me closer to give me a hug.

"Now," he said as he sat back down, "let's start figuring out what really happened to Kate."

"And so," Esther dropped her head down to her shoulders like a turtle pulling his head into his shell, and lowered her voice dramatically, "the merry band of super spies gathered together, determined to find out what kind of evil lurks in Shykoff's fiefdom."

"I think it's more of a monopsony than a fiefdom, actually," Bear said as he lit his pipe.

"What the hell are you talking about?" Rob asked.

"A monopsony, a firm that is the only buyer of labour in an isolated community. We're isolated and we supply our labour to the only buyer in town — Dan." Bear leaned over to me. "I'm not just a pretty face; I play the piano and educate my intellectually challenged co-workers."

"Dude, get your ego in check," Pam spoke up. "And you're wrong on that monopoly ..."

"Monopsony," Bear corrected her.

"Yeah, whatever you call it, you're wrong. We work for James, too."

"But Dan's a much more likely suspect than James," Esther added.

Pam jumped up, ran over to the electronic equipment, and pushed some buttons. "We need a soundtrack for this."

Children's voices came out of the speakers, sounding as if they were laughing and playing in an inner city park. Simple guitar strumming overlapped their voices. Then a woman started singing about how hard it was to live in the devil's playground.

"Good one, Pam," Esther said as she took two fries off of Rob's plate. "It matches the mood and setting. You ever heard of Gram Rabbit, Ria?"

I shook my head.

"They've got a song that would be perfect as the theme song for this show — 'They're Watching.'"

"It aired on NBC's show *Life*, episode two-fifteen, 'I Heart Mom.'" Bear instantly identified the television tie-in. "I liked that show. I wish they hadn't cancelled it."

I was beginning to understand how my new friends thought. Everything in their world was somehow tied in to either a movie or a television show, right down to the episode number. So what was Kate's tie-in?

played the part of the audience, while Bear, Rob, Esther, and Pam supplied the dialogue.

```
EXT. POOL PATIO — LATE NIGHT/EARLY MORNING


The last WAITER on duty had cleared our
table. The lights in the hotel rooms above
us had all gone off as the guests went to
bed.


                    ESTHER
          You're talking out of your butt. She
          came here on a mission, to get Dan
          to take her to Hollywood. When she
          figured out he wasn't going to do
          that she quit and left.


                    PAM
          You are so wrong! It was the other
          way round — Dan was using her. I bet
          that's what they were arguing about
          that night. She thought she had a
          relationship with him and he told
          her the real facts of life.


                    ESTHER
          So why would he bother to kill her?
          If he'd just dumped her his job was
          done.
```

PAM

Same thing if she dumped him. He'd
have no reason to kill her. There's
no way Dan cared enough about her to
be that upset.

ESTHER

Nobody did anything. She's back in
Toronto like the cops said.

BEAR

How do we know they actually talked
to her? Dan could have hired a double …

ROB

Or the story about the cops in
Toronto could be pure fiction, written by Dan.

PAM

If she was killed, Dan's the most
likely suspect I guess. He's the one
who had the screaming match with
her. Euw!
        (gags and then shivers as if
        shaking off a bad thought)
The foot couldn't have been real,
could it?

ME

Hopefully my father will be able to
tell us.
        (changing the topic before
        Pam can throw up for real)
Did she get into arguments with anybody else other than Dan?

ESTHER

Most of us tried to avoid her; she
was annoying, always asking who we'd
worked with …

PAM

I liked her. So did Winnie. I saw
them together a couple of times and
she even made Winnie laugh once.

>   ESTHER
> Winnie's capable of laughing?

>   PAM
> She's not that bad! And neither was
> Kate. She smiled a lot, especially
> when she heard that Chris was com-
> ing.

>   BEAR
>   (to me)
> Kate worked with Pam on one of the
> crews that's shooting Ted.

>   ROB
> But she wasn't originally scheduled
> to work on that crew. She started
> off working with us on a Judy crew.

>   ESTHER
> She got Dan to switch her over to a
> Ted crew.

>   ME
> Why?
>   (wondering why Kate wanted
>   to get away from Judy)

>   ESTHER
>   (shrugs her shoulders)
> Moth to a flame? Ted looks like a
> movie star.

>   PAM
>   (nods)
> Yeah, he's yummy, for an old guy. He
> reminds me of someone, but I can't
> put my finger on who.

>   BEAR
> Let's stay focused on the foot,
> shall we? We can worry about the fin-
> gers later.

>   ME
> Where was everybody the night she
> disappeared?

ROB

Our crew …
          (he points at Esther)
… was shooting Judy prepping for her
commercial.

PAM

Our crew had the night off. Kate
took the fancy boat back over to
Dan's place when we wrapped for the
day, then she came back with Dan and
James and Mandy. They had dinner
together in the kitchen.

BEAR

I was in the pseudo control room
most of the day and finished around
ten. Then I met up with Pam and
everybody, setting up the dinghy
explosion, and we were doing that
until well after midnight.

PAM

It was earlier than that, wasn't it?

BEAR

No, remember? Zack radioed me from
the north end to tell me that one of
the construction guys had knocked
the camera up there. That was the
last disc change on his rounds. The
earliest he would have got there
would have been around twelve-
thirty, probably later.
          (turns to me)
The day before Albert comes is
always a busy one for me — I have to
make sure all the discs have been
logged accurately and that dubs have
been made. And I go over the footage
from the security cameras to see if
anything's been caught on them that
could be interesting.

ME

What are dubs?

                    BEAR
Copies, duplicates. But the ones
we make down here aren't broadcast
quality. Your brother elected to
allocate his limited budget funds
toward giving Albert more frequent
flyer miles than George Clooney had
in *Up in the Air,* because apparently
that's got more production value
than replacing his antediluvian cameras or bringing an Avid down. You
can bet Mark Burnett doesn't shoot
his shows this way.

                    ME
What's an Avid?

                    BEAR
A keen or enthusiastic …

                    ROB
Stop messing around, Bear.

                    BEAR
It's an editing suite. Albert comes
down a couple of times a week, picks
up the camera originals and then takes
them back to Toronto, where they're
being edited on an Avid suite.

                    ME
And he brings you more blank discs
when he comes down, right?

All four characters turn and look at me

                    BEAR
He doesn't bring anything down with
him.

                    ESTHER
Except for his cheery personality.

                    PAM
He doesn't even bring clothes. He
has an extra set of beigeness that
he leaves in the laundry bag outside
his door for pick-up.

                    ROB
That guy's skin is so white I could
do a white balance on his legs.

                    BEAR
          (interjects, for my benefit)
A white balance is done on all the
cameras before they start shooting
for the day. A cameraman fills his
screen with something that's true
white which then allows the camera to
calculate the colour temperature …

                    ROB
TMI, Bear.

                    ME
He does bring something, though — a
bag full of DVDs. I saw it. He left
it at James' place.

                    BEAR
Maybe he brought James some movies
to watch? There's some sweet equipment in his villa.

                    PAM
Winnie would know what he brings,
but she won't tell you anything.

                    ROB
Does anybody know where he came
from? I've never seen him on one of
James' shoots before.

BEAR, ESTHER, and PAM all shake their
heads.

                    ME
Was he here that night?

                    ROB
No, he came down the next afternoon.

                    ME
Did anyone actually see Kate go back
over to Virgin Gorda after their
dinner?

                    PAM
              (shakes her head)
We saw the fancy boat leaving while
we were bringing the dinghy around
the north end, but we weren't close
enough to see who was in it.

                    BEAR
Ted may have seen who got in it.

                    PAM
Yeah, he might have. Dan called him
back up to the hotel while we were
rigging the boat on the back docks,
so he might have still been there
when they all left the kitchen.

                    ME
What about the next morning? When
did you find the foot?

                    ESTHER
Our call was six thirty, but —
              (looks at Rob)
— wasn't that the morning you showed
up late?

                    PAM
              (cuts in quickly, after a notice-
              ably nervous glance at Rob)
The foot was already there when
Esther's crew arrived on location.
They called me in and I got there
before seven.

                    BEAR
If we still had the discs down here
I could go through them to see if
any of the stationary cameras caught
someone putting the foot in the
water, but Albert took those discs
up to Toronto in the last shipment.

                    ME
But didn't you say you made copies?

                    BEAR
Only of selected shots.

```
                    ME
Who selects them?


                  BEAR
    Dan.

HARD CUT TO BLACK.
```

Thrust into complete darkness it took a few minutes for my eyes to adjust. It wasn't the darkness that told me we'd had a power failure though, it was my ears. I recognized the silence — a complete lack of electronic sound.

"Who's got a flashlight?" Esther asked.

"I do," Pam answered and then I heard a zipper unzipping.

"We should probably call it a night anyway." Rob's chair scraped on the patio stones.

Pam turned her flashlight on and held it under her chin, the beam washed up over her face. "What time should I come over tomorrow, Ria? My call's at noon."

"Nine?" I hoped that Dad would still be at home.

"Okay." Pam lifted her small canvas backpack up from under the table (the same backpack I'd seen her slip the gift from Rob into earlier). "I call shotgun."

"Who's got wheels?" Esther asked.

"Bear does," Pam offered.

Walking side by side, all of us using the beam from Pam's flashlight to lead the way, we walked through the dark lobby of the hotel as two Butler employees began lighting candles on the reception desk.

"I'll drive Ria's cart for her, she's never driven the island at night," Rob said as he started down the front steps of the hotel.

Did he want some time alone with me? Why? After seeing the kiss he and Pam had shared the only logical answer to that question was that he had something to tell me that he didn't want to say in front of everyone else.

"Then either you or Esther are going to have to drive, Pam." Bear stopped at the top of the steps. "I need to go check on the generators. It looks like we might need them tomorrow. I'll grab one of the groundskeeper's carts later."

"That means you're driving, Esther." Pam took the steps two at a time. "I don't drive at night around here. The one time I did I ran over a land crab and the crunching sound it made was gross! Those things are like a nocturnal army of hard bodied spiders on steroids."

"I'm not driving! Remember? I don't have my licence."

"Like you're going to get pulled over and asked for your licence, insurance, and ownership!" Pam scoffed. "These aren't real roads and the golf carts aren't real cars."

"And I'm really not driving." Esther said firmly.

So much for getting a chance to talk to Rob. "You go with them, Rob. I'll be okay."

They quickly loaded their equipment into one of the two golf carts parked near the front doors of the hotel and drove off, all three of them wishing me and Bear a goodnight.

"I lied." Bear said quietly.

"You what?"

"I made an untruthful statement that was intended to deceive others."

"Thanks for the definition. So, what untruthful statement did you make?"

"I don't have to check on the generators. I wanted to talk to you alone. Mind giving me a lift? I can walk down to the crew quarters from your place."

He didn't say another word until we were out of earshot of any of the hotel rooms. In fact, the first thing I heard, other than the whine of the almost-engine, was the sound of a land crab being crunched under the tires of the golf cart.

"There are some cameras that nobody knows about."

"Where?" I hoped he wasn't going to say the secret cameras were hidden in my villa.

"In Judy and Ted's rooms."

"Why?"

"We had them in all of the contestant's rooms. Dan wanted to see if anybody hooked up."

"He wouldn't be able to put that on TV, though, would he? Aren't there censorship rules or something?" Not to mention invasion of privacy rules.

"Editing is a beautiful thing. They could put something together that could go to air. But nobody hooked up."

"What happens to the discs when the show's over? Does James erase them?"

"James doesn't know about them. Those cameras were Dan's babies. Sometimes working for two bosses can get a bit tricky. On this shoot it's like walking a tightrope. Dan keeps the discs. Something happened in Ted's room that night, but I don't want you to misunderstand it."

I missed the turn-off to the road that led to my villa and made a seven-point U-turn — the golf cart's steering wasn't the best.

"Someone went in and took a pair of his shoes the night Kate disappeared. And then she —"

"She?" I forced myself to pay attention to what I could see of the road.

Bear didn't answer me. "She put the shoes back in his closet the next morning, a couple of minutes after Ted left to go watch the dinghy explode."

"Who was it?"

"The image isn't that clear, and the room lights were off and the camera wasn't focused on the closet ..."

"Who was it, Bear?" Why was he stalling?

"Winnie."

"Winnie?" Why would Winnie surreptitiously borrow a pair of Ted's shoes? Then I remembered Donnella's radio conversation with one of her staff about Ted complaining about sand on his shoes. Sandy shoes weren't exactly a smoking gun, even if they did give off a hint of smoke.

"I don't for a minute believe that Winnie did anything to Kate. Like Pam said, Winnie and Kate got along and Winnie doesn't make friends easily. But Winnie takes care of Dan, fixes his problems, and we know that he had some sort of problem with Kate that night."

I'd already seen Winnie's problem-solving skills play out in front of me. But would she kill for him? "What about the other cameras, the ones all over the island? Is there some way I could see what's on them? Maybe they recorded something ..."

"Albert already took all of the footage from that night and the next morning up to Toronto."

"But you said the footage was logged. Doesn't that mean someone watched it all and wrote down exactly what happened in each shot?"

"It doesn't work that way. All we log is the date, time, which camera, the scene and take, and a general description of what's in the shot. If there's something out of the ordinary the crew makes note of it, but there wasn't anything like that on the log sheets from that night or the next morning. And there's no description for the footage from the stationary cameras. The only people who will watch every single frame are the editors — and they're in Toronto with the discs."

"Could a friend of mine look at the discs in Toronto without Dan or James finding out about it?" Even if Bear said there was a way, I had no guarantee that Glenn would be able to fit it into his busy, busy schedule. And even if he did, I had no guarantee that he'd let me know what he'd seen. Apparently, he hadn't been able to find the time to call me back.

"I'll make a call. If my bud, Dex, is slotted into the editing schedule this week he could put something together for your friend, but I'll have to tell him which bins and folders you're interested in."

"What are tho —"

A blur of black dashed across the road in front of the golf cart. I slammed on the brakes. The blur stopped moving and took shape — the shape of a lycra clad woman in extremely good shape. Her muscles were so well exercised that they look sculpted. The beams from the pretend headlights on the cart were aimed so low that I couldn't see her face.

"Watch where you're going!" The woman yelled and jogged up to Bear's side of the cart. "Oh, hi, Bear." She sounded surprised, and pleased, to see him.

I was just plain surprised to see her.

"Good evening, Miss Winnie. Out for your evening ambulations?" Bear asked cheerfully. "Dan all tucked in?"

The woman talking to Bear didn't look anything like the Winnie I'd met earlier that day. The woman jogging in place beside the golf cart was capable of using muscles she'd shown no sign of having before — her facial muscles. They contracted into a big smile for Bear. Instead of a tight bun, her hair was pulled back in a loose ponytail that hung down to the middle of her back. Her clothing clung to her sculpted body, instead of hanging over it.

"He left the island a little while ago."

"And how many laps have you done since then?"

"This is my fourth."

Bear turned to me. "Winnie's training for a marathon. She runs laps around the island every night. It probably helps her burn off the frustration known as Dan."

Winnie's smile fell and she nodded at me. "Miss Butler."

"Sorry about almost hitting you, Winnie. I didn't see …"

"I've already contacted mechanical about the power failure." Winnie, the problem solver, let me know that she had already dealt with the issue that was affecting my ability to see what was on the road in front of me. "Now, if you'll excuse me, I'll finish my run."

"Are we still on for later?" Bear asked hopefully.

"Check," she called out as she ran away into the darkness.

"Checkmate!" Bear yelled back.

I pushed down on the accelerator slowly. "You've got a date with Winnie?"

"A chess date but, the powers of lust willing, I'm hoping it'll turn into a real date. She's hot!"

Bear was right about Winnie's body, but I wasn't so sure about her personality.

"I've got a thing for older women. If you're romantically unencumbered feel free to invite me in for a nightcap, I've got a free hour before I hook up with Winnie."

Older women? Winnie looked old. At least she had when I'd first seen her by the pool. I'd guessed her to be in her mid-fifties. I wasn't that old! (Close, but not there yet.) To avoid an awkward rejection of his offer, I simply ignored it. "Doesn't it bother you that the woman you're trying to date might be involved with Kate's disappearance?"

"Winnie's good people. She's a lot like James."

Even more so if she did end up getting to know Bear in the biblical sense. Like Mandy, he had to be at least twenty years younger than the person he was attracted to.

"I know what you're thinking ..."

I doubted that.

"... you think Winnie used Ted's shoes to walk on the beach and put the foot in the tidal pool, and you could be right. But if she did do that she did it because Dan ordered her to. Like everyone else around here she needs her job.

She's tied to Dan, but he's the one directing the action — not her."

I found it interesting that so many people saw Dan as some sort of all-powerful being, capable of controlling the women in his life. Having never met Kate I didn't know if Pam was right about Kate's innocence and gullibility, but I had met Winnie. She didn't strike me as being anyone's puppet. In fact, from the little I had seen of her interactions with Dan, it looked like she had more control of him than he had of her (or himself). Was Bear's assessment of Winnie's culpability clouded by lust?

"Dan's yanking everybody's chains on this shoot, including James'. James acts like an exec producer — he usually stays out of the way and handles the business end. But Dan? He's micromanaging everything and everyone. I can understand why James has been down here for the duration; it's his first shot at U.S. network and it came at the perfect time for him to escape his domestic troubles back home."

"You know about that?" I couldn't see James opening up about his personal issues to his employees.

"Ria, there aren't any secrets on a set."

"If that's true, why doesn't anyone know what really happened to Kate?"

"Oh, someone knows. More than one person probably ..."

"Dan and Winnie, right?"

"Probably. Maybe even another person or two. But they're not talking. That's what makes this extra strange. We're like castaways on this island. All we have is each other all the time, so all we usually talk about is ourselves. The people who are talking are talking about how strange it is that we don't know what happened. And they're talking about you and Rob, wondering whether you're just friends or if you're friends with benefits."

"You've all been talking about that?" I'd been talking about it, too, but only to myself and my gecko friend.

"So? Which one is it?"

"We're friends." Could we even be classified as that? There I went again, struggling to define or label a relationship. "Besides, I think he and Pam ..."

"You noticed that, huh? Yeah, they're close, but that relationship isn't what you think. At least, what I think you think it is anyway."

"What is it then?"

Bear smiled and shook his head. "Uh-uh, that's not for me to say."

"I thought you said there were no secrets on a set?"

"This is an exception to the general rule. It's private and it'll stay that way until Pam feels like talking about it. I only know about it by accident. Very few of the others know anything, but they've got their suspicions, just like you do."

"That sounds like the whole Kate situation — people have their suspicions but only a few of them know the truth."

"The truth's always out there. The trick is to get it into focus."

Even with two pillows held tightly over his head, Glenn could still hear Brandon and his friends laughing loudly at whatever they were watching on TV in the living room. Maybe some silence in the condo wouldn't be such a bad thing after all?

His frustration at not being able to get in touch with Ria wasn't doing much to facilitate peaceful slumber either. He'd tried to call her at the hotel ten times. Each time he dialled the hotel's number he got a busy signal. His six calls to her cellphone went straight through to voicemail, but he'd only left three messages. Call number seventeen was to Cable & Wireless, the only phone company he could find on the Internet that serviced the British Virgin Islands. That call had been answered by a very nice woman who informed him that Soursop was experiencing technical difficulties with its telephone service. In other words, there currently wasn't any phone service to or from Soursop.

Brandon and his friends burst into loud male laughter again.

Glenn flung both pillows onto the floor as he sat up and then tripped over one of them as he made his way to the door without bothering to turn on the lights in his room. All of the lights in the living room were on and he had to squint hard when he opened his bedroom door. "Would you guys mind keeping it down?"

Brandon leaned his head backwards and talked to Glenn upside down, his blonde curls hanging down the back of the couch. "Sorry, Dad."

His friends, their long limbs draped and flopped over the arms and backs of the rest of the living room furniture, all turned to look at Glenn. The coffee table was littered with the remnants of their pizza dinner and numerous empty beer bottles.

"What's so funny, anyway?"

"A&E's running a *Parking Wars* marathon and you should see this one lady. She must think she's on *America's Got Talent* or something. She just did a song and dance routine in the Philadelphia Parking Authority office."

"Some people will do anything to be famous," one of the guys said, but Glenn didn't know who he was.

Glenn backed into his room and closed the door. Scooping up his pillows, he flopped back into bed. Then he noticed that the little red light on his cellphone was flashing, telling him that he'd received a voicemail.

The numbers on his phone lit up as he dialled in to his voicemail. There was only one message.

"Hi." Ria didn't sound happy. "Glenn, please call me back. I really need your help on this. Thanks."

He tried her cellphone first, but again his call went straight to voicemail. Then he dialled the hotel, its number permanently burned into his short-term memory having already dialled it so many times that day. This time his call was answered.

Ria didn't do a very good job of hiding her anger, but it dissipated quickly when Glenn told her about his repeated efforts to reach her, all of which had been foiled by technology, not his lack of action.

"So, are you with me on this, then? Or are you too busy with your white-collar story?"

"I'm in. What've you got?"

It was hard to keep track of the many names, especially when he couldn't put faces to most of them. Glenn turned on his bedside lamp and started to jot down notes. "Why would Winnie want her dead, though? And even if she did do it, why would she go to the trouble of putting the foot in such a visible place? Whoever killed Kate hid her body well enough. Why take off a foot like that?"

"I don't know. What I'm hoping is that you'll see something in the footage."

"What time are you calling your dad tomorrow?"

"Nine. Why?"

"Think he'd mind if I dropped by to listen in? He might be able to give us some insight into the whole mutilation thing." Doc Butler had a clearer view of human behaviour than any sighted person Glenn had ever met. The trick was learning to ignore Doc's sarcasm and brusqueness to see the truths he laid bare.

"He wouldn't mind at all."

"What about that boat explosion? Do you think it has anything to do with Kate?"

"How'd you hear about that?" Ria sounded surprised.

"I didn't hear about it, I saw it. Our entertainment guys are trying to figure out if it's real."

"It's fake."

"It looked pretty real to me. Wasn't the guy in the boat hurt?" From the few seconds Glenn had seen, it looked as if the man had been blown up right along with the boat.

"That was a dummy named Albert. And speaking of Albert ..." Ria explained who Albert was, why he wasn't hurt in the explosion, and how she planned to find out what exactly it was that he brought down to James whenever he came to the islands. "Whatever Albert's up to, he couldn't have anything to do with Kate's disappearance. He wasn't here and he didn't get here until hours after the foot was found."

"But you still think he's up to something."

"I know he is."

Glenn hoped his next question wouldn't get Ria all uppity about Bobbie again. "While you're snooping around James' place don't forget to check out the room that Rob said he saw Kate's suitcases in."

"I already planned to," Ria said without any testiness.

"Okay. So we're good?" Talk about a loaded question, Glenn thought to himself as he turned the light off.

"I guess so." Ria didn't sound like she wanted to hang up, either.

The telephone made their silence awkward. The full moon over Toronto had turned Lake Ontario a shimmering dark grey and it reminded him of the night they'd lain together on the lounge chair outside of their room in Machu Picchu watching the stars. That night the silence between them had been heavenly.

"What about her sister?" Ria broke the silence. "Maybe she was lying? Maybe she knows where Kate really is?"

"No. She really thinks Kate is with Chris."

"Are you going to tell her...?"

"Not yet. Let's see what we see tomorrow."

"I guess I'll talk to you tomorrow then."

The silence in his room after hanging up lasted only a minute and was replaced by barely muted laughter from the living room. Glenn buried his head under the pillows again.

CHAPTER
NINE

The sun peeked over Gorda Peak on Virgin Gorda early the next morning and woke me up by blasting my bedroom with brilliant light.

Carefully holding an empty can of Diet Coke to clearly show the label, I managed to run only one lap of the island. Before I reached the halfway point my foot started to remind me of the twist I'd given it on Huayna Picchu. My quads complained bitterly for the uphill last quarter of the run. Without bothering to change into a bathing suit I collapsed into my pool with only one thought in my head — how the heck did Winnie stay upright for four laps? Bear said she ran her laps every night after Dan left the island. Her resting heart rate was probably in the low forties. Running the hilly island once, let alone four times, was an excellent cardiovascular workout.

I floated on my back, enjoying the refreshing chill of the water. Even though it was still early the air was already thick with humidity. My sweat combined with the salty moisture in the air made me wonder if running through an island -sized vat of French onion soup would have felt the same. My legs had sure ended up feeling like wobbly stretched and melted cheese. No wonder Winnie chose to run at night. I hadn't passed many people during my run, mostly hotel groundskeepers. At night,

Winnie could potentially do her entire run without seeing any-one. What had she done under that cloak of darkness the night before Kate's foot was found? She could have easily nipped off the path down onto the beach and dropped the foot into the tidal pool without being noticed. Heck, I hadn't noticed her until she was between my headlights.

But what about the rest of Kate? Where was she? Winnie was in great shape but even she couldn't have run around car-rying the weight of a ninety-nine percent whole person.

Using only my arms, giving my quads more time to for-give me, I swam over to the side of the pool and hooked my elbows over the infinity edge. There were some signs of life in the crew quarters below me. A group of equipment-laden people got into three golf carts and drove away. Room service delivered breakfast to a room at the end of the cell block. Then I saw Rob, wearing only a bathrobe, come out of a room on the ground floor and walk up the stairs to a second-floor room far-ther down the building. He knocked on the door and I instantly recognized Pam's pink bangs when she opened it. She wrapped her arms around his neck, pulled his head down to hers, and planted a big kiss on his lips. Any possibility of something hap-pening between Rob and myself ended with a much louder bang than the door made when Rob closed it behind himself.

The urge to move hit me again. I got out of my wet clothes, dried off quickly, changed, and let the wind blow-dry my hair as I drove to the hotel.

A large buffet had been set up by the pool. The majority of the people on the patio didn't look familiar to me so I guessed they were members of the incoming movie crew. I easily rec-ognized Bear and Winnie (once again dressed to spinsterly perfection). They were sitting together at a table in the middle of the throng. Winnie sat facing me. She was as still as a Great Blue Heron waiting for its prey, only her eyes were moving

— they followed me as I made my way to the buffet table. Bear had his back to me and was bent over, making notes on a pad of paper as he flipped through the pages in a three-ring binder. He stopped writing, looked up at Winnie, and talked to her as he spun the binder around so she could see what it was he was pointing to on the page.

Judy, followed closely by her merry band of a television crew, joined me at the buffet table while I stabbed some pine-apple slices.

"Good morning, Ms. Butler," she said cheerfully as she began to load up her plate, keeping her back to the camera (much the chagrin on the cameraman — he kept trying to shoot her from the side, but she kept turning away from him).

"Hi, Judy." A piece of mango was giving me a hard time; it refused to stay on the serving fork. The cameraman had moved to aim his camera at me and I pulled my secret weapon out of my back pocket — another empty can of Diet Coke (slightly mangled from being forced into the pocket). I couldn't do anything about the microphone that was being held in the air above us, but I would do something about the camera trying to shoot me. I put the Diet Coke can on my plate and pushed the pineapple slices into position to hold it in place.

Judy smiled when she saw the can and stood a little closer to me. "I'd like to apologize to you for last night. I should have talked to Mr. Shykoff in private, but I was just so …"

"Don't worry about it." I would have been screaming mad, too, if someone had just thrown up on me. "It's not like you did it in front of paying guests."

"No, I did it in front of my future employer."

"Who? Me?" Why wasn't my message getting through to anyone? "Judy, I don't have anything to do with running the hotels. Honest. Even if I did I wouldn't hold last night against you."

"Thank you." She handed her plate to one of the chefs behind the table. "Just a poached egg this morning, Paul." Turning to see who was coming through the doors from the lobby, her face fell. "Oh, no."

Despite his big sunglasses it was easy to spot Chris Regent. There was a loveable rogue aura about him that was unmistakable. The cameraman focused on Chris as he looked around the patio area, spotted Judy, and headed straight for us.

"I'm really, really sorry. Mike told me what happened yesterday." He flipped his sunglasses up onto the top of his head, revealing two extremely bloodshot eyeballs, one of them circled by the spreading blue bruise from Judy's punch. "Please, let me make it up to you? I don't even know your name …"

Judy straightened her spine stiffly. "Judy. Judy Ingram."

"Judy." Chris took both of Judy's empty hands in his and kissed them. "Please? Forgive me? I promise it won't happen again."

"Apology accepted, Mr. Regent." She forced a smile onto her face. "And I apologize for …" she pointed at his black eye, "that."

"From what I hear, I deserved it. Call me Chris." He looked up and down the buffet table. "What a spread! You run a nice place here, Judy."

"Actually, I'm only the acting manager right now." She glanced nervously at me. "But I hope to make it a permanent position. Is everything to your liking in your room?"

"It's fucking awesome!" Chris pinched a strawberry from the fruit platter and popped it into his mouth. "Seriously, isn't there something I can do to say thanks for putting up with me? What about a car? Can I buy you a car?"

A novel way to apologize. I smiled and scanned the drool-inspiring selection of baked goods.

"That's not necessary, really. If —" she stopped and corrected herself. "*When* I get the manager position what would I do with it here?"

"Good point. Okay, when you win I'll get you a suped up golf cart. Deal?"

"Again, that won't be necessary …"

"Morning, Ria." Bear walked up beside me, a binder and pad of paper tucked under his arm. "Nice breakfast," he nodded at my Diet Coke can as he handed me a sheaf of papers from the pad. "Here's the info for your friend. Tell him to talk to Dex."

"I owe you an even bigger apology," Chris walked around Judy to stand by Bear. "I was incredibly rude to you."

"Whatever." Bear waved Chris away. "I'm used to it."

"Hi, guys," Esther had come out onto the patio. Holding an empty plate, she elbowed her way between Chris and Bear, completely ignoring the star in her midst. "The usual, Paul," she said as she handed her plate to the chef. "You know what you should get here, Ria?"

"What?" Was she going to recommend something from the menu?

"A Timmy's." Esther turned to face the camera crew. "You won't be able to use this conversation, guys. Dan doesn't have a placement deal with Timmy's."

"That would be sweet!" Bear obviously liked Esther's idea. "We could have Iced Caps and maple glazes every day." He turned to look at Judy. "No offence, Judy, but the craft services here aren't quite up to par. I haven't seen a doughnut in weeks."

"What about the beignets?" Judy went on the defensive. "The chefs started making those fresh, every day, specifically to address the doughnut issue on the snack table."

"Craft services table," Esther corrected Judy (and answered my unasked question about what craft services were).

Bear nodded his head with next to no enthusiasm. "Yeah, they're good …"

"But they don't have holes. They're kind of like Timbits injected with growth hormones." Esther's description didn't match any beignet I'd ever eaten, but I understood her comparison.

"And they aren't Timmy's," Bear summed up succinctly.

"What's a Timmy's?" Chris asked.

"Tim Hortons," Judy explained. "It's a chain of coffee and doughnut shops in Canada."

"So, is a Timbit just a bit of a doughnut?" Chris looked from Bear to Esther and then back to Bear.

"A Timbit is the doughnut hole, they …" Bear started to explain.

"How can you eat a hole?" Chris looked very confused. "And why call a hole a bit? If it's the whole hole, wouldn't it be the whole thing, not just a bit of it?"

Esther spoke directly to me, turning her back on the whole hole episode between Chris and Bear. "Seriously, a Timmy's down here would be awesome."

"Why are they telling you all this?" Chris' interest shifted from holes to me. "Who are you?"

"Ria Butler," Bear offered a little too quickly with a wicked grin on his face. "She owns the place."

"Oh!" Chris was impressed.

"I don't …"

Chris turned back to Bear. "Are you working on the television show or the movie?"

"*Check-Out Time*. I'm the TD."

"And he's not technically a dwarf, okay? He's just vertically challenged." Esther made it extra clear how little she thought of Chris. "So, don't be an ass around him again."

"I've already tried to apologize."

Judy's poached egg was ready. She reached out to take her plate from the chef just as Winnie joined our motley crew.

"Judy? I need to go over the phone logs. The long distance charges are getting out of control. Do you have a minute?" Winnie asked.

Judy looked relieved to have a legitimate excuse to get away from the whole Timmy's hullabaloo.

"You can count on that golf cart, Judy!" Chris called out as Judy and Winnie left us and disappeared into the hotel, a camera crew in tow.

"What golf cart?" Esther asked.

"I'm going to buy her one when she wins, sort of like an apology gift. I offered her a car, but …"

"Does Bear get a car?"

"Sure, if he wants one." Chris looked at Bear. "Do you want one? I'd really like to …"

"I've already got a car." Bear picked up a muffin. "A double-double from Timmy's sure would go good with this, though."

"You could buy him a dentist's chair." Esther kept at Chris. "He doesn't do recliners, he does dentist's chairs."

"Okay, a dentist's chair it is."

"Why don't you buy a Timmy's franchise for the hotel?" Bear suggested. "We'd all appreciate that."

"Okay! If it's okay with you, that is," Chris asked me.

"I don't own …"

"Would you like anything from the kitchen, Miss?" the chef asked me.

I had been contemplating an omelette but knew that my sanity was more important than my hunger. Listening to the whole bizarre Timbit conversation was making me dizzy. "No, thanks." I grabbed a Danish and put it on top of the fruit I'd managed to get onto my plate.

I made my escape while Esther and Bear explained the virtues of Tim Hortons versus Starbucks to Chris, deciding to deliver my own room service and eat in my villa.

The elevator doors in the lobby opened just as I was walking past them. Ted and his camera crew practically filled the dwarf- (but not midget) sized elevator and they reminded me of a bunch of circus clowns tumbling out of an overstuffed car as they unsuccessfully tried to extricate themselves from the elevator gracefully. Ted must have thought the smile on my face was caused by pleasure at seeing him. He plastered an even bigger smile on his face, waited for the television crew to get themselves organized back into a cohesive working unit, and then walked slowly toward me.

"Good morning, Miss Butler. Another beautiful day in paradise, isn't it?" He turned, ever so slightly, to give the camera a better shot of his face.

"Yeah, it's nice." I kept moving.

Ted picked up his pace, but not so much that he'd lose his crew. "Did you sleep well?"

I half expected him to start into a dissertation on the merits of my bed, complete with the intricate details of how the individual air chambers in the mattress had been inflated by exhaling world champion freedivers, but instead of talking more his mouth stopped moving and fell into a frown. He'd spotted my can of Diet Coke.

"Oh, dear." He moved to use his body to block the camera's view of my plate, leaned in close to me and spoke softly. "Did no one inform you of the placement deal Mr. Shykoff signed with Pepsi?"

I kept moving. "No, I'm informed and I'm choosing to ignore it."

Ted stopped moving, as did his camera crew, and I was finally able to make it all the way to my golf cart. I put my plate on the bench seat beside me and then put the Diet Coke can on display on the almost non-existent dashboard.

The drivers of all but one of the golf carts I passed as I drove to my end of the island didn't look at me. The only one who did also waved me down.

"Hey!" Rob said as I slowed down and stopped beside his cart. "I just dropped Pam off at your place."

"I thought we agreed to meet at nine?"

"Yeah, but Pam got up early and said she saw you fall into your pool, so she knew you were already up."

"I hope she waits for me ..."

"She will. The servants' entrance to your villa wasn't locked. She's hanging out by your pool until you get back."

Did anyone in production respect, let alone recognize, the boundaries of personal space?

"Are you going to be part of the dinner shoot tonight?"

"Not if I can help it." I wasn't sure when I'd get back from Virgin Gorda, but planned to make sure it was after the shooting started.

"I'm not working it, so why don't we have dinner together? We could set something up by the west beach bar ..."

"I have to do the Albert run, remember? I don't know when I'll be back."

"Once again, our timing sucks." He smiled and winked (a lusty wink). "Can't blame a guy for trying and, just so you know, I plan to keep on trying."

There was no rear-view mirror in my golf cart so I didn't watch him drive away. I looked ahead, and hoped that I wouldn't feel as awkward around his location lover, Pam.

Glenn turned onto Riverview Drive and smiled. The tiny countrified enclave of mansions on the winding road in

North Toronto always made him feel as if he'd entered a secret world. Half-century old maple trees, their limbs laden with thick green summer foliage, lined either side of the street. Doc Butler's house, and the three acres it sat on, backed onto a ravine and one of the country's most exclusive golf clubs, making it feel like a country estate.

After ringing the doorbell for the sixth time and still getting no answer, Glenn decided to walk around to the back of the house to see if Doc was out there. The French doors to the kitchen were hanging open. Doc's Seeing Eye Dog, Stephanie, a big blonde German shepherd, lay motionless on the flagstone patio, a soggy well-chewed stick between her front paws. Her eyes opened at the sound of Glenn closing the gate, but she didn't lift her head. She said hello with her tail — it thump-thump-thumped against the flagstones. Doc was sitting in one of the chairs by the patio table, a set of headphones over his ears, his long legs crossed and wrapped around each other like a pretzel.

He must have felt the reverberations from Stephanie's happy tail because he reached up, took the headset off, and said "Who's there?" as he tried to flatten down the wispy white hair that matched his Einstein-level IQ.

"It's me, Doc," Glenn said as he took a seat.

Doc's Butler blues (as Ria called them) pointed in Glenn's general direction, but their aim was off. If he could have seen he would have been staring at Glenn's shoulder. "That moniker could apply to anyone, Glenn. Try to be more specific when you're dealing with a cripple."

"You're the least crippled person I know," Glenn laughed, "and you don't seem to have had much trouble identifying me."

"Given the fact that I've known you since you were three and heard every creak and crack of you maturing into that distinctive FM-DJ voice, that's not surprising."

"And I did call to tell you I was coming."

"Nevertheless, for future reference, identify yourself more clearly when the person you're greeting can't see you!"

"Point taken." Glenn watched Doc wrap the wire mostly around the headset and then put the mangled mess on top of the talking book machine on the table. "What are you reading?"

"John Gould's *Seven Good Reasons Not to Be Good*. Have you read it?"

Glenn shook his head and then backed his visual response up with words. "Never heard of it."

"The critics were right. It's a damn-near perfect book."

"Oh." It was the only response Glenn could think of. "Where's everybody else?"

"Up at the cottage."

"Why aren't you there?" Doc usually spent all summer, every summer, at the family's cottage in Muskoka.

"I came down to the city for a transfusion and decided to stay for a bit." Doc popped open the top of his Braille watch and felt the metal hands inside. "It's a good thing you called to tell me to be home." He snapped the watch closed. "Stephanie and I had a date to go hiking part of the Bruce Trail this morning."

"You're up to that?" Subtlety wasn't Glenn's strong suit and with Doc Butler he didn't even try to fake it. He knew that Doc would respect honest bluntness more. The fact was Doc had some weird-named cancer of the blood. But he sure didn't act like someone with a terminal illness. Yeah, he was looking a little pale and maybe a bit thinner (if that was possible), but his spirit was as strong as ever.

"I wish you'd all stop obsessing about my Waldenström's macroglobulinemia." The two words (or maybe three?) hadn't tied Doc's tongue up in a knot the way they would have Glenn's. "We're all dying, Glenn. Some of us will just take longer to do it than others. As for my demise, it's a long way off, I assure you. Now, tell me again, why am I about to do a telephone autopsy on a foot?"

Glenn brought Doc up to speed quickly, checking his own watch every so often. Ria would be calling in a few minutes and Glenn wanted the chance to pick Doc's brain before the phone rang. "If it is a real foot, what I don't get is why someone would cut it off."

"There could be numerous explanations for that."

"Care to name a few?"

"Well, for one, she might have cut it off herself or had someone do it for her. Back when I was practising, the desire to become an amputee was classified as a sexual deviation. That was a psychiatric classification, though, and as we all know Freud put sex into everything. He should have just had sex with his mother and been done with it, in my opinion. Since my time a few psychologists who, on the whole, aren't quite so sex-centric, have studied a phenomenon or unclassified condition that they've named Body Identity Integrity Disorder."

"Are you serious?"

"Dead serious. I remember reading a case study on one patient in particular who had always wanted to get rid of his leg. He tried to find a doctor to amputate it for him, but there weren't any takers. As far as I know there's been only one documented case of a doctor removing healthy limbs. Smith, I think his name was, but I doubt he had anything to do with the girl in the Caribbean. He was doing his thing in Scotland back in the nineties. As for the patient in the case study, he eventually did get his wish, his leg was amputated, but only after he'd frozen it in dry ice for several hours. He deliberately inflicted the damage that made the amputation medically necessary, not cosmetic."

Because of his job, Glenn had heard about some weird stuff over the years — but this stuff was the weirdest yet. And Doc wasn't done.

"Then there's somatoparaphrenia, a neuro-psychiatric disorder, usually caused by a brain malfunction brought on by stroke. Sufferers truly believe that their left arm or leg doesn't belong on their body. Although, it's only a temporary condition, so I doubt your girl had that."

"You're talking real fringe stuff here, Doc. Shouldn't we stay more mainstream, like in the realm of normal?"

"Attraction to amputation isn't that out there. John Irving is a bestselling author, read by millions of mainstream people, and dismemberment is a recurring theme in his books. In *The Fourth Hand* a TV reporter has his hand eaten off by a lion. Hmmm, maybe that's connected somehow? A TV person, amputation … two similar elements."

"I don't think there are any lions in the British Virgin Islands."

"How about some tigers or bears?" Doc tried, unsuccessfully, to look as if he wasn't joking around, but even Glenn recognized Doc's attempt at *Wizard of Oz* humour.

"Can we get back on track?"

"Oh, my." Doc gave his joke one last shot at getting a reaction from Glenn.

Glenn didn't give him one. "Will you be able to tell by just a description if it was cut off before or after death?"

Doc shook his head. "I'd need to see it and we both know that's never going to happen. I won't even be able to say with one hundred percent certainty if it's real or fake, but I'll give you my best guess."

"Why would somebody do that? Kill someone and then cut off a piece of them?"

"To get attention? Because he's careless and didn't realize he left it behind when he chopped up the body to dispose of it? Cutting up a body isn't easy. Maybe he started with the foot and then gave up when he discovered how much effort it was going to take to do the whole job? Or maybe he's just plain crazy? I don't know. All I'm doing is guessing in a void of information. Now that's something I'm an expert at — stabbing around in the dark."

Glenn was used to Doc's sarcastic comments about his blindness, but he never failed to detect the sadness in them.

The cordless phone that had been lying on the table rang and Doc handed it to Glenn. "You answer it. I don't know which button turns the speakerphone on."

Once on speakerphone, Ria introduced Pam to Glenn and her father and then let Pam have some uninterrupted airtime to describe what she'd found. The details she remembered were gruesome and, for some reason, she was shouting them into the telephone. Some of her over-amplified words came out distorted. Doc leaned forward toward the table and cut into her description while she was taking a breath.

"PAM!" He shouted as loudly as he could.

"YEAH?" She matched his decibel level.

"I'M NOT DEAF! My ears work just fine. Please stop yelling."

"Oh. Sorry."

Glenn took the opportunity allowed by the break in Pam's monologue to ask a question. "Pam, Glenn here. What was the one thing that instantly made you think the foot was fake?" Sometimes the most obvious things were the most important.

"There were two straws."

"Straws?" Doc asked.

"Yeah, you know, the things they used for bones. There's only supposed to be one, right?" Pam started to sing, "The leg bone's connected to the ankle bone …"

Doc rolled his eyes. "Was the foot cut off above the ankle?"

"The cut was through the leg bone that connects to the ankle bone, but there were two of them."

"The fibula and tibia," Doc muttered. "What kind of bugs did you see?"

"Bugs?"

"Yes, bugs, insects, maybe some flies …"

"None. There was a starfish. Does that count?"

"I've heard enough." Doc ran his hand along the top of the table, found the phone, and pushed the disconnect button. "The leg bone's connected to the ankle bone indeed!"

Glenn smiled, wondering how Ria was going to explain Doc's brusqueness to Pam. "So? What do you think?"

"Anatomically, it sounds like a real foot — the right bones in the right places, the waxy appearance of the skin, the thin layer of muscle, or meat as Pam called it, the marrow in the straws — all of that makes me think it was real."

Glenn nodded. Even before the telephone description his gut had been telling him that the foot was real.

"However, the lack of insect activity puzzles me."

Glenn stopped nodding and started feeling queasy. He knew too much about the bugs that Doc was wondering about, he'd been to too many crime scenes to not know about them. They were the main reason he'd included his wish to be cremated in his own will. That wish only intensified as he listened to Doc think out loud.

"Blowflies and flesh flies will start laying their eggs almost immediately after death, usually around the moist orifices like the nostrils, mouth, and eyes. An open wound of that size would have been like an all you can eat buffet for them. Because of the climate, Pam should have seen ample evidence of larvae activity — maggots. There is a way to slow it or even stop it — refrigeration or freezing, and Pam did mention seeing ice crystals on the muscle. So, if real, the foot would have to have been frozen immediately after dismemberment. But the same issue still arises — once it was removed from the freezer it would have warmed up quickly in those conditions. It could only have been in the tidal pool for a very short amount of time. You'd be looking for someone who had access to the foot and the tidal pool within less than an hour, probably significantly less than an hour, of when the foot was found."

"And the foot would have had to been in the freezer long enough to freeze it solid, right?" Glenn asked. "Which means she was probably killed the night before, right?"

"That would be a fairly safe assumption, but again, without examining the foot and the conditions there's no way of saying anything with certainty. You're dealing with guesswork here."

"I've started off with less before." But Glenn planned to add some facts to that guesswork.

He couldn't, or wouldn't, believe that not one camera on an island permanently under the watchful eye of multiple cameras had captured the action, or actions, that led to Kate's dismemberment.

Ria had said she'd send him a list of the camera tapes that had been recorded the night before Kate disappeared and on the morning of her disappearance. There had to be something on those, right? How could someone kill and cut up a girl without being noticed by at least one of the cameras? And if there wasn't anything on the tapes? The killer and the cutter (if they were the same person) had to be someone who knew an awful lot about the placement of those cameras.

A short, tense buzz along Highway 401 took Glenn to the top of the Don Valley Parkway. Morning rush hour had cleared out and afternoon rush hour hadn't yet started. It was one of those rare times when the highway wasn't earning its nickname — the Don Valley Parking Lot. The southbound lanes were almost empty. The roof was down on his trusty '76 MG. The sun was shining bright. He pushed an eight-track into the player under the dashboard. Lynyrd Syknyrd's "Free Bird" started playing in mid-chorus. Brandon would have recognized it from one of his "Guitar Hero" games. That saying, everything old is new again, was sure true. The classics from Glenn's teenage years were hits again on Brandon's video games and even on some of the television shows he watched. The *CSI* series used music from The Who — *CSI* used "Who Are You" from 1978 (Glenn had the original red-vinyl record safely tucked away with the rest of his albums in the milk crates in his storage space), *CSI New York* used "Baba O'Riley," and *CSI Miami* used "Won't Get Fooled Again," both from 1971.

As much as he felt like a free bird buzzing down the highway with the top down, Glenn wasn't in a Lynyrd Skynyrd mood. He was in a thinking mood and there was nobody better to think and enjoy a steady drive with than Carlos Santana. He changed eight-tracks tapes and rolled down the highway that ran through the heavily forested valley on the eastern side of Toronto while Carlos did his jazz, salsa, rock guitar thing on "She's Not There."

Where was Kate?

If someone had killed her, had they hidden her body somewhere in the hotel? Unlikely. Someone on the housekeeping staff would have found it or, at the very least, they would have found some sign of a murder. You didn't need a CSI team to recognize blood splatter and there'd be an awful lot of blood spread around when a limb got cut off.

If she'd been hidden somewhere outside the groundskeeping staff would have found her. Butler Hotels were famous for their landscaping. Glenn could safely assume that the entire island was crawling with an army of gardeners.

If not in the hotel or on the grounds — where? The only obvious answer was in the water.

But why cut off her foot? The killer had hidden the body well enough to avoid it being found. If he or she had left the foot attached they'd be dealing with just a missing person, not a missing body.

So who on the crew had spent enough time with Kate to work up a hate strong enough to kill her, who knew where all the cameras were, and who knew enough about the workings of the hotel and its staff to be able to pull off a murder (and dismemberment) without anyone noticing a thing?

And what about her stuff? Ria was going to confirm whether or not it was at James' place on the other island. Who would have been able to hide it there without anyone asking any questions?

One person fit the bill — James.

He knew all about the production.

He knew all about the hotel.

He had his own boat to get back and forth between the two islands.

It would kill Ria if James was guilty of something like that.

James. James? Glenn just couldn't picture it. He had a temper, to be sure, but a murderous temper? The worst thing Glenn had ever seen him do was belt someone in the face — and the guy deserved it, he'd said something pretty damn rude about Ria.

Glenn quickly added James' partner to the short list. He knew just as much as James did about the production. Maybe James was just an accessory? It wasn't much better, but it was some better.

Anybody else? The woman who worked for James' partner — the one with the strange name.

Damn, it would be so much easier if Ria was here, Glenn thought. They'd be able to talk it through without the distance of a less-than-reliable phone service between them.

Maybe he should go there?

The driver of the dump truck in the lane beside Glenn realized at the last minute that his lane was ending and he cut Glenn — and his line of thinking — off.

Glenn took the Richmond Street exit and slowed down to a crawl as he hit the city traffic. While sitting at a red light he looked around to see if there were any cops nearby, then held his BlackBerry in his lap and checked to see if Ria had sent the email with the tape information yet. The car behind him honked. The light had turned green.

By the time he'd inched (or centimetred, to be more metrically Canadian) up to the next red light, her email, with attachments, had downloaded. He had the list. Now all he had to do was find the place where James' company did their editing.

CHAPTER
TEN

VideoPost was in an old factory building on the outskirts of the Distillery District, the largest preserved collection of Victorian industrial architecture in North America. Parking was already at a premium in the trendy area and Glenn wondered how much worse it would get when the athletes' village for the 2015 Pan American Games was built just east of the district.

The receptionist at VideoPost wasn't as young or as pretty as the girls James usually hired for his production office. And she was a stickler for the rules. She insisted that Glenn sign in. He didn't want to put his name on any piece of paper that James might see. He wrote down an investigative journalist's name, it just wasn't his name — C. Bernstein. Satisfied, the receptionist buzzed the editor to tell him that Glenn was on his way and then told Glenn how to find the editing suite in the catacombs.

As he walked down the low-ceilinged underground hallway, Glenn could understand why the receptionist had called the basement the catacombs; it was like a subterranean cemetery. He had to stoop slightly to avoid banging his head.

A short bent-over man, who was wearing possibly the worst hairpiece Glenn had ever seen and had a face that closely resembled a pug, came walking toward him. "Are you Bear's friend?" he asked Glenn.

"Yeah, I'm Carl." Glenn held out his hand.

"Dex. Follow me."

Dex led him into a dark little room, illuminated only by the three twenty-one-inch flat screens sitting just above a long electronic console and a bigger fifty-inch flat screen that hung on the wall above the console. A slow-moving big blue Butler *B* against a white background was the screensaver on all the televisions.

"You got a list for me?"

Glenn opened up the email attachment on his cellphone and showed it to Dex.

"Jesus!" Dex scrolled through the information. "Bear didn't say it was this much. This is gonna take forever." He sat down in one of the padded swivel chairs in front of the console, pointed for Glenn to sit down, and started to click his mouse.

One of the small screens flashed and on it appeared a long list of what looked like places and activities: Kitchen/Cooking Challenge, Pool Patio/Elimination 11, Beach/JI Commercial (Albert Go Boom), to name just a few.

"Help me here" Glenn asked. "I don't know what I'm looking at."

"There's a folder for each scene shot at a specific location. Inside the folders are the bins. The bins hold all the footage from the cameras shooting that scene."

It made sense, sort of. "Why don't we start with whatever Bear put at the top of the list and work our way through that way?"

"Fine, but I'm hoping you'll be able to shorten the list down a bit. Let me know if you see whatever it is you're looking for." He started clicking and opened the folder called EXT. Kitchen

Tree Camera/Day 37. After checking the list on Glenn's phone again, he clicked on Scene 4, the last bin in the folder.

The big screen came to life and the eerie unlit image looked like something seen through night-vision goggles. The camera was pointing at a small patio area outside of a closed door on the ground floor of a building. There was a light on the wall over the door and Glenn watched bugs flying into the light for a few minutes. Then it got really exciting — a large dark crab slowly crossed the patio.

"Want me to speed this up?" Dex asked. "Unless you're researching a documentary on the nocturnal habits of land crabs I'd like to get out of here before midnight."

"Go for it." Glenn got more comfortable in his chair.

The bugs flew faster. Another crab (or possibly the same crab) set a land crab speed record as it crossed the patio in the opposite direction. The door suddenly opened and a man and a woman walked outside in high speed Charlie Chaplin style.

"Whoa! Let's see this."

Dex slowed the images down, rewound to the door opening, and then let the footage play.

The man had his hand on the girl's elbow and was forcibly pushing her out the door ahead of him.

"That's Dan Shykoff, right?" Glenn recognized him from the photos in Kate's digital picture frame.

"That's him. I don't know who the girl is, though."

Glenn did. He was looking at Allie's unpierced twin — Kate.

They could hear voices, but the volume was way down. Dex slid something on the board and the volume increased.

"Don't try to pull a stunt like that on me again!" Dan Shykoff was angry. He and Kate stood on the patio, a few feet away from the door and close to the camera.

Kate smiled a nasty smile. "Oh, Dan, that was no stunt. You will be getting me a job in LA."

"Like fuck I will!" He screamed. "Listen, you little bitch, you knew exactly what you were getting in to!"

"Not quite. I know stuff now that I didn't know when we hooked up."

"Is that supposed to scare me?"

"It should!" Kate, too, was screaming. "I can make sure that this show of yours goes nowhere. You'll lose a fortune."

"And just how are you going to do that? Let me guess, you've dug up some dirt on me …"

"Better than that. If I open my mouth you'll be in the middle of the biggest scandal to ever hit reality TV!"

"Yeah, right," Dan scoffed. "Darling, my life is an open book. I'm a walking scandal."

"Ain't that the truth," Dex muttered.

"I'm well-known because of my scandals. Who the fuck do you think lets the press catch wind of them? Me! Controversy keeps me current." He turned and started to walk back to the door. "We're done. Don't come back to Virgin Gorda tonight. Winnie will have your crap sent over here tomorrow." He opened the door and looked at Kate. "Finish this shoot if you want, but know that you'll never work for James again and you sure as hell won't get a job in LA, I'll make sure of it."

"You'll be sorry!" Kate was close to screeching. "And so will James! His little hotel chain won't look so good then. I bet he'd be more than interested to hear what I have to say."

Dan let go of the door, turned around slowly, glanced at the camera, and crossed his arms over his chest. "I don't what you're talking about. You're making no sense …"

"So that's how you're going to play it? What are you going to do? Save it for a shocking big reveal in the grand finale?"

Dan spoke with deadly calm. "Again, I don't know what you're talking about."

"Want me to spell it out for you?"

"I'm done with this." He turned and reached for the door handle.

"I'm not."

Dan went into the building and slammed the door behind him.

Kate walked right up to the camera and held her middle finger up dead centre in the lens. "Screw you, Dan! Maybe you don't care about your image, but we both know that there's someone here who cares a hell of a lot about their image! He won't risk this show not going to air!" She walked out of the shot and the bugs continued to fly into the light over the closed door.

"Do you know what that was about?" Glenn asked.

Dex just shook his head. "I haven't watched any of this stuff yet. Is this what you're looking for?"

"I don't know. Maybe." Glenn wanted to see the rest of the video that Ria's source had picked out for them. What bothered him about what they'd just seen was that both Kate and Dan knew the camera was there. Being threatened could push someone to murder for silence, but Dan hadn't seemed that worried and, more importantly, Kate had walked away … on both feet.

Dex moved the cursor up to close the KITCHEN TREE camera folder when Glenn remembered what Doc had said about the foot being refrigerated or frozen. There'd be freezers and refrigerators in a kitchen. "Hang on. Can you show me some more footage from that camera?"

"It's not on Bear's list."

"I know, but I'd still like to see it. We can watch it fast. I just want to see who came and went that night. And early the next morning."

Dex obliged. They watched the rest of Scene 4, but Glenn didn't see anything out of the ordinary. All of the people who entered and exited the kitchen were wearing kitchen whites with a Butler *B* embroidered somewhere on their uniforms.

Dex started playing Scene 1 from DAY 38 at high speed, but Glenn got him to rewind and play it at normal speed when someone raced into the picture and through the door to the kitchen. The person was a woman, her sculpted body clad in lycra, a long ponytail swinging as she ran. All Glenn could see was her backside ... and she had a great backside. Dex sped the footage up again. The morning kitchen shift started to arrive just as the sun was lighting up the day. Then a second non-Butler-uniformed woman came out from the kitchen. Her hair was pulled back from her stern face and she was wearing a dowdy suit. What Glenn really concentrated on was what she holding in her hands — a Butler *B*'d white dishtowel that was wrapped around something. He stared at the object. It was so well wrapped up that he couldn't tell what it was ... but he could make a pretty good guess.

"Okay, let's get back to Bear's list now."

They sat through many hours of dark shots from the night of Kate's disappearance, but the only things Glenn saw on the sped-up material were more fast-moving crabs, people driving to and fro in golf carts that would have had to been fuelled by nitrous oxide to actually go that fast, an extremely fit, tall woman running along an unlit road in the dark at sprint speed (was she the woman who ran into the kitchen?), a group of drunk people singing off-key as they stumbled down a paved road that led to a block of hotel rooms (with their voices sped up they sounded a bit like Alvin and the Chipmunks), and one sex scene. Dex didn't slow the footage down for that. Even so, they could easily see a young man and woman having a *From Here to Eternity* moment on a beach, complete with waves crashing, passion that took them further than just kissing, minus the bathing suits. Then things got interesting again.

EXT. Rear wharf camera/Day 37. Once again Ria's contact had selected Scene 4. A group of people were doing something to a small dinghy that was docked at the end of a long wharf. Unfortunately, the camera wasn't close enough to show exactly what they were doing. They couldn't make out what the people were saying to each other either, but they could clearly hear the laughter. Whatever those people were doing they were enjoying it.

"What happened on the island that night that you're so interested in?"

"I won't know what I'm looking for until I see it."

"That was weak." Dex raised his eyebrows (the muscles on his forehead pushed his hair piece up a bit) and restarted the footage.

A man walked into the shot. He was heading down the stairs to the wharf — and he was carrying a limp body. Dex sat up straighter in his chair and slowed the images down quickly. He didn't need Glenn to tell him that they were watching something out of the ordinary. The man carried the body to the end of the wharf and, with the help of a group of people there, he put the body in the dinghy.

"Yo, Ted!" Someone close to the camera yelled out. "Dan's looking for you. He wants you in the kitchen, like now!"

"Coming!"

Someone, possibly the man who'd carried the body to the dinghy, ran up to the camera.

He yelled over his shoulder to the group on the wharf, "I'm going to turn the camera off so Mr. Shykoff and Mr. Butler won't know for sure who's here."

He got so close to the camera that his face filled the screen entirely.

"Idiot! Sticking his face right in the camera was a sure fire way of making sure James and Dan know he was there."

"Who was that?"

"Ted Robarts, one of the contestants."

The screen went black.

Dex looked at the list on the screen of Glenn's phone, then clicked open some folders and bins on his screen, and then looked back at Glenn's phone. "There's a disc missing. Bear wrote down Ext. North End Tree Camera/Day 37, but it's not here."

"What do you mean, it's not here?" Glenn tried to sound less interested than he actually was.

"I mean it's not here. We didn't get it in the last shipment."

"Are you sure?"

"Positive." Dex started to write a note at the same time Glenn did. "I'll ask Bear about it. That camera was installed on day thirty-seven, so maybe they had some problems getting it up and running. The disc Bear wanted you to watch would have been the first disc from it."

Glenn planned to ask Ria about it.

His note written, Dex closed all the bins in the folder labelled Day 37. "That was all the footage from day thirty-seven. The rest of the stuff on the list is day thirty-eight. They managed to send the next disc from the north end camera. Let's start with that."

Glenn and Dex watched the sun light up a new day at record speed. The camera was pointed at a small backhoe that was parked beside a stack of lumber in what looked like a clearing on the top of a hill. The bucket on the front of the backhoe was filled with sand. Dex said the disc had six hours of footage on it — and during those six hours there was absolutely no human activity. The only exciting moment came when a large spider crawled across the lens of the camera. Dex opened the folder named Beach/JI Commercial (Albert Go Boom) next.

"What does JI stands for?" Glenn asked.

"Judy Ingram, another contestant."

Glenn knew that the production was close to being finished. "Are she and Ted Robarts the finalists?"

"The confidentiality clause that I signed precludes me from confirming or denying that comment." Dex put his hand on the mouse and opened the bin labelled Camera 1/RC.

The big screen came to life. A large television crew were milling around on a beach, Glenn couldn't identify anyone in the shot but they all looked like they were waiting for something. An incredibly sexy woman in a bikini was standing waist-deep in the water; a man in scuba gear stood near her.

A male voice loudly said "Recording!"

"Hang on!" Another man, this one wearing large headphones and holding a long pole that had a microphone on the end of it, shouted and pointed to the sky.

They could hear the whine of an airplane nearby.

The cameraman who'd shoot the footage they were watching pointed his camera up toward the sky and they could see a propeller plane flying high above the water. Then, in jerky movements, the camera spun around one hundred and eighty degrees to show an extreme, and out of focus, close-up on a man's face. He looked a bit like a younger Clint Eastwood and had a long scar that ran along the left side of his jawbone.

"Da plane! Da plane!"

"Rob! What the hell are you doing?" An unseen female laughed.

He laughed and started to turn the camera back around to face the beach. "Tattoo, from *Fantasy Island*, right?"

"What are you talking about?"

"I bet Dex gets it," the man replied off-camera.

From the smirk on Dex's face it looked like he had got the joke. So had Glenn.

Had that been Bobbie? Glenn hoped not. He didn't want to put that face next to the name that made his blood pressure rise. It was too good looking. Camera 1/RC — Rob Churcher. Damn.

"Do the slate!" someone off-camera yelled.

A girl wearing a floppy sunhat ran into the water and held up the slateboard. "Judy Ingram's Butler Hotel commercial, scene three, take one." She held the slate up for a minute or two and then walked back to the beach.

The diver put his hand on the shoulder of the hot babe, gave her the secondary mouthpiece from his oxygen tank, and then they too went under the water.

Someone yelled, "Action!"

The woman rose out of the water and started to walk slowly toward the beach. The camera that had shot the footage they were watching stayed aimed at the water as the woman walked out of the shot. Then it zoomed in on a small boat coming around the rocks just offshore. A big orange ball of fire shot up out of the boat, the person who'd been sitting in the boat blew up and out, and the bow of the boat immediately pointed down into the water. The boat sank quickly, bow first. Once it was completely submerged the screen went black.

"There are four more cameras on the list for this." Dex didn't seem even slightly fazed by the surprise explosion.

The fourth video of the explosion was shot from some-where behind the stern of the boat. The camera also captured a group of people who were standing on a point as the boat pulled away from the shore, heading out to the rocks. They were laughing (without sound). One of the men was holding what looked like one of Brandon's video-game controllers. The boat pulled away and, from the angle of the camera, Glenn could see that the supposed person in the boat was strapped into place with duct tape. Even his beige hat was attached to his head with a strip of the silver tape. The now familiar ball of fire rolled out of the boat, the stern rose out of the water, and someone knocked on the door of the editing room. Dex froze the image on the television screens.

"Hey, Dex," the receptionist came in holding a big box, "this just came for you. I need your signature."

While Dex signed the papers the receptionist had handed him, Glenn stared at the big screen. The fire ball was frozen in the air just above the boat. The head of the person had separated from the body and was in the process of exploding; the hat that had been taped to it was flying through the air. The body, too, was in mid-flight, one arm dangled off the torso. So what? He'd seen the boat explode already and Ria had told him that the head and the body were made out of Styrofoam. What did this have to do with Kate? Her foot had been found before this was shot and it hadn't been near the exploding boat.

The boat. Glenn stood up and looked more closely at the screen. Why was there so much duct tape on the bottom of the boat? Was that how the special effects team had attached the explosives? But the tape covered almost all of the surface area that was still sticking out of the water. And it looked like it had been strapped over something lumpy. The lump was too big to be just explosives. That much fire power would have obliterated the boat, but the boat had sunk pretty much intact. So what was strapped on the bottom of it? It couldn't be. Could it?

"Hey! That's Phil," the receptionist pointed at one of the men standing with the group on the screen. "What's the date on that?"

"Last Friday." Dex let the last few minutes of the scene play out.

"That is so cool. He made it to the final."

The boat sank quickly, taking the duct-taped lump with it, and the man the receptionist had called Phil laughed and slapped high fives with two of the people who'd been standing near him and then walked out of the shot just before the screen went black. Glenn recognized the man's face, he'd been the one who'd carried the body to the dinghy the night before

Kate's foot was found, and he was the person who'd turned the camera off. But Glenn couldn't shake the feeling that he'd seen him somewhere else. He couldn't remember where, though. "I thought his name was Ted?" The hairs on the back of Glenn's neck bristled.

"Oh, yeah," the receptionist started to back out of the room. "Phil's just a nickname. His real name's Ted."

"He's a friend of yours?" What kind of nickname was Phil?

"We go way back. It would be so awesome if he won, but I'll have to wait like everybody else to find out if he does. Dex's the only one who'll see the final shipment of camera originals. Right, Dex?"

"Yeah, just me and the hundred or so other people working on the show who signed confidentiality agreements." He waved his hands to shoo-shoo the receptionist out of the room. "Now get out of here and forget what you just saw."

"My lips are sealed." She closed the door.

Dex clicked to open another folder and the screens came back to life.

Glenn saw more than he wanted to of the show in production. It was obvious that the crew shot more footage of their goofing around than material that would actually end up in the final show. They'd be able to put together one heck of a blooper reel! Some of the footage had sound and Glenn recognized James' voice a few times, but he never showed up in any of the shots. The aerial footage over the beach where Kate's foot was found didn't really show anything useful. In the first shot the cameraman had zoomed in on a small white object in a tidal pool. The foot. It had to be. In his second shot it was blatantly obvious that he was more interested in the girl raking smooth the footprints in the sand than he was in the scenery. He'd done an extreme close-up on her body, moving slowly from her head, down her body to her feet. Her back was to the camera and through her thin T-shirt he could see that she wasn't wearing a bra. As the image moved down her legs Glenn acknowledged to himself that she had great legs. Then the shot widened out or pulled back, or whatever camera people called it, and he could see the tidal pool again. When the girl looked up and smiled and waved at the cameraman, Glenn recognized her face from her starring role in the *From Here to Eternity* scene. (She was fully dressed for the beach scene and without the night-vision camera he could see that she had Day-Glo-pink bangs.) She picked up the white object and threw it out into the sea. The cameraman followed the path of the object, but he wasn't zoomed in close enough for Glenn to see it clearly.

Dan Shykoff showed up in a lot of shots. In the daylight shots Glenn could see his face more clearly. In one of them he was wearing the same shirt he'd been wearing in the picture on the slideshow in the digital picture frame in Kate's apartment.

That's where he'd seen the other guy! The one who'd slapped high fives with another crew member after the boat explosion, the friend of the receptionist, the contestant named Ted Robarts (a.k.a. Phil to his friends). Well, that made sense. Kate's digital picture frame was full of pictures of her with television and movie people. As a finalist, Ted Robarts would be a fairly famous television face once the show aired. He'd get more than his fifteen minutes of fame, that was for sure. The other contestant, what's-her-name, Judy? Kate had probably sent a picture of herself with Judy to the frame, too. He'd check that out when he got home.

"Morons!" Dex clicked through many screens of folders. "They've forgotten another disc."

"What's on it?" Glenn wasn't so sure that the missing discs had been accidentally left out of the Toronto shipment. Those discs were important enough, valuable enough, to pay someone to fly back and forth between the islands. Without those discs James wouldn't have a show. Every penny he'd sunk into the production was on those discs and Glenn was willing to bet that James' staff double and triple checked to make sure that they all made it safely to the editors.

"Ext. East Beach Aloe Camera/Day 38. Bear wanted you to watch Scene 1 on it."

Glenn quickly wrote down the missing disc information. "That would have been more of the boat exploding stuff, right?"

Dex shook his head. "It might have caught some of the crew set-up, but that camera's down at the other end of the beach, where Pam was raking, so it would have long shots only."

"Day thirty-eight, though, right? It would have stuff from the same morning."

"Mostly before the shift started. For the stationary cameras the day is broken down into four scenes, each one six hours long because that's all you can get on one disc. Scene one would have been shot between midnight and six in the morning." Dex jotted the information down. "I'm going to call Bear and tell him to get his act together down there." Dex clicked the mouse and the Butler *B* screensaver floated across all the television screens. "That's a wrap. Did you see what you were looking for?"

"No." Glenn exhaled. He'd seen a lot, but not enough. What had he expected? A perfectly focused, well-lit shot, with sound, of Kate being killed? Her killer cutting her foot off and putting it in the tidal pool and hiding the rest of her body? If that footage did exist, Glenn bet it was on the missing discs. He and Ria were no further ahead — they still had a missing body, that was missing a foot, and the foot was missing, too. Now they could add missing discs to their list.

—>—

Pam left quickly after our phone call to Dad, and I spent the next hour perfecting my impersonation of a lion slowly going insane in a small cage — pacing back and forth, back and forth. My gecko friend got bored with watching me and scuttled across the patio to disappear under a red Hibiscus shrub. To change things up I swam some laps, but they were basically pacing in water instead of on the flagstone patio. Glenn hadn't called me after leaving Dad's place. The hotel phone system was working, but my cellphone still wasn't getting any reception so I was stuck waiting for his call. I was just about to call him and leave a decidedly curt message when my doorbell rang.

I opened the door and then looked down. "Hi, Bear. What's up?"

"You alone?" He walked past me and out onto my patio. "We might have a problem."

I followed him and watched as he walked around the edge of the patio, spreading open many of the bushes and plants. "What sort of problem?"

He didn't answer, he just kept looking through the bushes. "Son of a bitch." He leaned over and most of his upper body disappeared into a bush. When he stood up he turned around and I saw what he'd lifted out of the bush. A camera.

I protectively wrapped my arms around myself. I felt violated. Someone had been watching me!

"I just found out about this this morning, so don't blame me!" He pushed some buttons on the camera and took out the disc. "In fact, you've got Winnie to thank for me finding it."

"When? How?" I was so shocked that I couldn't form multi-word questions.

"It was put in yesterday, just before you got here. Dan told one of my assistants to do it."

"But Winnie? Why?" Someone had been watching me. Recording me. Without my permission or knowledge. No, they had my permission. I'd signed their damned release form.

"When I was going over the log sheets this morning I told her how wrong I thought it was that Dan had secret cameras in the contestant's rooms and she agreed with me, said it was a lawsuit waiting to happen. Her conscience was really bothering her, and she thought about it all morning and then called me. She told me to disconnect all the secret cameras. We're going to tell Dan that the X-lites on them are acting up. He won't know what I'm talking about — his technical knowledge hasn't moved beyond black and white. In reality, an X-lite is an electronic device that dentist's use to check for oral cancer. I told her I'd get right on it and get the cameras out of Judy and Ted's rooms, and then she dropped the bombshell and told me there was one here. I haven't looked at the log sheets for the last few days, so I didn't know about it. Ria, please believe me, if I'd known I would have ripped it out right away."

"But what about the stuff it recorded?" I pointed at the camera Bear was holding, lens pointing down to the patio.

"That's the good news. Winnie said Dan hasn't looked at any of it yet and Dan will never see it — not now." He handed me the disc he'd taken out of the camera and then reached around behind his back and gave me the three discs he'd pulled out of his pocket.

"But what if she's lying? Maybe Dan has seen what's on these? Maybe he even made dubs?"

Bear shook his head. "Didn't happen. Dan doesn't know how to make dubs, he needs me for that and I give you my word I haven't done that with these. And Tony, my soon-to-be-deaf-because-I'm-going-to-blast-him assistant, didn't get around to giving Winnie these discs until this morning. She hasn't looked at them. Like I said, Winnie's good people. Doesn't the fact that she came clean about this and handed over the discs tell you that?"

"I guess so." But I wasn't convinced. I knew I hadn't done anything embarrassing on my patio. I hadn't gone skinny dipping. Even if Winnie or Dan had watched the footage, what would they have seen, anyway? Me talking to a gecko? Me swimming laps? My heart sank. I looked at the microphone that was attached to the camera. What they might have heard was more upsetting — me talking to Rob, me talking to Glenn on the phone.

Bear apologized profusely a few more times and did his best to reassure me that it wouldn't happen again, but I couldn't shake the feeling that I'd been violated. It felt like I was covered in a layer of dirt that I couldn't wash off.

I threw the discs into the deep end of the pool and watched them sink to the bottom. Then I tore through every bush, not caring how much damage I was causing to the landscaping. I got the hotel supplied binoculars out of a drawer in the living room and scanned every tree I could see. I was in the master ensuite, looking carefully to see if there was a hidden lens behind the grate of the steam vent in the massive shower, when I heard an army of housekeepers invading. Donnella was leading the charge.

Her cleaning crew spread out and attacked every room, while she came and found me in the bathroom.

"I know you say you got nothing to do with running the hotels, but you be the one I'm coming to with this." She closed the door and looked at me quizzically. I stepped out of the shower and didn't bother explaining why I'd been standing in it fully clothed. "I can't go calling Ms. Whitecross about it; it's three-thirty in the morning where she is." She handed me a laminated identification card. "The girls found it in Mr. Ted's room this morning, behind the dresser."

I looked down at the card. Ted was looking back up at me, his expression stern and serious. I didn't recognize the logo on the ID badge — a small red Canadian maple leaf in a white square, with thick prongs of blue shooting out from it and a golden crown sitting on top — but I did recognize the name of the government agency: Canadian Security Intelligence Service. CSIS. Canada's version of the CIA. Ted was a spy? The photo on the card was of Ted's face, but the name was different. Who was Jake Purcell? Ted's twin brother? Ted had a twin, too? What were the odds of that happening? The title printed under Jake's/Ted's name was intelligence officer. What the heck was a CSIS agent doing pretending to be a contestant on a reality show, the goal of which was to be hired to manage a hotel?

"What do you know about this?" Donnella asked, but she didn't wait for an answer. "I like working for this company. Your aunt is a fine woman, but if this hotel is involved in something fishy I want to know about it. I've seen a lot of strange things going on with all those television people. With all the boats coming and going, and big boxes with I don't know what in them coming to the island, and now this. I have to wonder — just what's really going on here? We got enough troubles with drug runners using our islands. If you Butlers are involved in that I want no part in it!"

She thought we were drug runners? I would have laughed if the situation hadn't been so serious, and confusing. "Donnella, I promise you, Aunt Patti runs hotels — nothing else."

"So what's that about then?"

"I have absolutely no idea." I met her questioning stare. "Honest." My bafflement must have been plastered all over my face, because she slowly started to nod.

"I believe that." She crossed her arms mostly over her chest. "Tsk, tsk, tsk." She held up one hand and waved her index finger. "I told you he was no hotel manager. The man knows nothing about PMS. Nothing!"

I wanted to give my head a shake. Maybe if I knocked my brain around a bit it would be able to make sense of Donnella's comment about premenstrual syndrome?

"He say he got all this experience, working all over the world in fancy hotels, and he don't know how to work the systems?"

"What systems?"

"Property management systems — PMS." She smiled at me. "You really aren't part of the hotels, are you?"

"I told you I'm not!"

"I knew there was something about that man. All your people been eating here for how long?" I didn't know. They weren't my people. "Must be over two months now. Not one of them has had a single complaint about the food — except for Mr. Ted. He tried to say our food made him sick! And didn't he just have to do all his vomiting in front of the cameras, telling everyone it was because of something he ate? That won't help your aunt book any rooms if your brother puts that on his show!"

"When was he sick?"

"Oh, last week sometime. The day they blew up that boat and found the foot. See what I mean about seeing some strange things? Then he starts accusing someone of stealing his shoes. Nobody stole his shoes! He's just looking to get a free pair of new shoes. The fool should have watched where he was walking. Saltwater and leather don't mix so good."

"I thought he was only complaining about sand on them?"

"That's what he said, but I've seen them with my own eyes. They was in the water all right."

"Are we replacing them?" I accidentally used the royal we, as in *we* the Butlers.

"No, Mr. Dan is. He stuck his nose into it, just like he does with everything else.

"Now, what are we going to do about that?" She pointed at the ID card in my hand.

"I'm not sure." I wanted to show it to Glenn and knew exactly how to do it. "Aunt Patti should see this. Let me keep it for a bit. I'll scan it and send it to her." Maybe she already knew? I doubted that. But she would know about Ted's background. There was no way she would have agreed to let him be on the show, be a contender for the top job at her newest hotel, without having done a thorough background check on him. "I'll give it back to you after I've done that and then you can put it back where you found it, so he won't know that we've seen it. Okay?"

"I like the way you think, girl."

"Have you mentioned any of this to my brother?"

"Why would I?" She shook her head sadly. "That man got enough problems, he don't need no more from me."

I continued to look for hidden cameras inside the cottage, trying not to be too obvious about it as Donnella's team finished their cleaning mission. (They offered to fish the discs out of the pool for me and proved they were great Butler employees when they didn't question why I wanted the discs left right where they were.) The front tires of their golf carts had barely touched the main road when I snatched the cordless phone on the patio.

"There's been a hidden camera on me here, in my villa, the whole time I've been here and Ted Robarts is a CSIS agent. Call me." Simple. Succinct. Clearly angry and/or frustrated. Would Glenn hear the fear in my voice?

The phone rang within less than a second of me hanging it up. "Finally!"

"Huh?"

The voice on the other end of the line caused my blood pressure to spike so high that if I'd been wearing a blood pressure cuff it would have blown off my arm like the ripping sleeves of the Hulk's shirt when he got angry. "Hello, Mandy."

"Wow, you sounded like such a bitch there."

She had no idea how bitchy I could sound and if she didn't get to the point of her call soon I was more than willing to show her the full extent of my bitchiness.

"I'm here."

And I cared because … why?

"So, everything's set. Dan's private jet is waiting at the airport in Virgin Gorda for Chris' arrival scene and the crew's loading up the boat. Your call time is in half an hour. Malvin will be waiting for you down on the front dock."

"What are you talking about? Chris arrived last night by boat."

"Yeah, but they can't use any of the stuff they shot from that! You saw him, he was wasted. Instead, they'll get shots of him landing in Virgin Gorda on Dan's plane and then they'll shoot him coming over here on the helicopter."

"Why does he need Malvin and the boat? Can't he take the helicopter over to Virgin Gorda?" As much as I wanted out of my villa I wanted to stay by my phone even more.

"They're using it right now to bring over the losing contestants for the scene where Judy and Ted find out who they're going to be working with on the final challenge. That'll take a couple of hours and they have to get Chris' flying into the Virgin Gorda airport stuff shot before they lose the light. They want the sun just setting when he flies over to Soursop in the helicopter."

"Why don't I just take the crew ferry over later? Albert's flight doesn't get in until around five, right?"

"He's coming in on the earlier flight; it gets in at three-thirty. The crew ferry was just leaving when we pulled in and I don't think there'll be another one for a couple of hours."

"I'll be there." I grabbed a Diet Coke can and ran out the door.

CHAPTER
ELEVEN

I had just enough time to scan Ted's CSIS badge, email it to Glenn, and then give the original back to Donnella before my call time on the front dock.

Chris' arrival was going to be covered by a crew that was twice the size of the crews I'd seen shooting Ted and Judy. The large group, and all their equipment, was already on the boat by the time I stepped onboard.

"Hi, Ria! Hey! Where are you going?" Chris ran out onto the stern deck and started to follow me up the stairs to the wheelhouse. "What's up here?"

"Oh, no you don't!" One of the women from the crew ran after him. "You're staying down here in this living room with us, buster! I'm only doing touch-ups on Virgin Gorda and if you stick your face in the sun all my handiwork will melt off and I'll need another bucket of foundation to hide your black eye."

"But ..." Chris started to plead (and whine a little).

"I mean it!"

"Oh, all right." Chris smiled up at me and shrugged his shoulders. The eye that had been darkening by the minute at the breakfast buffet showed no sign of Judy's impact.

I went out onto the upper deck and enjoyed the view as we bounced over to Virgin Gorda … right up until the view included Pam's pink bangs.

"Hi," she said as she sat down on the padded bench seat next to me. "So? What did your dad say? Was it real?"

"I haven't heard anything yet." I hadn't heard anything from Glenn, but I'd heard too much from Bear and Donnella and I'd been hoping to have some time to myself to sort through my thoughts.

Pam pulled her legs up under herself and sat cross-legged. "Bummer."

We sat in uncomfortable talk-free silence for a few minutes. I started to feel guilty. Her relationship with Rob aside, Pam didn't deserve to be on the receiving end of my angry silence. "Aren't you supposed to be working on Ted's crew?"

"Yeah but Sarah's sick — she's the PA who's supposed to be working this shift. I don't mind working a double. This will be an easy one and working my Ted shift will go pretty smooth, too. He's a dream to shoot and he never flubs his lines."

"But it's reality TV. It isn't scripted." Unless Ted the spy was working off some clandestine script.

"Yeah, well, not scripted scripted, if you know what I mean." I didn't know what she meant. "But it's sort of scripted. Esther says Judy's a real pain. I mean she's nice enough, but she's always messing up, saying the wrong things."

The awkward silence between us returned and we both looked around at the scenery. We were halfway between Soursop and Virgin Gorda so our visual options were limited — there was an island in front of us, an island behind us, and a whole lot of water everywhere else.

"So, you and Rob, huh." What Pam had said didn't really qualify as a question, so I didn't quantify it with an answer. "He likes you. A lot. I can tell." She said it without any hint of jealousy. "He's one of the good ones, you know? You two should hook up."

Maybe it was a generational thing? Was she offering to share? "I thought you and Rob were, you know…"

"Shut up!" She slapped me on the arm. "You thought I was doing Rob? Are you serious? He's nice and everything, but he's older than my dad!"

"My mistake." Or was it? Maybe Pam just didn't want anyone to know about her relationship with Rob — and she did have a relationship with him, I'd seen that with my own two eyes.

"Don't get me wrong, I think he's awesome." She shimmied, turning her whole body to face me, reminding me of a little girl getting ready to share her deepest darkest secret with her BFF. "Don't tell anybody, okay?" Oh, God. She was going to share a secret. I really didn't want to hear the juicy details about whatever was going on between her and Rob. "So, like, the thing is …"

It turned out that my eyes had seen clearly, but my brain had blurred the facts into the wrong image. Pam wasn't *doing* Rob. She'd been doing Adam, the aerial cameraman. She hadn't wanted to "freak him out" (her words) when she thought she might be pregnant, so she'd turned to Rob, the closest thing to a dad she had on location. The package that Rob handed her by the pool had been a pregnancy test that he'd picked up for her when he was in St. Thomas, shooting Chris' drunken arrival. Pam's kiss that night had been one of gratitude, not lust. And the big smile and hug she'd given him when he'd come to her room so early in the morning? They'd been fuelled by relief, not lust.

"See what a sweetheart he is?"

"I do now." And I felt pretty dumb for jumping to the wrong conclusion so quickly based solely on visual images that I'd misunderstood.

"So? Will you hook up with him?"

"I don't know about that." All I did know was that I wanted to change the topic of conversation. Thankfully, the geography did it for me. We'd slowed down and were driving past the breakwater into the Virgin Gorda Yacht Harbour.

The damn door to the laundry room at James' villa was locked. None of the keys Mandy had left for me would open it.

"Great. Just bloody great!" With my luck Albert's bag would be locked too.

I leaned in close to the door and tried to get my head at an angle that would allow me to see between the wooden slats of the shutter on the inside of the window. No matter how I contorted all I could see was the slats. Now what?

I had two hours to kill before I had to be at the airport to meet Albert. I spent the first hour pacing, without a gecko audience. A bird's nest hung over a small wrought-iron bench behind the pool. A pair of tiny yellow-bellied black birds, who were barely larger than hummingbirds, darted in and out of the nest as they brought food to their babies, amusing me just long enough for me to be able to identify them.

Another hour to go.

I felt useless. I wasn't getting anywhere — even though I'd probably covered a couple of miles with all the pacing I'd done that day. I had to do something useful. Using my fingers, I tried to count out my best guesstimate of the time difference between Virgin Gorda and Sydney. Sixteen hours? Maybe seventeen? James was probably talking to Aunt Patti a lot so he wouldn't notice the call on his phone bill.

Aunt Patti answered on the fourth ring. I'd woken her up.

"What is it? What's wrong?" she asked before knowing who was calling. (She'd inherited the Butler worrying gene.)

"Hi Aunt Patti, it's Ria."

"Is Blake all right? Has something happened?"

I spent the next few minutes reassuring her that Dad was fine and apologizing for calculating the time difference wrong. Aunt Patti needed those minutes to wake up enough to consciously join the conversation.

I told her how nice the hotel was and asked who she thought should win the competition.

"They both came with excellent recommendations. They're equal in experience, but I think Judy's got a slight edge. She's worked at a more varied selection of international properties. Ted, on the other hand, is better at dealing with the guests. He's more polished, smoother, you know what I mean?"

She hadn't said anything about Ted being a spy. Did she not know? Maybe he was spying on her? Maybe she was doing something shady with the books, ripping Dad off ... at the rate my brain was working I'd be hiring Oliver Stone to make a movie about all the conspiracies my mind was theorizing about. "Could I look at their applications?"

"I'd love you to! Nothing against James, but I don't put one hundred percent faith in his assessment. He's looking at their entertainment value, while I'm more interested in their management value. You should know that the votes from the department heads at the BVI site are unanimous — they all prefer working with Judy over Ted and that carries more weight than James' vote, in my opinion. Jean Philippe, our head chef, even threatened to quit when Ted tried to put a padlock on one of the refrigerators. James' partner has commandeered it for his own use and he wanted to keep his food separate from everyone else's. It's Jean Philippe's kitchen! It took a lot of talking and a pay raise to convince him to put up with the creative types for a few more weeks. I can understand why Ted's doing all he can to impress the producers of the show, but he seems to have forgotten that he'll have to work with the department heads at the hotel if he gets the job. I'll be very interested to hear what you think. I'll email their applications to you just as soon as I get to the office."

"That'd be great." But what if Ted really was a spy? Would he be able to see what was coming and going in my email account if I logged on at the hotel? My Internet knowledge was limited enough to worry me. A new conspiracy line started to wriggle through my head … if he could access my account, had he seen that I'd sent Glenn a copy of his CSIS card? "Actually, could you send the information to a friend of mine? My email program's been messing up a lot lately."

"No worries. What's his address?"

I gave her Glenn's personal email address as I watched an Air Sunshine plane coming in from the west. "Aunt Patti, I have to go meet a friend at the airport. I just saw his flight coming in." As if Albert and I would ever be friends!

There was no sign of the television crew and there wasn't a private jet on the tarmac when I got to the airport. They must have finished shooting Chris' supposed arrival.

"Where's James?" Albert said the minute he stepped out of the airport building. He was carrying the same metallic silver briefcase he'd left Soursop with. He clutched it close to his chest, with the Toronto morning paper on top of it. Glenn's paper. The nightclub shooting that happened just before I left for Machu Picchu was still making news; the cover picture was of the three men who had been arrested.

"Over on Soursop. He asked me to pick you up." If the damn case was locked I planned to break it open by running over it with the Jeep.

Albert raised one eyebrow. "Why didn't he send Mandy?"

"She's in the scene they're shooting tonight, so she's getting her makeup and wardrobe done." I turned around and opened the driver's door. "Come on, Albert. I'm James' sister. He trusts me completely."

I heard, and ignored, his grunt of agreement as he begrudgingly got into the passenger seat beside me and clutched his briefcase in his lap for the ride to the marina. It wasn't until we were both standing on the dock beside the boat that he finally released his grip on it and let me take it. He kept his newspaper, though.

Like James, I sat in the car waiting to see the boat pull out. I wanted to make sure that Albert really left.

When I got back to the villa I ran down the stairs, two at a time. My hands were shaking as I opened the non-locking briefcase. It was full of plastic DVD cases. The brittle plastic cover almost snapped in my hands when I split the first case open. The DVD popped out and then I saw what had been hidden beneath it.

For the third time Glenn's call went to the voice mailbox for Ria's room. Where the hell was she? He'd been trying to reach her for hours, ever since he'd got back home from the editing suite. The message she'd left for him was a doozy — Ted Robarts was a CSIS spy and someone had been spying on her?

He'd given up on calling her cellphone. Those calls went straight through to voicemail; her phone was either off or not working.

For his fourth phone call he didn't ask for her room — he asked the person who answered the phone to find out where Ria was, only to learn that she was *"off island"* and wasn't expected back until after sunset. Didn't they have clocks down there? He wanted a time, something specific. Their messed up communications, on so many levels, were driving him crazy. It took two cigarettes, one right after the other, to calm him down enough to be able to sit at his desk.

There was an email from Ria, with attachments, but she sure didn't waste any words in her message — there weren't any.

Glenn double clicked on the attachment. "What the fuck?" Ted Robarts' serious face was looking back at him from the scan of a CSIS ID badge. But the name on the badge didn't match the picture. Jake Purcell? Ted Robarts was definitely tweaking Glenn's curiosity. The receptionist at the editing place had called him Phil. Ria knew him as Ted. CSIS knew him as Jake. Glenn zoomed in on the badge and carefully looked up close at every inch of it. It looked real enough, but anyone with a laminator and Photoshop could put together something like it. But why would they? His printer didn't sound very healthy as it turned the visual image on his screen into a solid, physical object. He picked up the printed sheet and stared at it. How was he going to check this out?

He clicked on Send/Receive one more time and was surprised to see what had to be a big file coming in. He had high-speed service, but it still took almost a minute for the email to load. It was from Ria's aunt, the president of Butler Hotels. He opened it and read Ms. Whitecross's cheery note, explaining that Ria had asked her to send the attached information. He double-clicked on the first attachment.

It was Judy Ingram's application package for the show. Her resume was impressive. She had a bachelor of commerce degree and an MBA. Glenn recognized the names of a lot of the hotels she'd worked at — mainly because he read Ria's travel articles religiously and she'd written reviews on most of them. Could Ria and Judy have possibly met before? The video that Judy had sent with her application looked so homemade and amateur that it was almost painful to watch. The focus was off, the lighting was terrible, and the open collar of her crisply starched shirt kept scratching against the small microphone that was pinned to her blazer. Despite the technical weaknesses of the video Judy herself came across as confident and competent.

The second attachment was Ted's application package. He, too, had an impressive resume. Like Judy he had a bachelor of commerce degree, only his wasn't a general degree it was specifically a B. Comm. — hospitality and tourism management. Unlike Judy, Ted hadn't gone on to earn an MBA. Glenn didn't recognize as many of the hotels on Ted's resume as he had on Judy's, but the technical quality of his video blew Judy's out of the water. Ted's performance, if you could call it that, was much smoother than Judy's. He smiled, he looked right into the lens of the camera, his shoulders were relaxed, and his body moved naturally with his dialogue.

Glenn felt a familiar quick pulse of adrenalin shoot through him. He wasn't stumbling around, trying to figure out what to do next. He knew what to do. With Judy and Ted's pictures both frozen on a split-screen on his monitor, he put their now-printed resumes on the desk in front of him, picked up the phone, and started to call each and every one of the references they had listed. All of the people he spoke to believed him when he identified himself and the newspaper he worked for and then claimed to be looking for background information for a story he was putting together on *Check-Out Time*.

Judy's references sang her praises and said they hoped she was going to win the job at The Butler BVI. From what they said, and from the career progression he'd seen on her resume, it seemed like the most logical and deserved next step-up on her career path.

Ted's references were just as enthusiastic about him. Glenn was getting nowhere, learning nothing. With a heavy sigh he dialed the number for Ted's last reference — the Crystal Hotel in downtown Toronto. He'd driven by it many times, but had never been in it. All he knew was that it was rated five-star and always packed full of movie stars during the Toronto International Film Festival. The human resources manager wasn't available, but the assistant manager was more than willing to answer Glenn's questions. Everyone at the hotel had enjoyed working with Ted; it was because of Ted and the changes he implemented that their hotel had been bumped up from a mere four-star rating. They'd all been sorry to lose him to the hotel in Dubai.

Dubai?

Glenn double-checked Ted's resume. There was no mention of a hotel in Dubai. "Which hotel was that?" he asked. It was a place he'd never heard of but, according to the assistant manager of human resources, getting the job of managing one of the few six-star hotels in the world was a real professional coup. Ted was so well thought of in the industry that he'd been poached for the job — he hadn't even applied for it.

"That's why we were so surprised to get a call from the production company about Ted's application for the reality show. He must not have liked living in Dubai. Maybe his wife had a problem adjusting to being a female in a Muslim country?"

Ted was married? Again, Glenn read through his application. There was no mention of a wife.

He quickly ended the call and then started clicking with gusto, finding the website for the Dubai hotel easily. Two clicks away from their homepage he found the general manager's welcoming letter. It said all the right things — and was signed *Ted Robarts, General Manager.*

Maybe the page hadn't been updated since Ted left to go to the BVI? Possible, but unlikely. Ted, or Jake, or Phil, had been on Soursop for over two months. A high-end hotel like the one in Dubai wouldn't wait that long to update their website.

A few more clicks — Glenn learned that Dubai was nine hours ahead of Toronto. The general manager of the hotel would be gone for the day. He didn't want to leave a voicemail and started typing up an email.

The open DVD cases were spread out in a circle around me on the floor of the great room. Each one held the exact same thing — a disc and, under each disc, one one-hundred dollar bill, one fifty-dollar bill, one ten-dollar bill, and one five-dollar bill. One hundred and sixty-five dollars per case, times sixty cases. Albert had brought James $9,900.00 in Canadian bills. Was that how James paid his employees? That didn't make sense. The salaries of so many employees must have added up to almost ten times that much. Even if the money did have something do to with the production, why the big secret? I slowly closed all the cases and put them back in the briefcase, while trying to think of an explanation for Albert's cash deliveries. By the time I clicked the briefcase shut I was no closer to understanding what I'd found.

And there was still the locked room under the outside stairway of the building across the pool patio. There had to be a way to open it.

I rummaged through all the drawers in the kitchen, but didn't find any keys. What I did find, however, was a collection of metal skewers. In almost every spy movie I'd ever seen someone picked open a lock with a long skinny object at least once. It was worth a try.

The baby birds were hungrily squawking for their parents to bring them more food when I walked by their nest. I knelt down in front of the door and tried to stick a skewer into the lock. It was too thick. I tried a slightly thinner one. It went in and I started to fiddle. Nothing happened. I tried an even thinner one. It went into the lock more easily and I was able to really move it around. I put more force into my fiddling.

"Want me to give it a try?"

I dropped the skewer when I heard Chris' voice and watched it roll under the door before turning my head around to face him. "What are you doing here?"

"I was bored."

"Aren't you supposed to be shooting your arrival?" With difficulty I stood up. My knees were mad at me for kneeling on such a hard surface.

"We've done the airport stuff. Now we're just waiting on the light. We won't start shooting the helicopter bit for another hour and a half. Everybody's at the Bath and Turtle. They'd heard that Jimmy Buffett wrote "Cheeseburger in Paradise" about the burgers there, but I'm trying to amend my carnivorous habits. I just had a salad." His shiner was shining through his makeup. He'd need another touch-up before shooting the helicopter scene.

"I know of four other places in the Caribbean that make the same claim about Buffett's song."

"There's a shocker — false advertising." He feigned a shocked look, but the bruised skin around his left eye didn't open as wide as the skin around his right eye. "I wonder which one's real?"

"You'd have to ask Jimmy Buffett that."

"Okay. I'll tell Mike to get his number for me. Anyway, I left to check out some of the cars in the parking lot, they really know how to pimp their rides here, and there was this one Beetle, bright red, extra big shiny spinners for rims, big yellow flames detailed on the sides, and slammed really low to the ground — awesome, awesome car. I started talking to the guy who owns it. He's a singer. His name's Elvis."

"Of course it is. Was Keith Moon sitting in the backseat?"

"Who?"

"Exactly. Keith Moon was the drummer for The Who. And he's dead. Just like Elvis."

"No, really, the dude's name is Elvis. He gave me a ride over here and he gave me a copy of the CD he's trying to get released. It's pretty good, too. He played it for me on the way here. I'm going to see if Mike can get someone to listen to it."

"So, Elvis left the building with you and gave you a ride here. Why?"

"I told you. I was bored. Pam said you were here so I figured I'd come over and see what you were up to." He pointed at the door handle. "But you were down there. Want me to open it for you?"

"I can't find the key."

"Obviously." He reached into the back pocket of his designer jeans and pulled out a small black leather case that looked about the right size to hold a pair of sunglasses, but that's not what it held. When Chris unzipped the case and opened it flat in his hands I saw a collection of metal picks, some short, some long, some straight, some squiggly. "I learned how to use these when I was shooting *Crosshairs*. Did you see it?"

"No, I'm not a big fan of spy movies." Maybe I should have brought Ted over to Virgin Gorda with me? If he was a spy he'd know how to pick a lock and, from what I'd seen, he was willing to go out of his way to please a Butler. Chris wasn't a real spy, but he had played on one a movie screen. "Why do you carry those with you?"

"Because they're cool!" He dropped to his knees, picked a tool, and then picked the lock. "There you go," he stood up and opened the door. "You broke in to do laundry? Is there something wrong with the laundry service on Soursop?"

"I'm looking for something." I walked past him into the small room. Sitting right where Rob had said they'd be against the back wall of the laundry room were two *Partridge Family* lunchboxes, sitting on top of an *Around The World in 80 Days* suitcase. I lifted up the name tag on the suitcase — Kate Bond, Toronto.

"Are these hummingbirds?" I heard Chris call out from somewhere on the patio. "They look like hummingbirds."

I couldn't open the suitcases with Chris around and knew that I'd seen enough anyway. James wasn't just hiding money, he was also hiding Kate's suitcases. I lifted one up to feel if it was empty. It wasn't. It was surprisingly heavy.

Chris was standing up on the wrought-iron bench, his face mere inches away from the squawking baby birds in the nest.

"They're bananaquits." I picked up all the skewers and closed the door to the laundry room.

"Oh." He stepped down off the bench. "Hey, these are pretty!" He ran across the patio to the planters of red bougainvillea flowers and reached out to touch one. "Ouch!"

I was starting to wonder if Chris had a touch of ADHD. "They've got thorns."

"I noticed. Kind of like roses, huh?" He sucked the wounded finger. "I like roses. They smell good."

"I thought you were scared of red flowers?"

"Nah, that's just something my agent puts in my contracts to pump up my mega-star image." He bolted over to the door that led into the great room. "What's in here?"

Chris reminded me of a little kid let loose in the FAO Schwarz store on Fifth Avenue in New York as he ran around exploring every corner of James' villa. "What do you want to do now?" he asked me when he finally stopped moving and sat down on one of the couches on the covered veranda.

"Drive you back to the marina?"

He checked his watch. "They won't be looking for me yet."

I tried to make conversation and quickly discovered the antidote to Chris' perpetual motion — talking about himself.

He behaved like a grownup when he was answering questions about his life and career.

"In this one I'm playing a really interesting character. The audience won't know until the very last scene who he actually is — he might be a history scholar, or a journalist, or Rebecca's illegitimate son. He's come to dig up the truth about Rebecca's death. It's a great role. I was a little worried about working with Ariel, though. She's a real bitch-a-rooney-dooney!"

The look on my face must have conveyed my silent question — *a what?*

"Red Forman, from *That '70s Show*. One of his best lines."

"Oh."

"Her fans think she's a real sweetheart, but the whole world's a stage and everybody's just play acting, right?"

"Is that the way you like your Shakespeare quotes?"

"Huh?"

"Never mind."

"Ariel only appears as a ghost in my scenes so I don't have to do any lines with her, thank God. All her scenes are flash-backs that took place when my character was just a kid. Gail Watson's playing Mrs. Danvers, Rebecca's crazy housekeeper. I'm really looking forward to working with her. She isn't coming to Soursop, though. All her scenes are being shot in-studio back in LA, once we're finished shooting here. The rest of the location cast should be flying in soon, but I'm not supposed to say who's coming. Nobody's supposed to know who they are until the masquerade ball."

I didn't dare interrupt Chris' monologue by asking what ball he was talking about. He'd been stationary for almost ten minutes.

"That's not part of the movie, but you already know that. It should be an awesome finale for the TV show, don't you think?" I simply nodded. "Everybody wearing masks and period costumes. We'll take our masks off when we come out of the voting booth — the big reveal — which stars are in the movie and who won the reality show. Dan's really good at coming up with ways to promote his product and, with this one, he'll be killing two birds with one stone. Are you going to stick around to watch Manderley burn? We're shooting that first. It'll be awesome."

"You're shooting the burning of Manderley? Here? It was the de Winter's mansion in Cornwall."

"It's Maxim de Winter's plantation in the Caribbean now. Mrs. Danvers torches it. I'm not in the scene, but I can hardly wait to see it. That's why I asked to be in a cottage at the north end of the island. I'll be able to sit out on my patio and watch the whole thing. Hey! You want to come over and watch it with me?"

"I don't know if I'll still be here." They'd built a plantation at the north end of the island for the sole purpose of burning it down, and that fire was going to be ignited by someone who wasn't really on the island, but who would appear to be on the island in the finished product. I found myself wishing that movie people followed the principle of the line I disliked so much — it is what it is. From what I'd seen, nothing in their orbit was real; it was just a distorted illusion of reality.

CHAPTER
TWELVE

When *Check-Out Time* aired the television audience would see Chris' arrival on Soursop. They'd see him step out of the helicopter, shake hands with Judy, and then walk out of the shot with her. What they wouldn't see was the not-yet-fifty-year-old woman with long red hair who'd hitched a ride over from Virgin Gorda with him. That woman, namely me, did as she was told; staying squished up against the back wall of the helicopter and scrunched down in the seat, making sure that the top of her head stayed below the lower edge of the side window once the helicopter was within visual range of the cameras on the island.

The sun hadn't been low enough in the sky to make the shot of the helicopter landing picture perfect so we'd circled the island a few times. I got to see how big it really was and was amazed by how many secluded beaches there were on its shoreline. At the north end of the island I looked for the Caribbean version of Manderley. My eyes followed the winding dirt road that cut through the thick vegetation. A large area on the very top of the northern plateau was in the process of being clearcut; sunlight reflected off the shiny blades of the scythes that several gardeners were swinging back and forth through the dense bush. No plantation had been built, though.

In fact, nothing had been built, although it was obvious from the piles of lumber and the construction vehicles that something was about to be built.

The makeup woman who'd spent the day covering up Chris' black eye (and who repeatedly offered to show me how to cover up my freckles) gave me a ride to my cottage. The sun dropped below the horizon as we drove and a line of automated lights came on over the road. The porch light over my front patio was already on when we pulled into the driveway. I'd left my golf cart by the main dock, but someone must have arranged for it to be returned to my cottage. It was parked by the front stairs, the key left in the ignition.

I turned on the hallway light once I was inside; it supplied all the illumination I needed to make my way into the living room without crashing into any furniture. The flashing red light on the side of the phone was like a beacon of hope — I hoped that it meant Glenn had called and left me a message. Even more, I hoped that he, not his voicemail, would answer when I called him. I picked up the receiver and then froze; a man had just cleared his throat. That throat, and presumably the man attached to it, was somewhere very close to me.

"Do you want to explain to me why Glenn's snooping around for dirt on my show?" James asked.

"You first. I'd like you to explain to me how you got into my cottage. My locked cottage." I reached in what I hoped was the direction of a lamp. It was, but I knocked the lamp off the table and from the sound of glass breaking as it hit the tile floor I knew it wouldn't be shedding any light on the situation.

"I borrowed Winnie's master key." A light came on, the lamp on the end table nearest to James. He slowly lowered his hand from inside the shade. "Your turn." He was sitting on the biggest sofa. The lamplight sparkled off the empty etched-crystal highball glass in his hand. Draped over the back of the couch was a white tuxedo jacket. An untied, or not-yet-tied, black bowtie hung around the open collar of his white shirt.

"I don't know what you're talking about." Even though I was telling the truth I still felt guilty and made a point of not looking at him as I sat on the sofa opposite his. I didn't know what Glenn was doing, but was pleased to hear that he was doing something. "Why don't you call him and ask him?" Maybe, just maybe, James would open up to his best friend. He'd have to hit rock bottom to open up to me and he wasn't there yet.

James exhaled an almost laugh. "Yeah, right. Call Glenn. Like that's going to happen. As I'm sure you already know we're not exactly on speaking terms right now."

I didn't know. Glenn hadn't said anything about being at odds with James. "That's news to me."

"Oh get off it, Ria! You expect me to believe that you and Glenn didn't natter away about me being with somebody on this shoot?"

Glenn knew about James having a mistress on the shoot? And he didn't tell me? Then again, he wouldn't. He and James were best friends, and best friends protected each other's secrets. But he could have warned me! Oh. No, he couldn't have — because I hadn't told him I was going to the BVI. "Natter? You actually used the word natter?" I tried to steer the conversation away from what Glenn and I may or may not have talked about.

"Nice try. Answer the question."

"We didn't natter about you."

"This shoot is turning into a fucking nightmare." James bent over, dropped his head into his hands, and talked to his knees. "Ted got a call from his sister. She said a C. Bernstein was asking a lot of questions about the show." He sat up and looked straight at me. "C. Bernstein? We both know who that is." He leaned into the cushions on the back of the sofa. "You spend a week with Glenn, then you suddenly have the urge to come here, and while you're here Glenn starts snooping around in my post-production facility. Am I supposed to believe that's just a coincidence?"

I glanced longingly at the flashing red light on the phone and kept staring at it.

"You're doing your 'look everywhere but at me' thing."

I looked down through the glass coffee table at his shiny black leather shoes. "I know about the money, James. I saw it this afternoon." I forced myself to meet his glare.

He jumped up off the sofa and yelled, "Fucking Mandy! She was supposed to —"

"Well, she didn't. I did. I met Albert."

James grabbed his highball glass off the table and I thought he was going to hurl it at the wall, but he marched out onto the patio instead, heading for the bar. "That stupid, stupid bitch!"

I followed him. The lights in the pool had been turned on and I was pleased to see that the camera discs were still soaking in the aquamarine water. "What's the money for, James?"

"It's … it's for the production. It was all Dan's idea." James instantly slipped into standard James behaviour — blame someone else. But his defiance and denial didn't last long. Tears were welling in his eyes. "Why is it all going so wrong?"

"I don't know, James. And I can't help you if you won't tell me what's going on."

He rolled up his dress pants. I rolled up my jeans. We sat, side by side, our feet dangling in the pool.

"It was all Dan's idea …" he started.

Dan came up with a way to hide some of James' money from Victoria and her lawyers, but it was James who had hired Albert. He brought James just under ten thousand dollars every time he came to the island, because anything more than that would have be declared at customs ... so it was legal, right? (James tried to limit his guilt liability.) Dan, with Winnie's help, then magically produced receipts for services rendered on the production that always added up to the amount of Albert's deliveries. Victoria, or her lawyers, would see the money leaving James' company accounts, they'd see receipts from the production to justify those amounts, and James would have a bank account in the British Virgin Islands that nobody knew about.

"I don't want to lose her, Ria, but I think I already have." A few more tears leaked out.

My mouthy nature was hard to control, but I knew that telling him his marriage would have been in much better shape if he'd kept his pants zipped up wasn't going to help matters any. Instead, I went with a more helpful suggestion. "Then get rid of Mandy. Fire her. Send her home. Sell her to Dan for all I care. Call Victoria and grovel — and I mean grovel. You've got a lot of apologizing to do."

"But ..."

I held my hand up in front of his face to stop his mouth. "Don't start with a list of buts. If you mean what you say, about wanting to work it out with Victoria, then do it. Just do it."

"Do you think she'd...?"

"I don't know what Victoria will or won't do. There's only one way to find out."

"Are you sure you and Glenn didn't compare notes? That's almost exactly what he said to me." James stared out into the dark horizon for quite some time. "Look at me, a middle-aged, balding, old guy, turning to my big sister to help me out of a jam."

I took a deep breath. "You're not quite jam-free yet, James. The money isn't the only thing I saw at your villa." As much as I hated to pop his positive outlook bubble, I knew I couldn't let him off the hook yet. "I saw Kate's suitcases in the laundry room, too."

James didn't burst, but he sure deflated.

If I wanted honesty from him I had to deliver the same. "That's why I came, because of Kate. Rob called me."

"You don't think I ..."

"I don't know what to think." And I wasn't going to give him the chance to deny or deflect. "What I do know is that one of your production assistants is missing. You and Dan told the crew she'd gone home, but she's not there." James looked honestly surprised. "And I know that you know something about it because (a) you've been trying to hide in a bottle, just like Dad, and (b) you threatened to fire Rob when he tried to talk to you about it. James, what happened to Kate?"

"But Dan said ... the cops said ... they said she was in Toronto!"

"She's not."

"Are you sure?" He spoke in barely more than a whisper.

"Positive. Glenn went to her apartment and talked to her sister."

"Oh my God." He swallowed hard and stared at the water in the pool as if in a trance.

"You really don't know what happened to her, do you?"

He shook his head slowly. "I mean, I wondered, especially when Dan told Mandy to put Kate's suitcases in the laundry room. But then the police, they said the cops in Toronto had checked, that they'd talked to her, so I figured she'd just quit, like Dan said she had, and she'd gone back home in a huff."

As much as I hated to do it, I knew it was the perfect time to hit him with the information about Ted. If James had anything, anything at all, to do with Kate's disappearance the only way he'd admit it was if he was hit when he was down. "There's something else, too. Ted Robarts is an intelligence officer with CSIS."

"What?" He shook his head. "This can't be happening."

"It is. And, James, I need you to hold it together. If you want to go on the bender to end all benders do it later when you're back on Virgin Gorda. Right now, I need you here and sober."

James stood up and walked slowly, determinedly, toward the bar. I couldn't watch. I didn't want to see him with a bottle in his hand. When he handed me one of the two Diet Cokes he'd got out of the refrigerator I knew he was going to stay in the now of the crisis, instead of flooding it with alcohol. "Tell me what you need."

"Answers."

"Shoot."

"Ted. Did you know who he was when you signed him on for the show?"

"No! Dan's people checked and double-checked his references. This is Dan's fourth reality show, so his team have had lots of experience checking applicants out. And before we made the final selection all of the applicants went through psychological testing. Ted passed with flying colours. He can't be here because of the money. That whole scheme of Dan's didn't come into play until long after we'd chosen the contestants."

I elected to hold off on correcting James' blame placement for the incredibly stupid money scheme. Who came up with the idea was unimportant. James had been the one to do it. "And speaking of Dan, let's talk about him for a bit."

"Do we have to?"

"You're the one who teamed up with him, not me. Straight up — do you think he killed Kate?"

"He couldn't have."

Damn. There went the most likely suspect. "Are you sure?"

"Positive. Mandy and I were on Soursop when Dan and Kate had a big fight. We'd all been in the kitchen, Dan made us dinner, and then Kate started riling Dan to get specific about what job he was going to get her in LA. Dan tried to bluff, he stayed vague, but Kate kept pushing. She said he'd better come up with something solid, and fast, or else she'd put both Dan and I out of our jobs. Nobody threatens Dan — nobody. He yanked her outside and they yelled at each other for a couple of minutes and then Dan came back into the kitchen alone. He was with us for the rest of the night except for about five minutes. He had something he wanted to straighten out with Ted, but I could see them the whole time they were talking. He rode back to Virgin Gorda with us. He stayed at my place bitching about Kate for a while. He must have been at my place for over an hour and he would have stayed longer, but then Winnie called."

"When was that?"

"I don't know, maybe around twelve-thirty or one?"

"What did she want?"

"I'm not sure, but when Dan left to go to his place he said something about to having to find some information in a file for her."

"At one in the morning?"

"We don't exactly work nine-to-five, in case you haven't noticed."

Even so, one o'clock in the morning seemed like a strange time to be doing some filing. Another thing was strange about it — Dan plus filing. The two didn't add up. "Why would Winnie be asking Dan about a file? The man dictates emails. He doesn't strike me as someone who'd be office savvy. Does he keep a lot of files in his villa?"

"No. Now that you mention it, it does seem strange. Winnie handles all his paperwork. She won't even let him touch an original of a document because she says he loses them all the time."

"What about Winnie? Could she have done something to Kate?"

"I doubt it. She and Kate got along, which was kind of surprising, actually. She's been with Dan since his Toronto days and she's never liked any of his fiancées."

Had Winnie spent her entire professional life hoping that she might, someday, become Dan's last fiancée? "Winnie was on Soursop, right? She had opportunity ..."

"But Kate didn't fight with her or threaten her job."

"Not directly, anyway. If she took Dan down, Winnie would be out of a job, too."

"I guess so."

"Any idea what Kate had on Dan?"

"No. You name it, he's probably done it — at least twice." He sighed heavily.

"Could Ted be here to investigate something to do with Dan?"

"It's possible, I guess."

A thought occurred to me and I quickly tried to push it out of my head — but it wouldn't go. What if Dan had set James up? What if he'd been the one to twig CSIS to James' tax evasion? If James was out of the picture Dan would reap all the rewards — both fame and finance — from the show. I couldn't fit Kate into that scenario, though. Unless she'd figured out what Dan was up to and threatened to expose him to James.

I listened to Glenn's phone ringing as I watched James drive away from my cottage. He answered on the second ring. After doing a quick verbal polka around the *"Where the hell were you?"* question (we both asked and answered it), we easily slipped into working together and quickly shared what little information we'd each managed to find. We were so caught up in the questions about Kate that neither of us had the time, or desire, to worry about the questions regarding our personal relationship.

"Frozen? Dad said it might have been frozen?"

"To keep the bugs at bay. If your dad's right, it was a real foot and someone stuck it in a freezer right after it was cut off and then got it out and took it to the tidal pool just before it was found. And on the footage I watched …" Glenn explained the two women he'd seen going in and out of the kitchen.

"That sounds like Winnie! She runs at night and dresses like a frump for work. And we know that she's the one who took Ted's shoes."

"Which begs the question, did she do it and then try to frame Ted by leaving his footprints in the sand? It's a possibility. Ted's a front-runner, too — too many things aren't adding up about him. Like the call he said he got from his sister — it's pure fiction. I'm looking at his application for the show right now, the one you had your aunt send me, in the family information section he just wrote "*all deceased.*" There's no mention of a sister. My bet is that it was the receptionist at James' editing place who called him."

"Why would she do that, though?"

"Because they're old friends. She saw him on one of the monitors when we were in the editing suite and she called him Phil and said they went way back."

"Phil? Who is this guy, Glenn, and why is he here? Is he Ted or Phil or Jake?"

"You've got me."

"Could he be here investigating why James is moving so much money?"

"Uh-uh. If he really is a CSIS agent he wouldn't be there for that. CSIS only worries about national threats. James isn't a threat to anyone but himself. Listen, let's wait until I hear back from the hotel in Dubai before we go off on the Ted tangent. In the meantime, I need you to find out why two discs weren't in the shipment of camera originals that came up here. The technical guy, what's his name?" I could hear Glenn rustling through some papers. "Bear — weird name."

"You wouldn't think so if you saw him."

"Well, two of the scenes he wanted us to watch aren't here. Got a pen?"

"Yup."

"Exterior, north-end tree camera, day thirty-seven, and exterior, east beach camera, day thirty-eight. I don't know what the first one will have, but the second one might have caught whoever putting the foot in the tidal pool. It looks down the beach were the foot was found. The disc that's missing is the one that would have been shooting that morning."

"The missing discs are probably here, waiting to go in the next shipment. Bear's already said how busy his day is whenever the courier comes down to pick everything up. He must have just missed them when he was putting the ship-ment together."

"Maybe, but it's kind of strange that those are the only two that are missing, don't you —"

I waited for Glenn to finish his sentence, but he didn't. He didn't do or say anything. "Glenn?" No answer. No anything. I couldn't even hear him breathing. "Glenn? Are you still there?"

Crickets chirped from somewhere in the foliage around the pool. A few bars of big band music floated faintly through the air. The water in the pool was glass flat. Instead of shatter-ing it rippled when I hurled the useless cordless phone into it. It sank and landed on one of the discs.

"God damn it!" Glenn hurled the cordless phone across his home office. It bounced off the wall on the other side of the room and landed on the floor about halfway through its rebound trip to his desk. There was a new dent in the wall, but the phone was probably okay. It had been purchased for its ability to endure Glenn's occasional bouts with frustration.

The crappy phone system at Ria's hotel was driving him beyond frustration. He put his hands over the keyboard of his laptop and was about to pound out an email to her but stopped himself before hitting the first key. If the phones weren't working chances were that the island didn't have Internet access either.

As he exhaled on the balcony he watched the smoke roll up into the sky. Maybe he should try smoke signals? At least with them he felt as if he had some control. How were they ever going to sort this out without being able to communicate? Did people still send telexes? Telegrams? Glenn pushed aside a few squished butts in the planter and added another. A pigeon cooed from the balcony next to his. Maybe he should hire a carrier pigeon? Modern technology sure wasn't doing him any good.

Technology was entertaining Brandon in the living room. He was sitting on the couch, his hands on a controller, his shoulders set, his concentration entirely focused on the big flat-screen television. His character was walking through a futuristic factory of some sort and he was shooting aliens who looked like they had wishbones on their heads. They were carrying big blue shields that looked like man-sized albums — real albums, not little pretend albums called CDs.

"What was that bang a couple of minutes ago?" Brandon asked, without looking away from his game.

"I threw the phone."

"That's what I figured." His character walked past three dead bodies and then started blasting an alien spaceship. "Want to play?"

"Sure." Glenn had tried playing a few of Brandon's games and had only been able to master the art of shooting aliens and other invaders in the feet. He hoped that trying to improve his aim might also improve his mood.

Brandon won the mission. Glenn's contribution had been to shoot several feet, one wall, and two members of Brandon's team. He'd also shot Brandon's character once, but the wound to his foot hadn't been fatal.

Back in his office Glenn split his computer screen — the picture of Ted that Allie had sent him from Kate's digital picture frame on the right side, Ted's photo from the CSIS card on the left side. It was definitely the same guy, just a little sterner looking in the CSIS photo.

"Who are you?" he asked both photos.

Ted? Jake? Phil?

If it was the receptionist from the editing place who had called Ted, the man she'd called Phil, why had she felt it necessary to warn him about a reporter asking questions?

He went back to a full screen and pulled up the photo of Kate with Dan Shykoff. The smiling man with his arm around Kate looked happy and relaxed — a far cry from the angry man Glenn had watched yelling at her on the screens in the editing suite. Dan hadn't had time to kill and dispose of Kate, nor had he had the opportunity to place her foot in the tidal pool the next day. His secretary, Winnie, had the opportunity to do both, though.

His computer pinged to tell him that he'd got mail.

"These just came in but they don't make sense. They were taken today on Soursop and they came from Kate's phone. And you're not an entertainment reporter. What's going on? Where's Kate? — Allie"

Glenn quickly emailed Allie back.

"I don't know what's going on. That's what I'm trying to find out. I give you my word — I'll find Kate. Glenn"

It was a promise he planned to keep.

He opened the first photo attachment. It was a scenic shot that showed nothing but greenery. Lots and lots of greenery, that was very green, with a splash of red flowers. Ria probably would have been able to name some of the bushes and trees. His eyes scanned the image and focused on something not green near the edge of the screen. It was sort of golden, verging on beige. Only a little bit of it was poking into the shot. He leaned in closer and was able to make out thin lines of darkness between beige strips. Lumber. It was the corner of a pile of lumber, stacked up near a tree. Glenn focused on the tree. Its shape reminded him of an open umbrella. Its many branches were covered with green leaves that looked a bit like ferns. Bright red flowers lay over the whole tree like a blanket. But it was just a tree — a brown-barked, green-leafed, red-flowered tree ... with a tiny red spot in the *V* of its trunk. That wasn't a flower. His nose was almost touching the screen as he looked closer. The *V* wasn't empty. There was a box of some sort sitting in it. The red spot was near the top of the box — just above a round shiny lens. A camera that was shooting pictures of lumber? Glenn quickly flipped through the notes he'd written in the editing place. *North End Tree Camera — day 37 missing/ day 38 — top of hill, lumber, backhoe, bucket filled with sand, spider on lens.*

Glenn recognized the two men in the second picture. Dan and Ted (or Phil) (or Jake) were standing very close to each other on the side of a paved road. The photographer had been standing across the road from them. Behind them was what looked like a marina; there was a barge docked across the end of one of the big wharves and a large group of people where near and around it. Dan's mouth was open and from the angry look on his face they weren't having a cheery conversation. Ted's face, looking worried, was turned to look to the right side of the screen. Glenn followed his line of sight and saw what he was looking at. Ria. She was just a blur, but Glenn easily recognized the swirl of red hair that flowed out in a ponytail from the back of her head. She was running down the road. Running into the shot.

Someone was taking too many pictures of Ria! First with the camera on her patio and now this. Was she in danger?

The third picture really confused Glenn. It was a close-up of the front page of his own newspaper from the day before. Instead of trying to enlarge the image, he picked up his own copy of the paper from the recycling bin beside his desk. The story and pictures about the nightclub shooting had nothing to do with Kate! He lets his eyes scan the whole page, glancing back and forth between the physical page in his hand and the virtual page on his computer screen. That's when he saw that the person who'd sent the picture had drawn a thin circle around the Upcoming Features box ... and they'd double underlined *"Glenn Cooper Exposes the Dirty Side of White-Collar Crime."*

Was someone trying to send a message? To who? Allie? What was the message?

Look at the place where the lumber is (is that where the murder happened?) — look at Dan and Ted (was Ria in the shot by accident?) — Glenn Cooper (contact him? How would the picture taker know Glenn was involved?).

If someone had looked at the footage recorded at Ria's place, they'd know that Ria and Glenn were talking. If the Bear guy had been telling Ria the truth about Dan not seeing it, the only people who could have looked at it were Winnie and Bear himself.

Winnie knew that Allie was in Kate's apartment, she'd actually spoken to Allie. Winnie knew about the camera at Ria's.

If Winnie was the picture taker and the picture sender, Glenn could think of two possible reasons for her to do it: One, she knew who killed Kate and was trying to send Allie a message — if true, why didn't she just call the police? Two, she killed Kate and was trying to point the finger of blame away from herself — but by doing that, wasn't she at the same time drawing attention to herself?

There were too many questions piling up. The answers were on that island somewhere.

And the most frustrating question of them all: when would the fucking phones down there be working again?

He almost jumped out of his chair when his phone suddenly rang. "Ria?"

"No," the male voice sounded confused. "This is Ted Robarts. I'm looking for Glenn Cooper."

"You found him."

"I just got your email. I know who you are, I used to get your paper and I recognized your name. Care to tell me why you're supposedly looking for information on a reality-TV show that I've never heard of?"

"Where are you calling from?"

"Dubai."

CHAPTER
THIRTEEN

The golf cart outside my cottage hadn't been mine. It had been James' and he'd driven away in it. The phone at the bottom of my pool was just as useful as the other phones in the cottage — none of them worked. If I was going to find Bear I was going to have to do it on foot. A few golf carts passed me, heading for the crew quarters, but Bear wasn't riding in any of them. Even though the sun had been down for hours it was still sticky hot. I was thankful for the breezes I felt whenever the road swerved near a beach. Winnie passed me once — running almost as fast as a golf cart and heading in the same direction as the carts. I had to sidestep around one or two land crabs. The shadows cast by the road lights made them look bigger than they actually were.

I found Bear standing at the far end of the pool patio, talking to Rob and two other men. A group of production people were in the process of taking light stands down, winding up long lengths of electrical cable, and removing the table that had been set up over the end of the pool.

Rob spotted me and walked down to join me at the shallow end. "Hey, how did it go?"

"It's getting stranger by the minute."

"Why doesn't that surprise me? Welcome to my world. Production life is never — ever — normal."

"Two of the discs that Bear wanted my friend to watch weren't in Toronto. Is he busy right now?"

"He's just having some down time while they strike the set. BEAR!" Rob bellowed.

Bear looked over, smiled, and walked toward us. "So? Anything?"

I shook my head. "Two of the discs you listed weren't in Toronto."

"Which ones?" His smile flattened.

I handed him the note I'd written during my call with Glenn.

"That's weird." He handed the note back to me. "They should have been there. I packed the shipment myself and checked everything off before handing it over."

"Who did you hand it over to?"

He thought for a minute. "Winnie. She said she was meeting with Dan and Albert, so she took them for me."

"So she could have taken them?"

"Yeah, I guess so. I really think you're wrong about her, though."

"If she kept them they'd be in her office," Rob interjected. "She keeps that place locked up tighter than Fort Knox. Even Dan's not allowed to go in there by himself."

"Winnie wouldn't —" Bear started to say before he was interrupted.

"Hi, guys!" Chris came bounding through the doors from the lobby. "Just the man I was looking for," he said to Bear. "How does a Belmont Quolis Q-5000 sound? I don't know what colour you want, though, or where to have it shipped."

"I don't need another damn chair," Bear grumbled.

"A chair?" Rob sounded confused.

"A dentist's chair. That girl, the one with the long black hair, she said Bear liked them and I want to buy one for him."

"I told you, I don't want one. Do you mind? We're kind of in the middle of something here." Bear had little to no patience for Chris, no matter how many Oscars he'd won.

"Sorry!" Chris flipped his hands up in the air in quick mock surrender. "Excuse me for trying to be nice. I'll let you get back to whatever super important stuff you were doing." He turned to walk away, but I stopped him.

"Actually, Chris? I think you might be able to help me." Winnie was out doing her nightly run. Winnie locked her office. Chris was good an unlocking things.

"Cool!" He excitedly came back to us and looked like a puppy dog eagerly waiting for his human to throw a tennis ball.

"How would you feel about opening another locked door for me?"

"Oh, no! I'm not going to be a part of this." Bear shook his head.

"But if we can look at what's on those discs ..." I tried to explain.

"Nope! Don't want to know about it." He stuck his fingers in his ears and went back to work with the crew, chanting a mantra of "La-la-la-la-la," as he walked away from us.

"Are you thinking what I think you're thinking?" Rob asked me.

"Chris opened the locked door to the laundry room at James' place for me earlier today," I explained.

"You want me to break into another laundry room? Do you have a laundry fetish? I played this character once that had a fetish, but it wasn't for laundry. Actually, maybe it was more of an OCD kind of thing. He —"

"Chris? Stop talking. Just for a minute." I couldn't believe that I'd just told one of the world's most famous movie stars to shut up, but I had. And it worked. "Are you in, Rob?"

He shrugged his shoulders. "Why not?"

—>—

Winnie's office was on the third floor of the hotel. Her door was definitely locked, but there was nothing Chris could do to open it. His picks were useless. The electronic lock required a keycard to open it.

"What do we do now?" I asked Rob as we stood in the hallway.

Chris didn't join the conversation. Instead, he tried the door to the left of Winnie's office, but it was locked. Then he tried the door to the right of her office and it opened. As he walked into the room we heard him exclaim, "Do people really stay in rooms this small?" but neither of us bothered to answer him.

"Does James have a master key?" Rob asked me.

"I don't think so and even if he did it would be back on Virgin Gorda with him." Talking about James and master keys reminded me of something he'd said when he'd been at my place. He'd borrowed Winnie's master key to get into my cottage. Why did Winnie have a master key?

"Do you think Judy or Ted would give us one?"

"Ted might, Judy wouldn't."

"Hi there!" The door to Winnie's office opened — Chris had opened it, from the inside. "That was too easy."

"How did you get in there?" I asked.

"I climbed over from the balcony of that room," he pointed at the room we'd last seen him disappear into, "and came in through the balcony of this one. The door wasn't locked. People usually forget about locking their balcony doors. I learned that when I was making *Crosshairs*. Did you see it?" He asked Rob.

"Yeah, it was pretty good."

"You know the scene where I rappel down the side of …"

I heard a ding announcing the arrival of an elevator on the floor and pushed both men into the office, closing the door behind me. "Let's continue this discussion in here."

The room was the size of a standard Butler deluxe room, big enough for two king-size beds and a sitting area. Even though there weren't any lights on the beam from the full moon lit up the room well enough for me to see where the furniture was. Instead of beds there was office furniture — a couple of chairs and a small sofa, a desk, a big three-drawer file cabinet, and all the required electronic equipment. I tried the drawers in the file cabinet and the drawers on either side of the big desk, while Chris boasted to Rob about how he'd done his own stunt work on *Crosshairs*, including rappelling down the side of a fifteen-storey building.

"Everything's locked."

"Oh! That's why I'm here." Chris happily pulled out his lock pick kit and started opened drawers.

Rob and I looked in each drawer as soon as it was opened. We did the file cabinet first and, not surprisingly, saw a lot of files. I took the right side of the desk, Rob took the left. Chris opened each lock with the speed of a break-and-enter expert.

In the second drawer I saw a collection of discs that looked just like the ones Bear had given me earlier that day. "I think I found them, but I can't read the labels."

A small beam of light waved over the open drawer.

Chris was standing behind us, a miniature flashlight in his hands. "Does this help?"

The two discs we were looking for were at the front of the drawer.

Rob and I used the door to get back out in the hallway. Chris did his balcony hopping thing. Once we'd regrouped Rob led us to the emergency exit stairwell and down to Bear's technical control room on the main floor. We used his electronic keycard to open the door.

Chris' disappointment when he learned that his skills wouldn't be needed any more quickly disappeared when he saw the large and varied collection of electronic equipment in the room. "What's this?" he asked Rob repeatedly.

Rob answered in short sharp answers that sounded more and more exasperated by the minute as he turned on some lights and equipment. He shoved the first disc into the slot on the front of an electronic box and the small monitor above it came to life.

"Oh-oh," I heard Chris say.

I turned around to see that he was struggling to get what looked like a large nylon circle to bend over on itself.

"It's a reflector," he explained. "I've seen the lighting guys fold them up, but I can't figure out how they do it."

It reminded me of the floating beds that Dad had for his pool. While I showed Chris how to re-twist the reflector back on itself, Rob fast forwarded through most of the footage on the first disc.

Out off the corner of my eye I could see that the camera had been watching a long beach. The sun had just started to light the sky when Rob quickly pushed a button and stopped the playback.

"Look." Rob rewound a bit and then let the images play at normal speed.

Winnie stepped onto the beach. She was wearing another drab suit, but it was her footwear that really caught my attention — brown leather loafers that were obviously too big for her feet. She walked slowly toward the water, stretching her legs out to elongate her strides, and she put force into each footstep. In her hands she was holding something that had been wrapped in a dishtowel (one with a Butler *B* embroidered on it). She walked into the water until it was up above her knees, bent over, unwrapped the dishtowel, and placed something white in the water, holding it down just under the surface for a few minutes. She slowly pulled her hand out of the water, balled the dishtowel up, and made her way back to the treeline, leaving a second set of footprints in the sand. Her two lines of footprints formed a *V* that pointed right to the spot where she'd stood in the water.

"Wow, these things are heavier than I thought."

Both Rob and I turned to see what Chris was doing. He was holding a long pole high above his head with both hands.

"Stop playing with the Goddamn boom poles," Rob said firmly, and then went on to mutter, "He's like a little kid," under his breath.

"You know what that means, right?" I pointed at the monitor.

"Yeah," Rob took the disc out of the machine and slid the second one in.

The monitor came to life again.

"The lighting sucks on that shot," Chris shared his opinion with us.

He was right. It was like we were looking through night-vision goggles, everything was slight green-grey. I could just make out the shapes of some trees and bushes. Moonlight reflected off the Caribbean far below where the camera was positioned.

"Hey! That's up near my place." Chris leaned in, putting his head in the small amount of open space between my head and Rob's. "See that?" He pointed at the screen. "That's the little backhoe they're using up at Manderley."

I took his word for it. The backhoe was parked beside a stack of lumber in a clearing on the top of the hill; the empty bucket was resting on the ground and various long-handled gardening tools were leaning against it. A pair of weak lights flickered across the clearing, growing brighter. Then the front end of a golf cart drove into the picture from the right side of the screen. A pole moved diagonally across the screen, very close to the camera.

"Boom in the shot!" Chris called out.

"That's not a boom pole," Rob corrected him. "There's no audio on this."

The pole had stopped moving, but was still visible on the right side of the screen.

The driver got out of the golf cart and walked in front of it, her silhouette lit from behind by the golf cart's lights. Kate. Her head turned as she looked around. The pole flew across the screen and connected with Kate. Both dropped out of the picture. Then the pole rose up again. Moonlight flashed off of the long curved blade on the end of it just before it knocked the camera. The camera jerked forty-five degrees to the right.

Someone was running up the hill, toward the camera. She had an athlete's body and her hair was pulled back into a pony-tail. Winnie. She ran across the screen, her eyes glowing dark green like an alien's.

"Whoa, dude," Chris said in barely more than a whisper. "Nobody told me the Grim Reaper was hanging out here. Did you see that blade thing?"

"It was a scythe." Just like the ones I'd seen the gardeners using.

The screen went black.

"What happened?" I looked at Rob. "Why did it stop?"

"That's the end of it." Rob pulled the disc out of the machine. "Whatever came next would be on the next disc." He, too, was talking softly.

"That means that Winnie didn't …"

"But she saw who did."

Glenn had to think fast. The first thing to come to his mind was what he was supposed to be investigating. "I'm doing a piece on identity theft."

"No way!" Ted Robarts sounded less angry and suspicious. "Somebody's pretending to be me? Son of a bitch! It must be whoever stole my wallet."

How would the Ted Robarts (or Jake Purcell) (or Phil) in the British Virgin Islands have had the opportunity to steal the real Ted Robarts' wallet? "When was it stolen?"

"A couple of days before I left Toronto. I had to cancel all my credit cards and get new ones super fast, but thankfully the thief didn't have time to charge much on my Visa. She got away with an expensive visit to the salon across the street from the hotel. She got the works — cut, colour, massage, facial ..."

"She? How do you know it was a she? Did the police catch her?"

"I don't know. I haven't heard anything from them since I reported it stolen. I just assumed it was a she. But she must have sold it or given it to the man who's now pretending to be me."

Possible. But why would a CSIS agent use ID from a stolen wallet? It wasn't adding up. None of it. "Do you remember the date she went to the salon?" It was a long shot, but maybe the person who did all the fluffing and pampering on the thief would remember what the person they worked on looked like.

"It was the nineteenth of March, the day after I left. The credit card company let me off on the charges because I could prove I wasn't in the country. So, who's this guy and how did you find him?"

"It's a long story," Glenn started. He then edited and shortened the story drastically. The man on the phone said he was

Ted Robarts and maybe he was. Maybe he was even calling from Dubai, the display on Glenn's phone only showed "Long distance, Unknown Number." No matter who he was, Glenn wasn't going to tell him everything. Instead, he got creative and made up a story about coming across Ted Robarts' stolen wallet report to the police while researching the story he was working on and then accidentally stumbling across the same name being used by a contestant on a reality-TV show.

"I'd like to look the guy in the face and let him know how much trouble he caused me."

That could be arranged, sort of, if technology was on Glenn's side. "Are you near a computer?"

Within minutes, a cropped version of the photo of Ted Robarts/Jake Purcell from the CSIS card image was magically transported across the globe.

"It's here. Let me look at him." Glenn felt his heart rate increase slightly as he waited for Ted Robarts' reaction to seeing Ted Robarts. "Nope, he doesn't look familiar, but hundreds of people came through the hotel every day, so that doesn't mean much." Ted laughed. "He kind of looks like one of our waiters, actually. Like a distant cousin or something."

"Which waiter? Here or in Dubai?" Glenn tried to sound calm.

"Phil London. He was with us for years, in Toronto. He's probably still there. Maybe you should go ask him if he's got a cousin with sticky fingers?"

"Could he have stolen your wallet?"

"Phil? Nah! He was an employer's dream — on time, good at his job, excellent with the guests. He probably made a fortune in tips, too. Nobody schmoozed the guests as well as Phil."

Before hanging up Glenn was already Googling "Phil London." Something about the name rang a bell. Not just the first name, which had set off alarms, but the whole name. One hundred and eighty-three million results. Glenn clicked on a couple of promising links, but those promises fell short. He tried "Phil London waiter." One hundred and seventy million useless results. "Phil London waiter the Crystal" brought one million and eighty thousand results. Talk about trying to find a needle in a haystack! He clicked and read and clicked some more. The little numbers on the right side at the bottom of his screen changed over to read 2:30 a.m. Glenn knew that he could sit in front of the computer all night and it still wouldn't tell him anything. Google didn't know who Phil London was, at least not Glenn's Phil London. For the hell of it he searched Jake Purcell — sixteen million, four-hundred thousand results. He checked out some of the Facebook photos of various Jake Purcells, but none of them were Ted or Phil.

He couldn't go to the Crystal to ask about him — the restaurant Phil worked in didn't open until eleven. Same thing with the salon across the street from the hotel; according to its website it didn't open until seven-thirty.

His heart was racing. He was close, he could feel it.

He dialled the number for the Butler BVI again. The phones still weren't working.

Glenn stood up and walked out into the living room. "I'm going to the British Virgin Islands."

"Okay, bye." Brandon didn't look away from the television screen.

Glenn walked in front of the screen, blocking Brandon's view. "I need your help."

Brandon blinked a few times as if trying to come out of a trance. "Let me just finish this mission …"

Glenn didn't move. "I need your help — now. Come show me how to buy plane tickets online?" He walked away from the screen and into his office. He could hear Brandon following him.

"You're serious?" Brandon looked surprised as he sat down in Glenn's chair and started to click the mouse. "You're really going? When?"

"Today?"

Brandon looked up at his dad. "Have you had a stroke or something? You don't do stuff like this."

"Stuff like what?"

"You know, spur of the moment stuff. On top of that, you're scared of flying. Remember?"

"I am not scared of flying." Glenn immediately denied Brandon's accusation … and then clarified it a bit. "I'm scared of crashing. The flying part doesn't bug me that much."

"You go with that. But seriously, you've taken one trip in ten years, and you wouldn't even have done that if Ria hadn't talked you into it. What's up?"

"It's Ria, we're working on something together, well not together together …"

"But you're still together, right?"

"Yeah!" Glenn said with conviction, hoping it was true. "But she's in the British Virgin Islands and I'm here and it's like the right hand is in one place and the left hand is in another, and neither one can fully grasp the whole thing without the other."

"Wow. That was deep." Brandon looked at the computer screen. "What's the name of the airport you want to go to?"

"Virgin Gorda." Glenn felt rather proud of himself. His right hand/left hand description of his relationship with Ria had been kind of deep. He quickly jotted it down in point form, because he planned to use an expanded version of it when he was face-to-face with her to explain how he felt about them as a couple.

"When do you want to come back?"

"In a week? Get a ticket I can change, just in case."

"Credit card," Brandon held out his hand and then quickly typed in Glenn's credit card number once he had the card. "Done." The printer came to life. "Your flight leaves at eleven-thirty. You have to make a connection in Miami and then another one in San Juan. That one will be really tight, but if your other flights aren't delayed you should be able to make it."

"What time do I have to be at the airport?"

"Three hours before departure to clear U.S. Security."

"That'll work, just." Glenn began walking back into his bedroom. "Now show me how to get everything into a carry-on bag."

Brandon followed him into the room, pulled Glenn's backpack out of the closet and dropped it on the bed.

"Mind driving me to the airport?"

"Can we take the MG?"

"Okay," Glenn opened the top drawer of his dresser, grabbed a stack of boxers, and threw them on the bed. "We have to make one stop on the way, at the salon across the street from the Crystal Hotel."

"Who are you and what have you done to my dad?"

"What?" Glenn laughed.

"You don't do salons. If you tell me you want a mani-pedi, I'm taking you straight to the home and locking you up! I'm not ready to deal with pre-senile dementia."

Glenn tried to control the giggle that was bubbling up inside him. "Maybe I want a Brazilian wax?"

"You can stop talking now."

Glenn was waiting outside the doors of the salon when a white-coated technician unlocked them. She didn't recognize the man in the picture of Ted that Glenn had printed out, but with the help of the receptionist she found what services Ted Robarts' credit card had paid for on March nineteenth. He'd paid for a mani-pedi, a massage, and a cut and colour. (No Brazilian.) While the technician went to check the colour file of the person who'd received those services Glenn watched Brandon drive by three times as he circled the block.

"He went brown, dark brown." The technician walked out of the backroom holding an index card in her hand. "Looking at this formula, he must have been a blonde to start off with."

"He?"

She looked at the card again. "Definitely a he."

Glenn profusely thanked the girls who had helped him and promised, again, to recommend their salon to Ariel Downes and Chris Regent when they were in town on the press junket for the movie they were currently making in the British Virgin Islands. He even went so far as to say that movie might be pre-viewed at the Toronto International Film Festival, when lots of stars would be staying in the hotel right across the street and, being a senior producer at Butler Entertainment, he assured them that he'd use his connections to get their salon noticed by the right people.

It was during the turbulent two-and-a-half-hour flight to Miami that the puzzle pieces in Glenn's mind started to fit together and take shape. He barely noticed the turbulence.

He made two phone calls while waiting to make his connection in Miami. The first one was to James — and James picked up. With the arrangements made to get him from Virgin Gorda to Soursop, Glenn made his second call. Dex gave him the receptionist's name — Holly Stewart, aka friend of Ted/Phil/Jake. Following the detailed instructions Brandon had given him he tried to connect his computer to the airport's wi-fi. Technology was on his side, but time wasn't. His flight was called just after he'd entered Phil London's name into the IMDbPro search box.

"Well, hello, Phil Lunden!"

IMDbPro had found several people whose names were similar to Phil London, but Glenn now knew that he had to focus on Phil Lunden. He studied Phil's IMDbPro photo — he had blonde hair, lots of freckles, and a killer smile. Checking out Holly Stewart and Jake Purcell would have to wait until he was between flights in San Juan.

The only thing he had time for in San Juan was a full-speed sprint from his arrival gate to the Air Sunshine departure gate.

James was waiting for him at the airport in Virgin Gorda.

"You didn't tell anyone I was coming, right?" Glenn said as he jumped into the front passenger seat of James' Jeep.

"No one except Malvin. He's going to take you over to Soursop."

The sun was setting but there was still enough light left for Glenn to get a look at the island when Malvin circled it for him. Soursop was one nice island.

The only thing that didn't seem to fit was the over-sized bill-board that was being built on the north end of the island. Had the recession actually touched the Butler's to the point where they had to sell advertising space? As the boat rounded the northern point Glenn saw the front of the billboard and realized how wrong he'd been. It wasn't an ad. From the other side it looked like the front of a large plantation from the southern States, painted white with wide steps leading down from the veranda to what looked like a front lawn that went to the very edge of a cliff. It even had shutters beside the windows that had been cut out along the front of the fake building. Glenn was reminded of the movie sets he'd seen in the lakeshore studios in Toronto when he'd been investigating the death of a security guard on a movie shoot a few years earlier. From the front they looked like real houses. It was only when you walked behind them that you saw how fake they were.

I spent the day wishing Glenn was on the island with me. And pacing. And swimming. And picking up the phone to see if there was a dial tone. I walked to the hotel (to burn off more frustration) and sent him an email, but I had no idea if it actually went anywhere.

Chris and I had lunch together, but I barely heard a word he said. (And he used so many, many words!) The only words I paid attention to were: "I put those discs back like you asked me to."

It was while I was walking back to my villa that Rob and his crew pulled up beside me on the road.

"Want some company?" he asked as he slid off the back bench of the cart. "We just finished our shift."

"Okay."

Rob slipped his hand into mine as we walked down the pathway to beach. "So …" Rob seemed reluctant to finish his thought. "Maybe I've been reading your signals wrong, but I don't think I have. Ria?"

Uh-oh. It was moment of truth time, I could feel it coming. "Yes?" We'd danced around our mutual attraction for years, but we'd never had to really address it. Each time our lives had crossed paths one or the other of us had been married. This wasn't a hypothetical situation, something I could daydream about in an adolescent way, it was really happening. I had motive (he was incredibly sexy), I had opportunity (we were in the same place, at the same time) … but did I have the intent? If I said yes to Rob, I'd be saying no to Glenn.

"Once this whole Kate thing is all figured out, how would you feel about coming with me to St. Thomas for a couple of days? I've got two days off and …"

"Rob," I stopped him, "I'm seeing someone." It was the truth, sort of. I was in an undefined relationship that I hoped to define once Glenn and I were able to talk for longer than ten minutes without worrying about losing our connection.

"I know, James told me, but the guy's not here and we are. He wouldn't have to know."

Adolescent girls were attracted to bad boys. Given my track record (especially including my divorce), I too had a habit of finding them irresistible. When Glenn had talked about his white-collar criminal he'd said he was a grown-ass man who'd acted like a child. It was time for me to act like what I was — a grown-ass woman. "I'd know."

"Yeah, but …"

"It's not going to happen, Rob. Not now." I didn't put a time limit on that negative response.

"Got it." Rob looked around, as if he was looking for somewhere else to be.

Thankfully, Bear chose that moment to come trotting down a pathway from the road. "Hi, kids. How's it going?"

Neither one of us answered.

"I just heard some juicy gossip." Bear broke the silence, perhaps sensing the unspoken tension.

"Do tell." Rob sounded interested.

"Mandy's moved out of James' place and into Dan's."

"Good," I said out loud by mistake.

"I thought you'd like that." Bear smiled at me just as the radio on his belt crackled to life.

"Bear? You there?" a male voice asked.

"Bear here."

"We, ah, we have a little problem with Gary's camera."

"What kind of problem?" Bear's eyes closed to slits.

"He kind of lost it."

"Well, tell him to look for it. We're on an island, for Christ's sake. It didn't swim away."

"Actually, it sort of did. He was getting scenic shots from the speedboats and he got artsy, leaning over the side to get an angle on the waves. They hit a big wave." The man stopped talking.

"And?"

"And he lost his grip on the camera."

"I'm near the front dock. Bring him in there." Bear pushed a button on his radio and stuck it back on his belt. "I am surrounded by imbeciles! Can you believe it? He dropped a camera! In the ocean! Rule number one in cameraman school — don't ever drop the damn thing."

We heard the speedboat before we saw it. It rounded the northern tip of the island and flew past us, bouncing over the waves as it headed for the main dock south of us. Bear picked up the pace, and we matched his steps.

"Maybe I'll just kill Gary and toss his corpse out into the water to hide the evidence? Wow, did I just say that? Sorry. Call me insensitive. I'm pissed off. See ya." Bear broke into a run, leaving us behind.

J.E. Forman

"Well, I should get going. I have to white balance some cameras."

Maybe Rob really did have to do something with the cameras, or maybe he was just making an excuse to leave the painfully awkward situation — I'd never know. "Okay. See you later."

He sounded angry when he said "Sure" before turning and walking in the other direction.

I kept on walking toward the main dock. I could hear Bear screaming at someone and saw his little arms flailing around as he made his point. Bear's yelling was drowned out by the sound of a powerful boat motor. Like the speedboat before it, it came around the northern tip of the island and as it passed me I saw that it was the Butler *B* boat.

It gave me an idea, something to do. I could go over to James' villa and use his phone to call Glenn. With a burst of renewed energy and purpose, I jogged to the main dock.

Bear had his back to me as I walked down the dock. He was holding up a single digit salute as the speedboat pulled away from the dock and had just lowered it when the Butler *B* yacht arrived. "Good God, Gulliver's come to the island." Bear was staring at the Butler *B* yacht.

"Who?" I looked at the boat and couldn't believe what I was seeing. Glenn was standing on the stern deck, holding a rope, ready to jump onto the dock once the boat was close enough. "Glenn."

"No, Gulliver," Bear corrected me. "Look at the size of him! I'm going to feel positively Lilliputian standing next to him."

"He's not that tall, he's only six-four and a bit. And his name's Glenn."

The big smile that spread across Ria's face was exactly the welcome Glenn had been hoping for. He leapt off the boat a little

272

too early and almost ended up in the water, but managed to land on the dock without looking like too much of a spazz. The little guy standing with Ria had to be the one they called Bear, but they really should have called him Cub. Malvin took the rope from him and he started to walk toward Ria, who hadn't moved a muscle in either her body or her face. "Did you know that your phone's not working?"

Her smile turned into a laugh. "I had noticed that actually, but thanks for dropping by to tell me."

"No problem." He stood in front of her, not sure if he should hug her. "Mind if I stay for a bit?"

She made the hug decision by reaching up and wrapping her arms around his neck (after he bent down enough for her to reach it). Glenn hugged her back, hard, picking her up off the dock.

"I'm so glad you're here," she whispered into his ear.

"Me too." He put her down and smiled at her little friend. "You must be Bear. I'm Glenn."

"So I've been told, but I'm thinking there's more to this story than I've heard. That was quite the hug." They shook hands. "And I'd love to hear the rest of it now, but —"

"Bear?" A woman's voice came out of the radio on his belt.

Bear put the radio to his mouth as he was walking away. "Please tell me you're calling with good news?"

"Not exactly," the woman started.

"So? Should I check-in or something?" Glenn hoped she'd say no.

"I guess so. They didn't make me check-in, but they knew I was coming. Grab your bags and I'll take you to the front desk."

He smiled. "I've already got my bags. All of them." He slid the backpack off the shoulder it had been hanging from.

"No way! I'm so proud of you."

"Yeah, well, don't get too excited. The truth is Brandon did the packing."

The lobby of the hotel was a beehive of activity, people carrying movie equipment, people pushing racks of clothing around (most of them held what looked like fancy ball gowns to Glenn), even the guy behind the front desk was involved in the production somehow — a makeup person was dabbing his face with a little sponge. It wasn't until they were right at the desk that Glenn realized he was looking at Ted Robarts, a.k.a. Phil Lunden. Man, how he wanted to get Ria alone to tell her what he'd learned (and for a few other reasons that would hopefully come to fruition).

"Hi, Ria," the makeup girl said once she'd finished touching up Ted's face. "Here," she bent over, took a small glass jar out of her toolbox-sized makeup kit, and handed it to Ria. "This is the stuff I was telling you about. Try it. It does a great job covering freckles."

Glenn liked Ria's freckles. He liked them a lot. Especially the ones on her chest. If she covered them up he wouldn't get to play connect the dots again.

"Thanks." Ria took the jar. "Ted, this is a friend of mine from Toronto. He's going to be staying here. Do you need him to check-in?"

Ted ran a hand over his head to smooth his hair and smiled the fakest smile Glenn had ever seen. "Any friend of yours, as they say." He turned to either face the camera that was shooting him or get into position to put his hands on the keyboard that was sitting on the counter in front of him. "I'll need your name, sir, and home address."

Glenn gave Ted his address first, he wanted to save the best for last. If Ted was a newspaper reader the chances were that he'd recognize Glenn's name and maybe, just maybe, he'd feel a little uncomfortable. Watching people's reactions when they found out who Glenn was often told him a lot. "The name's Cooper, Glenn Cooper."

Ted's fingers froze over the keyboard for less than a second. "That's Glenn with two *n*s?"

"That's right." Bingo. Ted knew exactly who Glenn was.

"Would you prefer a room in the main building or perhaps one of the suites in the beachfront …"

"He'll be staying with me," Ria cut-in.

Jackpot!

Driving the golf cart was a blast. The bigger tires gave it great traction. Everything was bigger and better at a Butler Hotel — especially Ria's villa. Glenn felt as if he should have dressed better to fit in with the luxury surroundings. He left his backpack in the front hall, not sure of where it would end up spending the night.

They sat at the table on the patio by the pool and compared notes — Ria bringing him up to speed on what she'd learned and Glenn doing the same in return, neither one of them venturing into the minefield of a discussion about the current state of their relationship.

"I get that he's an actor, and that makes a lot of sense from what I've seen, but I still don't understand where the CSIS agent bit comes in. Do you?" She asked him.

"Not yet. I did a quick search on the name Jake Purcell before I left, but I didn't find anything."

"Well, you wouldn't if he's really a secret agent."

"He's not a spy, he's an actor with a career that was going nowhere who saw a chance to play the role of a lifetime and he went for it, including stealing the real Ted Robarts' identity. That reminds me, are your phones working yet?"

"They weren't the last time I checked."

Glenn stood up and walked to the patio bar. There was a base for a cordless phone, but no handset. "Where's your phone?"

"Down there," Ria pointed at the pool.

"Interesting place to keep it. Should I ask why?"

Ria shook her head. "There's another one in the living room. Who are you going to call?"

"If your phones are working it means we can get Internet access." He found the cordless phone in the living room and took the handset out onto the patio. It was a waste of energy, though. There was no dial tone.

"You know what bothers me?"

"The unreliable phone service down here?" Glenn put the useless phone down on the table.

"Why did Winnie do all that stuff? She stole Ted's shoes, left his footprints in the sand, and left the foot where it would be found. Maybe she's trying to frame Ted? Maybe she's really the killer?"

"But you saw that video, you said she didn't —"

"What if it was edited? To make it look like Winnie couldn't have done it?"

Ria's theory didn't sit right with Glenn. "I can see where you're coming from, except for one thing — why? Why would Winnie kill Kate? You said they were friendly with each other."

"To protect Dan. We know Kate had something on him …"

"But Ted's the one pulling the scam, we know that now. My bet is that Kate recognized him and figured out what he was up to. She was a TV addict, you should see her place. She even had a poster for his show on her wall."

"But our Ted is almost thirty years older than Phil Lunden, and he's dyed his hair. You really think she could have recognized him? You didn't recognize him and you and James used to watch that show all the time."

"Yeah, but I don't think like her. I'm not star crazy. And it fits. The whole premise of this show is respectable professionals who make complete asses of themselves as they compete for the chance to manage a real luxury hotel, right? A fake contestant would turn the whole thing into a joke before it even got broadcast. Ted wanted his second shot at stardom and if the show got killed he wouldn't get the chance to be famous again. When Dan fluffed Kate off she went to Ted and threatened to expose him."

"But why? What good would that do her? She wanted a job from Dan, not Ted."

"Good point." Glenn heard and felt his stomach grumble. It had been a long time since he'd had a real meal, almost twenty-four hours. "Dan couldn't have known what she had. There's no way he could turn this around to make himself look good. And if Dan didn't know, neither did Winnie."

"You haven't met Dan. He's cocky enough to think he can do anything. Winnie's super protective of him and we've got proof that she's involved somehow, which is more than we can say about Ted."

"We need more." Glenn opened the file where he'd stored the pictures from Kate's digital frame on his computer. "The person who sent these knows something."

"And we know that Winnie knew there was someone in Kate's apartment to see them. I'm telling you, it's Winnie." Ria pulled her chair closer to Glenn's. "Let me see them." She put her hand on the touchpad and quickly flipped through the pictures of Kate with Dan and James. She didn't spend much time looking at the pictures of Kate with Ted, either. But she looked long and hard at the picture of the camera in the tree. "That could be the tree by the front steps of the hotel. There's a camera in it."

"Are they building something there?" Glenn pointed at the corner of the stack of lumber. "See that?"

"I know where that is! That's up at the north end, where they're building Manderley. That's where Kate was killed."

The north end? Glenn ran into the villa and dug his notebook (his paper one) out of his backpack. "I watched a video from up there," he said as he flipped through the pages and walked back outside. "It was the one after the one Bear had listed. Here is it — all I saw was a backhoe. Its bucket was full of sand."

"When I watched the one that was in Winnie's desk the bucket was empty. The gardeners had left their tools leaning up against it."

"So somebody used it in between recordings. A backhoe would come in mighty handy if you had to carry a body somewhere ... like down to a boat that you knew was going to explode the next morning." Glenn held his hand out for Ria to take. "Come on. We're going around in circles and we're not going to find any answers here. Let's go find out how they rigged that exploding dinghy. If I'm right, Kate went down with it."

She took his hand without hesitation. She took his hand! The day just kept getting better and better.

Glenn drove like a race car driver. I slithered around on the slippery seat as he took the curves in the road too quickly. The tires squealed more than once. The crew members in the golf cart I flagged down didn't know where Pam was but they said I could find Esther up at Ariel's cottage.

Through Ariel's open front door I could see Esther, a cameraman and a camerawoman, two lighting people, and a man wearing headphones shooting Ariel and Judy. Ariel was standing on a low pedestal as two seamstresses did adjustments to her gown. I didn't want to knock so I waved my arms up and down. Eventually, Esther glanced over at me, held her index finger up, and mouthed *"One minute."* Three minutes later, one of the lighting men turned off his big light and the crew members started to move around. Esther ran out onto the front veranda.

"What's up?" she asked.

"We need to talk to the special-effects person who rigged the dinghy," Glenn immediately answered.

"That's nice." Esther stared up at him. "And who might you be?"

"He's a friend of mine, Esther. He's helping me sort this out."

"Okay. You want to talk to Ray." She unclipped her radio. "I'm not sure where he is, but Pam might know.

"Hey, Pam," she said into the radio, "do you know where Ray is?"

"Do I look like his coordinator?"

"You don't look like anything, I can't see you. Do you know where he is?"

"I think they're down on the back docks."

"Thanks." Esther hooked her radio back on her belt. "Tell him I sent you. He won't talk to you if you don't. James still doesn't know for sure who blew up Albert and we'd like to keep it that way."

Esther went back to work. Glenn went back to driving the golf cart as if it were a Maserati.

"Down there!" I yelled seconds before Glenn was about to miss the turn off.

He yanked the wheel to the left and the cart left the ground when we bounced over — and off — a bump. He slowed down just in time to avoid driving straight down one of the docks and into the water.

We walked over to the northernmost dock, the dock where Glenn said he'd seen Ted carrying Albert's dummy to the waiting crew. Both of the speedboats were docked there and two men were working inside one of them.

Glenn watched them for a minute or two. "Ray?"

They both looked up from the boat to Glenn.

"Not me," the one with the crewcut said.

"Who wants to know?" The almost-anorexic one with the long blond hair asked.

"I do."

I could tell from his tone that Glenn was starting to flex his macho defensive muscles and quickly jumped in to ask his questions for him, in a much friendlier tone. "Esther sent us. She said you rigged the dinghy for Pam's crew. We were just wondering if you could tell us how you did it. We don't know anything about special effects and we're curious. How did you make it sink bow first?" I hoped I'd remembered everything that Glenn had mentioned on the thrill ride from Ariel's cottage.

I'd been close enough. Glenn quickly warmed up to Ray as he explained the intricacies of blowing up a boat and dummy. The menfolk bonded over things that go boom. Ray dropped his guard so much that he stepped out of the boat and started drawing sketches for Glenn.

"… so we put the trap mortar here, in the bow. It's shaped to aim the fireball upwards for a directional charge. And we put a sheet of three-quarter-inch ply on the bottom of the boat to take the kick from the explosion. Pam wanted us to make sure there wasn't much debris, she said she'd have to clean it up, so we were trying to keep the boat in one piece. The bendy —"

"What's a bendy?" Glenn asked.

"The dummy, they bend, he was taped onto the seat with gaffer tape …"

"Duct tape." I added my one and only bit of technical knowledge.

"… yeah, gaffer tape. And here," he drew a tiny circle near the bow of the dinghy he'd sketched, "we put a little bit of det cord." He saw the confused look on Glenn's face and got more specific, "Detonation cord, to make a hole in the bottom of the boat so it would sink bow first."

"I think I get it." Glenn took the sketch from Ray and stared at it. "Did you use duct tape, or gaffer tape, anywhere else? Like on the bottom of the boat?"

"Nope, just to hold the bendy in place."

"And you set it all up the night before?"

"Everything but the charge. We drove it over to the other side that night, but didn't put the charge in until the next morning."

"How did you trigger the explosion? Was it on a timer or something?"

"Radio remote."

"Okay, I think that answers all my questions. Thanks." Glenn and Ray shook hands.

It wasn't until we were back in the golf cart that Glenn explained to me why he'd asked those questions and what the answers meant to him. "… and if I'm right, it makes Ted even more of a suspect. He was here that night. He knew the dinghy would be exploding the next morning, and he's the one who turned the camera off."

"Winnie would have known about the dinghy explosion. Rob said that Dan helped to plan most of the stunts. If Dan knew about it, Winnie would, too."

"When do I get to meet this Rob guy?"

"Later." Much later, I hoped. "He said something else, too."

"I'll bet he did," Glenn muttered loud enough for me to hear him.

I ignored his mutter. "He said that a bag of gaffer tape rolls went missing that night, which fits your theory about where Kate is."

"And it adds to my theory about Ted. He was there, with the special effects guys. He would have known where to find enough tape to strap Kate up."

"That doesn't preclude Winnie. Trust me, she knows where everything and everyone is on this island."

Glenn wisely changed the topic. Until they had more facts, they weren't going to agree on the most likely suspect. "Let's go look at the scene of the crime."

I held onto the handle of the glovebox as Glenn sped up the mountain road, and closed my eyes when the tires hit the gravel road at the end of the pavement. I didn't want to know how close the road went to the side of the mountain, especially when I felt us sliding a bit on the gravel. When the golf cart jerked to a stop I opened my eyes.

What had looked like a small cleared field from the air twenty-four hours earlier was now a manicured lawn that surrounded a big, extra big, billboard that was still under construction and had some rectangular openings cut in it. The lines between the strips of recently laid grass sod were easily visible.

"It looks much bigger up close than it did from the boat," Glenn said as he slowly nudged the golf cart forward onto a wide swath of freshly poured gravel that looked like a driveway of some sort.

The driveway curved around the billboard.

"I can't believe it! They actually built Manderley." The front of the billboard was painted to look like the front of a plantation with white wood siding. It even had a wide set of steps that came down from the front veranda.

Manderley had a resident. He was sitting on a folding lawn chair on the veranda, watching the sun set over the Caribbean.

"Hey! Ria!" Chris jumped out of his chair and ran down the stairs.

"That's Chris Regent," Glenn whispered. "That's really him."

"Chris, I'd like you to meet Glenn Cooper."

Terence Grey had been getting a feel for Manderley, according to Chris. Chris, on the other hand, had been getting bored. He was puppy-dog happy to see us and got even more excited when I asked him to help us by acting something out.

Finding the camera in the trees wasn't easy, it was well hidden.

Glenn picked up a rake that had been leaning against the back of the Manderley facade and walked over to stand by the camera. "So whoever was standing here, right?" He lifted the rake up and let it rest on his right shoulder.

"Whoa! I know what this is. You're re-enacting that Grim Reaper scene." Chris walked over to Glenn and repositioned him. "More stage right. Your head and shoulders will be in the shot if you stay there. And you've got your hands backwards; he had his right hand above his left hand."

"He?" Glenn asked.

"Yeah," Chris looked at me. "You saw the hands, didn't they look like dude hands to you?"

"I didn't look that closely." I should have.

"Hold that." Chris was done with Glenn. "You can be the girl in the golf cart." He pointed at me and then went to stand right beside Glenn. He held his hands up and put his thumbs and middle fingers together to form an almost square, which he then looked through. "Got it." He dropped his hands and ran out from the camera, stopping abruptly where he used his feet to scrape a line in the gravel. "There's your mark. Drive the cart up to this line and then stop. I'll be the running lady. On my cue, you drive into the shot, get out, and stand by the front tire." He turned to Glenn. "Then you wail down on her with the rake handle, but don't really do it, miss or something, 'cause I like Ria and we're just faking this. Then Ria will fall down and you'll bring the rake up again and hit the camera. That's when I'll come into the shot. Are we good?" He looked from Glenn to me.

We both nodded.

"Places!" he yelled out as he ran down the hill until he was out of site.

"Is he directing us?" Glenn asked.

"I think so." I got in the cart and backed it down the hill a little way.

"Ready?" I heard Chris yell.

"Ready!"

"ACTION!"

I drove up to my mark and got out of the cart. Glenn brought the rake down a few feet in front of me, and then lifted it up again. He didn't smack the camera in the tree, but we both looked in the direction that camera would have been pointed if he had.

Chris came jogging up the hill, his body slowly appearing above the rise. A shocked expression came over his face and he slowed down and began to walk like the Pink Panther sneaking up on someone.

"Did she slow down like that?" I asked.

"Yeah, in the last few frames you could tell she was trying not to be noticed."

I hadn't noticed.

"And that's a wrap. Good work people," Chris said proudly. "Why are you guys doing this, anyway?"

"Um …" I didn't know what to say.

"Ria's helping me do some research on a piece I plan to write," Glenn tried to sound nonchalant.

"You're a writer? Like a screenwriter?"

"Investigative journalist," Glenn said with pride.

"Wicked! My character, Terence Grey, one of his possible identities is a reporter! I'm hungry. Have you had dinner yet?"

I shook my head.

"Cool. Let's eat together." He ran over to the golf cart and hopped into the back seat. "To the pool patio, my good man!" he shouted, doing a very good British accent.

"Is he on something?" Glenn asked me quietly as we walked to the golf cart.

"I don't think so." Chris wasn't drunk, at least. I could spot someone over the limit a mile away.

The big band was nowhere to be seen. Their chairs and music stands had also disappeared. In their place was a karaoke station. Three girls I didn't recognize were doing a painfully awful rendition of Avril Lavigne's "Complicated." The patio was packed with more people than I'd seen on it at mealtime before and I couldn't see any empty tables.

When the terrible singing stopped, and after the booing had quietened, I heard someone calling "Ria! Ria! Over here!"

It was Glenn who was able to spot Esther's waving hand from his vantage point above the crowd.

We made our way through the throng to her table. She was sitting with Bear, Pam, and Rob. It was a small table, with four place settings. Bear moved the place settings around. Pam and Glenn went in search of three more chairs. Rob didn't move or speak.

Chris sat down in the first chair Pam brought to the table. "Hi, I'm Chris," he smiled at Pam.

"Like we didn't already know that," Esther was in fine friendly form.

"Esther, right?" Chris asked. "You work on the crew that's shooting Judy. So do you," he looked at Rob.

"Yup."

"I'm Pam, I work on Ted's crew." She was the only one to lean over to shake his hand. "And I was on the arrival shoot with you yesterday."

"Who are you?" Esther asked Glenn when he came back with two chairs.

"Gulliver," Bear answered. "He's a friend of Ria's."

Glenn and I almost played a game of musical chairs. He'd put the two chairs down between Chris and Rob. I didn't want him sitting next to Rob. I won the game.

"My name's actually Glenn," he corrected Bear as he plunked himself down into the chair between Chris and me.

Bear took over the introductions at that point, starting with Esther, then Pam, then Rob.

Glenn and Rob acknowledge each other's presence by leaning forward to look at each other from either side of me.

Glenn said, "Hey."

Rob said "Hey" back.

It was promising to be a really fun night …

Thankfully, Chris supplied enough entertainment to amuse us.

"You guys are way more fun than those guys," Chris nodded in general toward the tables nearest us. "I wish you were working on the movie."

I learned that the increase in bodies around (and in) the pool had been caused by the steady influx of movie personnel. They were moving in, eclipsing and ignoring the inferior television people who had been there before them.

Glenn started to yawn more and more as the evening progressed. He'd had a long day, flying down from Toronto, spending hours exploring the island.

Chris imitated every move Glenn made. When Glenn put his hand over his mouth to cover a yawn, Chris did the same. When Glenn lifted his right leg to cross it over his left, Chris performed a synchronized movement with a one-second delay.

The only original movement Chris made was a pout when I called it a night and he realized that he wasn't going to be able to play with his new little friend anymore.

I carried Glenn's backpack into the master bedroom. "Do you feel like a swim?" I wasn't ready to go to bed. Before anything started up between us I wanted to talk, but I didn't want that talk to get too serious. The pool sounded to me like the perfect place to have a serious, but not too serious, conversation.

"Okay."

"I'll meet you out there." I opened the sliding doors from my room and went out onto the patio.

I'd left my bathing suit hanging over the back of one of the patio chairs. It hadn't dried completely in the humid air and the thought of putting on a slightly damp suit didn't thrill me.

Why not? It wasn't as if he'd never seen me naked before.

Then I remembered the camera in the bushes. I ducked behind the bar to change, squiggling, squirming, pulling, and snapping the wet suit into place with the same difficulty that women in previous generations had probably experienced when they shoved themselves into tight girdles.

I floated. I sat on the steps in the shallow end. I dove down and retrieved the cordless handset (but left the discs were they were). Still no Glenn.

I stood dripping in the open door to my room and smiled. He'd sat on the edge of the bed, his bathing trunks in his hands, and had made the mistake of lying back. The bathing trunks were still in his hands, but he wouldn't be putting them on. He was so sound asleep that he barely noticed when I heaved his legs up and slid him around to lie lengthways on the bed.

"Good night, old man," I whispered as I went back outside to turn the pool lights off.

Glenn woke up with a start, not sure of where he was. He felt the bed move and looked over to see Ria, sound asleep, snoring ever so slightly, all tucked in under the covers. He was on top of the covers and fully dressed. Gently lifting the covers up he took a quick peek at Ria. Wow. She'd stayed awake long enough to take her clothes off. It was tempting, very tempting, but he didn't want their first time together again to happen in an early morning fog. He wanted Ria to be an active participant.

As slowly as he could, he got off the bed.

A little green lizard clung to the stone wall of the shower and watched him lather up.

Ria slept through his shower, and his shave, and his unpacking (which didn't take long) and through him getting dressed.

Hearing a dial tone when he picked up the phone made him smile. It was all systems go.

I woke up to the sound of Glenn's voice, but he wasn't talking to me. He was sitting on the patio, his computer open on the table in front of him, talking on the phone. He smiled and waved when I sat down in the chair across from him.

He pointed at a carafe that was sitting on the top of the bar, beside a sugar bowl and a cream pitcher. "Look, James, I've got enough to print. I'm offering you the opportunity to make yourself look good, not just stupid."

I listened to him as I went to the bar and got a Diet Coke out of the refrigerator for me and then took the coffee carafe over to top up Glenn's mug.

"I'll see you there." He put the handset down on the table. "Good morning."

"It looks like you've been busy. How long have you been up?"

"A couple of hours. Sorry about last night. I was beat."

"Apparently."

"Rain check? Tonight? Unless you've already got plans, that is."

"I think I can squeeze you in." Not a bad teaser for an old broad, I mentally patted myself on the back.

"Don't do that to me," Glenn growled. "You hungry?"

"As a matter of fact, I am."

Glenn sighed heavily. "For breakfast, Ria, food." He'd caught my meaning. "It should be here any minute and we've got a busy day ahead of us."

"Do *we*," I used the royal we, "get to know what we'll be doing to fill this busy day?"

"Chris gave me an idea yesterday. We've been running around in all directions, right? Not sure of who did what. But someone's been trying to direct us, right? The person who sent those pictures."

"I guess so."

"No guess about it. Think about it. Winnie had access to the stuff that was recorded on the camera that was here. So let's assume she watched it and heard you talking to me. You mentioned something about Winnie going over the phone records because of the long-distance charges. She'd see that you dialled my number a lot. She could do a reverse lookup and bingo, she'd know exactly who you were talking to. And she knew that Allie was in Kate's apartment — so she knew that Allie would see those pictures. She couldn't have known if Allie and I were talking, so she highlighted my upcoming article on the picture of the front page."

"But why the secrecy act? Why not just call the police?"

"You yourself have said how Dan's the master of making himself look good. He's got visual proof that Winnie put the foot in the water. If she went to the police he could have used that to get her charged with an accessory or something.

Same with James, he had Kate's suitcases put at James' place to make it look like James was involved."

"But Dan didn't kill Kate, so what did he have to lose if the killer was caught?"

"His grand finale."

I nodded. "That sounds like him. That bit I believe. But I'm still not sold on Winnie being little Miss Innocent. She could have just called the police that night, she didn't have to take Kate's foot, or …"

"But she knows how good Dan is at twisting images around to make himself look good. She'd be risking her job if she called the cops, and from what you've said her job is her life. Dan's got too much riding on this show — not just because he's sunk a fortune into the production, but because of the free promotion it's going to give his two movies."

"Okay." But I still wasn't sold. "So why did she do anything at all?"

"Because she's got a conscience? Maybe she really did like Kate? Or maybe, just maybe, she's getting fed up with Dan? We'll never know. Maybe she wanted him to get caught, too?"

"But he didn't kill Kate! And you know what? I've heard too many people say that Dan's this all powerful being who controls the women in his life, but I think it's just an act. He didn't control Kate, did he? She stood up to him. You've never met Winnie, but I'm telling you — she's got more control of him than he's got of her. If you're right that she figured out we were talking, found you, and came up with a way to get your attention, those aren't the actions of a puppet on a string. Those are the actions of someone who's in charge, someone who's capable of directing others actions. I still think she could have done it."

"But you saw that footage, someone else was holding the scythe."

"Or someone edited that stuff to make it look like Winnie didn't do it. Yeah, Bear says they can't do editing down here, but he didn't know about the cameras watching me, so maybe there's some editing equipment that he doesn't know about? The fact is we don't have any proof of anything."

"You're right."

Why did he always do that to me? It got confusing when he agreed with me like that.

"And that's why we're going to rewrite the script and direct the next scene. James and Dan will be on Soursop in two hours to meet with us. If I'm right, that Ted's the killer and Dan knows it, he won't let himself go down on the same ship. I'll bluff, pretend we have all the answers."

"But we don't …"

"Not yet, but if I play my role well we'll get them."

"Go on then, rehearse, prove to me that Ted is the killer."

He took a big sip of his coffee and cleared his throat. "Get comfy — I'm about to give a soliloquy. I managed to find a few facts this morning. Phil Lunden played Billy Packham, the precocious little brother on *Packham Inn*, the same show that is prominently displayed on a big poster in Kate's apartment. Ten years ago Phil Lunden got a part in a low-budget TV movie, shot in Toronto. An actress by the name of Holly Stewart also had a minor role in that film. It was a cheap spy flick and Phil played a dark-haired CSIS agent. That fictional agent's name was Jake Purcell."

"So he's not an —"

"No heckling from the cheap seats." He continued, "Holly didn't get many roles after that movie, but she did stay in the business. She became the receptionist at VideoPost, James Butler's post-production facility. The audience may, and should, assume that while working there she heard about a new production in the works — a reality-TV show called *Check-Out Time*. At the same time, her old friend Phil Lunden was working as a waiter at the Crystal Hotel. The day after the general manager of that hotel left the country to take up a new position in Dubai, Phil Lunden became Ted Robarts. He used that identity to get himself on the show that his friend Holly had told him about." He looked very pleased with himself and spread his arms out in the air while he bowed his head. "You don't have to hold your applause, you know. Let her rip."

"But that doesn't prove that Ted killed Kate. He'd get to be famous either way — win the show and go *Surprise, I fooled you all!* or let Kate tell the world and he'd be at the centre of a big scandal and he'd get invited to go on every talk show there is, he could milk it for all it's worth."

"You're forgetting something — if Kate spilled the beans, the show would never be broadcast. Ted wouldn't get his face on television screens across the continent for one hour every week for thirteen weeks. Sure, he'd get some interest, but not the kind of press he'd get if he was able to save his surprise until the very last episode."

"I still think Winnie did it. She's a lot like Mrs. Danvers."

"Who?"

"The housekeeper in *Rebecca*. Completely devoted, to a psychotic level, to her employer, willing to do anything to protect him. Mrs. Danvers burned down Manderley, a place she loved, and she did it to hurt Maxim de Winter when she found out he might have killed her beloved Rebecca. Winnie found out that Kate could hurt Dan, so she hurt Kate."

"You read too much. This isn't a novel or a movie. This is real life."

"And we really don't know for sure which one of us is right."

"We'll know soon enough. But before that happens, you're going to get us one more fact."

"I am?"

The doorbell rang and Glenn stood up to go answer it. "Yes, you are! That's why I ordered you a light breakfast. You've got a date with some little fishes before we meet with the big fish."

CHAPTER
SIXTEEN

The dinghy was sitting on an angle, its stern resting on a rock, at thirty-eight feet down. A small white stingray shimmied out of its hiding place in the sand when I crouched down to get a better look at the bottom of the boat. Something with claws or sharp teeth had been tearing at the duct tape. The delicate fingers on the bloated white hand that had been pulled through an opening in the tape, the skin picked or torn completely off two of the fingers, made me want to throw up in my regulator. I quickly looked away and nodded at the dive buddy who'd come with me from the dive shop. I gave him the thumbs up signal to let him know that I was ready to ascend. My stomach didn't start to calm down until we made our five-minute safety stop at fifteen feet.

We drove back around the island to the dock and I changed in the bathroom of the dive shop and then walked up to the hotel. Glenn had waited there to meet James and Dan, just in case they came over earlier than expected.

It was quicker to cut through the kitchen than go all the way around the hotel. Two men in chef's uniforms were having a smoke on the patio by the back door of the kitchen. They nodded at me as I pulled the door open and went inside.

Ted burst through the swinging doors at the other end of the kitchen just as I passed the sinks. He stopped when he saw me. Then his mouth slowly spread into an unnerving smile.

"Hi, Ted," I kept on walking.

"Miss Butler," he nodded as we passed each other.

He grabbed my arm so fast that it took me a second or two to react. I saw a flash of shiny metal as he reached out with his other hand and grabbed a cleaver that was lying on the counter.

"Keep your mouth shut and act natural." His mouth was so close to my ear that I could feel the moisture in his breath. "One stupid move and I'll cut you."

The cleaver in his left hand, tucked inside the front of his Butler blazer, his right hand squeezing my elbow hard, we walked out the back door of the kitchen together.

Glenn had been right. I only hoped that I'd get the chance to hear him say *I told you so.*

"So what? You've got nothing." Dan scoffed. He calmly crossed his legs and picked a microscopic speck of lint off of his linen pants.

"You knew! All of it?" James looked like he'd just been kicked in the balls.

Glenn glanced at his watch again. Where the hell was Ria?

"Yeah, yeah, yeah, I knew." Dan leaned forward. "This show was all set to have a killer ending. Picture it — the costumes, the set, the dramatic mood of the masquerade, the anticipation of the results from the final vote. Ted wins the vote in the live finale. Then cue the powerful music, I walk onto the stage and confront Ted, tell him we've found out who he really is, a former child star with no career or talent, using a stolen identity to try to trick us."

"How long have you known?" Some colour was coming back into James' face.

"I recognized him from the eight-by-ten glossy that he sent in with his application. Hotel managers don't hand out eight by tens, actors do."

James stood up and walked to the closed sliding glass doors to the balcony of Winnie's office. "I can't believe this is happening."

"We've got the footage of Winnie placing the foot in the tidal pool." Glenn wanted to keep the conversation going. He wanted to know what was keeping Ria even more.

"Do you? I wouldn't be too sure about that, if I were you. I'll tell you what you do have, though — you've got some friends who might be charged with break and enter. I've got footage of them breaking into my secretary's office and stealing confidential items from her desk."

"What are you talking about?" James turned around and walked back to stand beside Glenn.

"I'm talking about your sister and your cameraman, and my star — but I'm not going to have him arrested. They were so busy looking for camera discs that they didn't bother to look for cameras — there are two of them in here, for security purposes."

Dan pointed up to the ceiling and Glenn slowly scanned the corners. He saw two very small cameras in opposite corners, aimed to get full coverage of the room.

"Too bad for you I had those cameras disconnected a few minutes ago. There'll be no record of our conversation. So tell me again, Mr. Investigative Reporter, what do you actually have?"

Glenn mentally scrambled to come up with something solid, something that was already up in Toronto that Dan wouldn't have had time to hide. "We've got footage of Winnie taking the foot into the kitchen and then bringing it out the next morning." For the first time Dan looked concerned. Glenn kept on going. "And we've got the footage of the foot. Your guy in the helicopter zoomed in on it."

"He sure did! Mark Burnett only managed to get a guy's burnt hands — I've got a severed foot! And I plan to show that footage to the police. Through the magic of modern technology we'll be able to zoom in even closer. I'm sure the local police will be very interested to see that. And I'll also give them the footage we have of someone reacting very badly to hearing that a foot had been found." Dan chuckled. "Ted puked his guts out when he heard about Pam finding it. We caught him doing it from three angles."

Glenn finally thought of something solid. "We've got Kate's suitcases."

Dan opened his eyes wide and feigned surprise. "Really? What suitcases would those be?"

"The ones at James' place."

"Look again, big boy. They're not there anymore. Like Mandy, they moved. But they served their purpose. If Jamie here had started to ask too many questions those suitcases would have shut him up."

"A girl died!" James spit out at Dan. "Doesn't that mean anything to you at all?"

"She brought it on herself. She got involved in something that was none of her business. If Ted hadn't hit the damn camera we could have made her immortal. I'm telling you, public executions are coming back. That's where reality TV is heading and we would have been the first to have one. Instead, all we've got is her foot — but it's better than nothing."

"What happened that night?" Glenn would let Dan fill in a couple more blanks and then he'd find out where Ria was.

"I don't know. I wasn't here, remember? I was over on Virgin Gorda with James."

"Dan, stop it." James finally sounded as if he taking charge of his show, something he never should have relinquished. "Your big dramatic ending isn't going to happen, so just tell us what we want to know. Then we'll call the police. We can script something for the finale, you can deliver the lines if you want, and then we'll announce Judy as the winner."

"You know what your problem is, James?"

"Why don't you illuminate me?"

"You think too small. The finale is going to be better than I hoped. Care of your big friend there," he pointed at Glenn. "I've rewritten the script — again. We'll be airing the," he counted out something on his fingers, "fourth draft. The first draft was the basic boring competitor-wins-competition version. Draft two came to me when I realized who Ted was. But Kate forced a rewrite on that one. I wish there'd been a camera on Ted's face when I told him Kate was on to him. He ran through a very dramatic array of emotions, real ones, before I reassured him that it didn't matter to me who he was and told him he was going to win, if he got Kate to shut up. I suggested that he talk to Kate in private, like up at the north end where no one had a room with a view, so to speak, but I couldn't possibly have foreseen that he'd use a gardening implement as a silencer. Imagine my surprise when Winnie told me what she saw him do? So draft three had to be written quickly and it would have worked if Pam hadn't thrown the foot away. Just picture it — unsuspecting production assistant comes across a severed foot. But she didn't follow the script, she improvised, and that meant I had to, too. Quite frankly, the fourth draft is the best, much more dramatic, and the big reveal about where the rest of Kate's body is will really add punch to the finale."

"How do you know where the body is if you didn't have anything to do with it?" Even if the conversation wasn't being recorded, Glenn had James as a witness that Dan had just admitted to knowing where Kate's body was. It was something — not much, but something.

"Please! Do you really think Ted's capable of coming up with such a visually dramatic hiding place? Between us, I'll take the credit for that. The stupid oaf didn't even realize that he'd cut her foot off and left it behind. I'm just glad that Winnie thought to keep it."

"I'm calling the police," James snatched up the phone from Winnie's desk.

"I've already called them." Dan waited until James put the phone down. "I called them right after you told me about this meeting and wouldn't be surprised if a contingent from the Royal Virgin Islands Police Force was already downstairs in the lobby. Here's how it's going to play out — a crew is going to get me explaining to the police that I think Ted killed one of our production assistants; we'll save the details about his true identity for the post-finale wrap-up show. I'll tell the cops that I think Ted's making a run for it. He is making a run for it, by the way. I told him that you were on to him and suggested that he take one of the speedboats to get off the island until I figured out a way to cover for him. The cops will chase him in their boat — we should be able to talk them into letting us send at least one camera with them. They'll catch Ted, bring him back here, and then we'll shoot Winnie explaining how she was out for her run when she thought she saw Ted kill Kate. Imagine Winnie's surprise, and mine, when the police in Toronto reported that Kate was just fine? Fools! All they had to do was read her info sheet. She clearly wrote *twin sister* in the family contact section. That reminds me — Winnie!"

The door that Glenn had thought led to a closet opened and Winnie came through it from a connecting room.

. "Did you get the rights to that *Packham Inn* footage? The price will go through the roof once this goes public."

"I secured them last month." She walked over to the filing cabinet and opened the bottom drawer. "I probably bought more footage than we'll need, but we'll have lots to work with."

"Excellent." Dan stood up and straightened his trousers. "Now, gentlemen, shall we go watch it all play out?"

"Actually, Dan," Winnie reached into the file drawer, slid all the hanging files together at one end of the drawer, pushed something that clicked, and then stood up with two discs in her hands, "there's been another rewrite." She walked over to Glenn. "Give these to the police." She turned and smiled at Dan. "Oops! I forgot to turn the cameras off in here."

"What the fuck do you think you're doing? I'll fire your ass!"

"No, Dan, you won't. Because I'm firing you. Or don't you remember why we had to move to the States? How many lawsuits were you dodging because of your questionable backend accounting? Three? Four? But they couldn't touch the company assets once they were all in my name, could they? And, as you told me so often, it wasn't as if you'd killed someone, it was just a white-collar crime, nothing serious." She walked right up to Dan and poked him in the chest, hard, with her index finger. "You went too far this time, Dan. I'm directing your finale, and this time the shit's going to stick to your white collar!" She turned to look at Glenn and James. "What are you waiting for? The police are already on their way to the back dock. Ted's acting out Dan's escape script, and he's added a dramatic twist — he's got Miss Butler with him."

A seismic jolt of adrenalin ripped through Glenn's body. He pushed Dan out of the way, knocking him to the ground. James jumped over Dan and followed Glenn down the hallway.

Glenn punched the down button on the elevator panel.

"Stairs!" James yelled as he ran past the elevator.

Glenn's legs were longer than James' and he got to the stairwell first.

"Through the kitchen, third set of doors on the left!" James called out directions as their feet clattered down the metal stairs.

"Sorry," Glenn called over his shoulder after bumping into a waiter in the kitchen, sending his tray full of glasses flying.

Two men were unloading boxes from the bed of a small pickup truck by the back door of the kitchen. They'd left the engine running.

James pulled himself into the passenger seat just as Glenn slammed his foot onto the accelerator. They both ignored the yelling men they'd left behind.

The truck's engine roared as Glenn did more off-roading than on-roading between the hotel and the docks. The Butlers could afford to pay to repair the swath of destruction the truck's tires had made in the landscaping. He had to pump the brakes to get the truck to stop just as the front tires hit the first plank of the dock. Two crew members who were carrying a large metal trunk jumped out of the way — into the water. One of the two blue speedboats was speeding away from the dock. It was easy to spot Ria in the boat, her red hair blowing in the wind contrasted sharply against the blue of the boat. "Fuck!" He ran down the dock and looked at the ignition in the boat's twin. The keys weren't in it.

Ray, the special-effects guy, came running down the dock. "Are you trying to kill somebody?"

"We have to get out to that boat. Where are the keys for this one?" Glenn didn't bothering trying to silence the panic in his voice.

Ray looked out at the boat that was heading for the northern point of the island. "He's not going anywhere."

It was then that Glenn noticed the control unit that Ray was holding. "Can you turn him around, bring him back here?"

"Sure, but Dan told me to keep him out there until all the cameras are in position for the police takedown."

"He's got my sister!" James' face was beet red and sweat was streaming down it. "He could hurt her."

"Then I'll blow him up. We armed the boat right after Dan called."

Glenn looked down the shoreline. There were cameramen spaced along the length of the island, all the way to the northern tip. The Butler helicopter swooped over their heads, a cameraman sitting with his legs hanging out the open side door, his camera pointing down at them. The Butler yacht came speeding around the northern end of the island, a camera crew on its front deck. "Directional charge?"

Ray had barely nodded his head when Glenn asked another question. "Which direction?

Ray pointed at the top toggle switch, "This one shoots out the front of the boat," he pointed at the bottom toggle switch, "this one shoots out the back, and this one," he turned a small dial, "controls the speed." The boat started to slow down.

Glenn did what any man would do when watching a show he didn't want to see — he grabbed the remote control and changed the program. Worst case scenario? He'd blow Ted's foot off.

ROLL TAIL CREDITS.

PHIL LUNDEN & DAN SHYKOFF
Long term accommodations supplied by:
Her Majesty's Prison, Tortola

JAMES BUTLER & WINNIFRED PAVLOVICH
Executive Producers — *Check-Out Time*
Canadian Screen Award: Best Reality
Program or Series

CHRIS REGENT
Oscar Nominee
Actor in a Supporting Role
For his portrayal of Terence Gray in
Rebecca's Story

RIA BUTLER & GLENN COOPER
Stay tuned …

ACKNOWLEDGEMENTS

No writer is an island, even if their story is set in the islands. I couldn't have written this without the support and help of many people and apologize if any accuracy was washed away by a wave of creativity.

Thank you to the characters who inspired and informed:

John — my best production ever!

Jane — hired for your ability to decipher hieroglyphics, you'll never be fired from your current position, 1st AD of friendship

Marilyn — for helping me hear a Who

Sandy — you were write (sometimes) and now you have it in writing

Angie (aka Sis) — for being there all the way from Spring to Sitka to Spanish Town

Robyn — for spotting me when I had to bench press the weight of doubt

Lyne — for suggesting that a production memo should grow up to be a book

Arthur Hiller — for encouraging the story of me

Officers Denise and Rich, the armed arm of the family — for answering all of my 911 calls

Germaine Fritz — for sharing her Dream

Gino Russo — for ferries and flight rules

Patrick Darrah, John Hektor, and Mike Twamley — for bringing me up to speed on Ickys, Avids, and gyros

Rudy Rivas — for making things go BOOM

Amanda Dunning — for giving me PMS

Dr. Susan Kuzmyk — for curling my toes with her severing expertise

Deputy Chief Forensic Pathologist, Ontario, Dr. Toby Rose — for performing a literary post-mortem on a pedal extremity

Sylvia McConnell — for opening the door to Dundurn

And all of the wonderful people on the other side of that door: Kirk Howard, Beth Bruder, Sheila Douglas (who sends the best emails), Margaret Bryant, Synora Van Drine, Caitlyn Stewart, Karen McMullin, James Hatch, the magical Allister Thompson, to name just a few … with a special curtain call for Cheryl Hawley and her gentle red marker

Bob, Brad, and Harry — where's Barry?

OF RELATED INTEREST

Spoiled Rotten
A Liz Walker Mystery
Mary Jackman
978-1-459701410
$11.99

Liz Walker is the quintessential broke all the time, cynically optimistic restaurateur. As the owner of a charming corner bistro in downtown Toronto, she doesn't mince words when glamour and romance elude her. Despite the foibles of running a notoriously risky business, covering cheques with her line of credit, and dealing with a fickle public, she wouldn't dream of doing anything else. Unfortunately, a missing chef, prickly health inspectors, and murder threaten to shut her down. When the body of her meat supplier, Mr. Tony of Kensington Market fame, is found dismembered, her star chef Daniel Chapin becomes the lead suspect, then goes missing. More problems arise when two people are poisoned at the place where Daniel has been moonlighting. Determined to get her chef back and clear her restaurant's name, Liz jeopardizes her life in pursuit of a ruthless killer, crossing paths more than once with Detective Winn.

A Green Place for Dying
A Meg Harris Mystery
R.J. Harlick
978-1-926607245
$17.99

Meg Harris, an amateur sleuth who drinks a little too much and is afraid of the dark, returns to her home in the West Quebec wilderness after a trip. Upon her arrival she discovers that a friend's daughter has been missing from the Migiskan Reserve for more than two months. Meg vows to help find the missing girl and starts by confronting the police on their indifference to the disappearance. During her investigation, Meg discovers that more than one Native woman has gone missing. Fearing the worst, Meg delves deeper and finds herself confronting an underside of life she would rather not know existed.

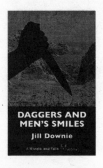

Daggers and Men's Smiles
A Moretti and Falla Mystery
Jill Downie
978-1-554888689
$11.99

On the English Channel Island of Guernsey, Detective Inspector Ed Moretti and his new partner, Liz Falla, investigate vicious attacks on Epicure Films. The international production company is shooting a movie based on British bad-boy author Gilbert Ensor's bestselling novel about an Italian aristocratic family at the end of the Second World War, using fortifications from the German occupation of Guernsey as locations, and the manor house belonging to the expatriate Vannonis. When vandalism escalates into murder, Moretti must resist the attractions of Ensor's glamorous American wife, Sydney, consolidate his working relationship with Falla, and establish whether the murders on Guernsey go beyond the island. Why is the Marchesa Vannoni in Guernsey? What is the significance of the design that appears on the daggers used as murder weapons, as well as on the Vannoni family crest? And what role does the marchesas statuesque niece, Giulia, who runs the family business and is probably bisexual, really play?

Nightshade
A Sam Montcalm Mystery
Tom Henighan
978-1-554887149
$11.99

Deadly nightshade — the poison plant par excellence — and in historic Quebec City at an important scientific conference concerning the genetic manipulation of trees it means *murder*!

Police, RCMP, and a mysterious FBI agent from Washington converge on the scene. But the sharpest eye belongs to Sam Montcalm, a despised "bedroom snooper" from Ottawa, whose primary concern is to clear a First Nations activist of the crime. Sam is middle-aged, tough, and sophisticated, yet he's also a lone wolf who feels displaced nearly everywhere, and his relations with his colleagues, the police — and with women — are always complicated. "You're a psychic wound without a health card," a friend comments.

The story moves to its surprising climax as Montcalm follows the trail of murder back to Canada's capital and into the Gatineau Hills, his deep sense of cynicism about human nature confirmed as he closes in on the killer and struggles to come to terms with himself.

Visit us at
Dundurn.com
@dundurnpress
Facebook.com/dundurnpress
Pinterest.com/dundurnpress